**Carola Dunn** is the author of several mysteries featuring Daisy Dalrymple as well as numerous historical novels. Born and raised in England, she lives in Eugene, Oregon.

*The Daisy Dalrymple Series*

Death at Wentwater Court*
The Winter Garden Mystery*
Requiem for a Mezzo*
Murder on the Flying Scotsman*
Damsel in Distress*
Dead in the Water*
Styx and Stones*
Rattle His Bones*
To Davy Jones Below*
The Case of the Murdered Muckraker
Mistletoe and Murder
Die Laughing
A Mourning Wedding
Fall of a Philanderer
Gunpowder Plot
The Bloody Tower
The Black Ship*
Sheer Folly*

*published by Constable & Robinson

# To Davy Jones Below

## A Daisy Dalrymple Mystery

CAROLA DUNN

ROBINSON

Constable & Robinson Ltd
3 The Lanchesters
162 Fulham Palace Road
London W6 9ER
www.constablerobinson.com

Published in the UK by Robinson, an imprint of
Constable & Robinson Ltd, 2010



A copy of the British Library Cataloguing in Publication data is available from the British Library

ISBN: 978-1-84901-519-6

Typeset by TW Typesetting, Plymouth, Devon

Printed and bound in the EU

1 3 5 7 9 10 8 6 4 2

Yo ho, yo ho, the frisky plank,
You walks along it so,
Till it goes down and you goes down
To Davy Jones below!

– 'Pirate Song' from *Peter Pan*, J.M. Barrie

# PROLOGUE

Caleb P. Arbuckle scowled. His long, bony face, had anyone observed it, would have conveyed extreme dissatisfaction. But his companion in the box at the Windmill Theatre, London, England, was not looking at him. Jethro Gotobed's entire attention was fixed on the stage.

To be precise, Gotobed's attention was on the third girl from the left in the front row of the chorus. He had pointed her out. She was a looker, no doubt of that. They all were, long-legged dolls with baby-doll faces, white-powdered and rouged, scarlet-mouthed; hair bobbed and marcelled; hemlines not a quarter inch below the centres of their kneecaps; necklines not a quarter inch above the level which would keep the Lord Chamberlain off the management's necks.

Arbuckle sighed. He was no Puritan. What got his goat was not the sight of twenty-some pairs of bouncing bazooms, or twenty-some pairs of long legs in the latest skin-coloured artificial silk stockings, high-kicking for his amusement – and that of several hundred others. No siree bob, to that he had no objection at all.

Nor was he dissatisfied with his company, not by a long shot. Gotobed was a mighty swell guy for a Limey, a business acquaintance who had become a real pal. Arbuckle knew from sad experience that a millionaire has few real pals. Those few were not to be sneezed at. Besides, Caleb P. Arbuckle was not the sort to ditch a buddy in trouble, and that Broadway beauty hoofing it on the stage spelled trouble or he was a Dutchman.

As the number drew to a close with a flurry of kicks and a flourish of garters, Gotobed leaned closer to nudge Arbuckle.

'T'lass – Miss Fairchild – has her solo next,' he whispered. The broad Yorkshire vowels which had at first flummoxed Arbuckle no longer puzzled him any more than a Texas drawl. 'She has a grand voice,' Gotobed continued. 'Might've bin an opera singer with the proper training. O' course, I'd pay for lessons like a shot, but she says it's too late. She doesn't make any secret o' being thirty, not to *me.* Hush now, and you'll hear summat worth listening to.'

The light from the stage reflected off his beaming face, the large, ruddy face of a hick farmer, not the 'cute customer Arbuckle knew him to be. Gotobed had made his millions in steel, and they were honest to God English millions, at five of Uncle Sam's greenbacks to the pound sterling. Yet the Fairchild floozy was jollying the poor boob along just as if he was the rube he looked. She was getting set to take him for every penny he possessed.

Listen to her now:

'"Darling, I am growing old,"' she crooned.

'"Silver threads among the gold . . ."'

No spoony gaze for Gotobed. She was too savvy for anything so obvious. Nothing but a half-laughing, conspiratorial glance flashed up at the box. *No grey hairs yet*, that glance said, *but you and I know I'm no spring chicken.*

And Gotobed, as if on cue, passed his hand over his grizzled head and said defensively, 'I know I'm twice her age, but it's not as if she's not old enough to know her own mind.'

Old enough to know her days in the chorus line would not last much longer, Arbuckle thought. If she admitted to thirty, she was probably nearer forty. A nice little voice, but not enough talent to go it alone, especially with vaudeville dying. After all, it was 1923 and in this modern age, picture houses were all the rage.

Yes siree, Wanda Fairchild had her eye to the main chance, and Jethro Gotobed was the sap elected to provide for her future. Tarnation, he might even find himself tied up in matrimony if he didn't watch out!

But not if Caleb P. Arbuckle had anything to say in the matter. A distraction, that was what was needed. The dawn of a plan glimmered in Arbuckle's mind.

# CHAPTER 1

'Mother will never forgive me,' said Daisy. She clutched her bouquet of rosebuds in one hand and smoothed the skirt of her cream linen costume with the other as the big, green Vauxhall pulled smoothly away from the kerb in a shower of confetti.

'For marrying me?' asked Alec softly, glancing at the chauffeur's back.

'Oh no, darling. She's been resigned to my marrying a policeman ever since she discovered you're a Detective Chief Inspector, not a humble bobby. Besides, an unmarried daughter of twenty-six is a fearful reproach to someone of her generation.' Daisy heard herself babbling but couldn't stop. After all, she had never been married before, and it felt most peculiar. 'Where Mother's concerned,' she continued, 'it doesn't hurt that *your* mother disapproves of me quite as much as mine disapproves of you.'

'I'm afraid so,' he admitted, 'but Belinda adores you. Amost as much as I do.'

When he looked at her like that, it was hard to believe those grey eyes were capable of making an erring subordinate snap to attention or freezing a criminal to the marrow of his bones. 'Alec, my hat!' she squeaked, as he enveloped her in a crushing embrace.

Though she was unable to speak for several minutes, her ears were unencumbered. She distinctly heard Bill Truscott chuckle as he drove the Vauxhall, its hood down on this sparkling October day, towards the Dorchester Hotel. That was the worst of old retainers.

The loan of the motor and chauffeur was the least of what Daisy's cousin Edgar, Lord Dalrymple, had provided. He had done them proud, in spite of the short notice. Coming over all dynastic, he had begged to give the bride away and to provide a bang-up reception. Daisy hadn't had the heart to refuse, knowing how guilty the ex-schoolmaster felt at having inherited Fairacres and the viscountcy after her father's death in the flu pandemic of '19.

Her father ought to have been there to give her hand to Alec, he or her brother, Gervaise, killed in the Flanders trenches. And it might have been Michael who placed the ring on her finger, if that landmine had not blown up his Friends' Ambulance Unit. A catch in her throat, Daisy blinked.

She loved Alec dearly, but her sight was misty as she glanced back at the following motor cars. The first bore Cousin Edgar, the Dowager Lady Dalrymple, and Daisy's maid of honour, her erstwhile housemate, Lucy Fotheringay. The second, Alec's cherished Austin 'Chummy', was driven by his sergeant, Tom Tring, who had stood as his best man. In the back seat, Mrs Fletcher sat poker-stiff with Alec's ten-year-old daughter, Belinda, bouncing slightly at her side.

It was a small wedding party, just what Daisy had wanted but not at all what her mother considered proper.

'She'll never forgive me the Registry Office,' Daisy sighed, 'since she had her heart set on St George's, Hanover Square. Darling, I'm frightfully glad Superintendent Crane gave you so little notice of your fortnight's leave.'

'So am I, since it pleases you, love.' Alec's dark, rather fierce eyebrows met in a frown. 'Yet I have a nasty feeling he's got something up his sleeve.'

'Oh, Alec, he *can't* ask you to investigate a crime while we're on our honeymoon!'

'That's why I suggested a week in Jersey. The Channel Islands have their own legal system, which is none of our business. And I haven't mentioned to anyone at the Yard that we'll spend the second week at home. No, I suspect the Super has something special in store for when I go back to work.'

'Let's not worry about it now, then, darling. Oh, here we are. You squashed my flowers. Is my hat straight?'

The reception was on a completely different scale from the wedding. In spite of the short notice, few of those invited failed to attend. The Dorchester's ballroom was crammed with Daisy's aristocratic family connections, Alec's Metropolitan Police colleagues, and an eclectic collection of friends.

Daisy made friends easily and, according to her mother, without discrimination. Standing in the receiving line, the Dowager Lady Dalrymple was forced to shake hands with, among others, an Indian doctor, an American industrialist, and a Russian Jewish violinist.

'I knew if you insisted on working for a living you were

bound to meet the most unsuitable people,' she moaned, 'but need you make *friends* of them?'

'Buck up, Mother,' Daisy whispered. 'Here come Lord and Lady Wentwater. I wrote an article about Wentwater Court, remember?'

In spite of their unfortunate connection with her work, an earl and countess could not fail to please. For the moment at least, Daisy was spared further reproaches.

Another 'suitable' guest was the Honourable Phillip Petrie, who had grown up on the estate next to Fairacres. Lady Dalrymple's only objection to him was that he had not married Daisy. It was not for want of trying. As Gervaise's closest chum, he had long felt honour-bound to take care of Gervaise's little sister, which led him to propose to her at regular intervals.

Daisy having refused him with equal regularity, he had recently married an American girl. He appeared to be utterly besotted with his golden-headed Gloria, whom he generally addressed – revoltingly – as Glow-worm.

Later on, after cutting the wedding cake, Daisy and Alec were talking to Phillip and Gloria when Gloria's father, Mr Arbuckle, approached. Curiously, he was accompanied by Detective Superintendent Crane, with whom he appeared to be on unnaturally friendly terms.

They were an oddly assorted pair, and the uniform of formal morning cutaways and striped trousers only served to accentuate the contrast. The American millionaire was short and spare, his long face lengthened by a receding hairline. The English policeman stood well above the regulation height, his bulk still muscular (thrice weekly games of fives, according to Alec), his sandy hair fading but still thick.

Mr Arbuckle looked smug, Superintendent Crane bland in a way Daisy had long since concluded all detectives must practice in front of their looking-glasses. She regarded him with suspicion.

'He *does* have something up his sleeve,' she muttered.

Catching her words, Gloria glanced back. 'Yes, Poppa's been up to something,' she said. 'I don't know what, but he's in cahoots with Superintendent Crane, I do believe. I've seen them with their heads together, haven't you, honey?'

Phillip's conventionally handsome face remained blank. In anyone she knew less well, Daisy might have supposed he was aware of whatever plot was hatching and was attempting to conceal his knowledge. In Phillip, however, blankness of face denoted blankness of mind. Put him down in front of a motor car engine and his capabilities amounted to near genius, according to his poppa-in-law. Little else, always excepting his young bride, was able to stir his brain cells into action.

'Er, yes,' he agreed uncertainly, smoothing his already sleek, fair head.

Arbuckle and Crane were upon them. The usual congratulations for the groom and wishes for the bride's happiness were repeated. During the brief pause that followed, Daisy caught a hint of embarrassment marring the Super's placid facade. He turned his head towards his fellow conspirator.

'Waal, have I got a surprise for you folks,' said Arbuckle, beaming. 'I'm tickled to death, Fletcher, to be able to tell you I've been pulling strings in Washington on your account. See, our noo President, Mr Coolidge, wants to clean up the Investigation Bureau of the Justice Department – that's like our national police – and boy oh boy, do they need it! Orgian stables isn't in it, trust me.'

He smirked, pleased with himself at this classical reference. After a momentary vision of mounted police indulging in orgies, Daisy translated it as Augean stables. Her school had not considered Greek and Latin suitable for feeble female minds, but tales from the myths, properly bowdlerized, were staples.

'I've heard rumours,' Alec admitted with caution.

'Graft's the word, right from the top. Burns, the Director, has been using federal employees to run his own 'tec agency. Waal, to cut a long story short, I got put on to this smart young guy who'll likely end up as the boss man. I talked to him on the transatlantic telephone and convinced him he needed to consult with Scotland Yard.'

'And the Sûreté,' put in Superintendent Crane dryly.

'Gotta be fair to our gallant allies, sir, or at least look like it. Anyways, as I was about to say, there's no police department back in the States that's worth a dime, not when it comes to big ideas for organizing things on a sound, honest basis. And once I'd talked round this J. Edgar Hoover guy, your Commissioner was easy as pie.'

'I hope you won't let him hear you say that!' Crane exclaimed, not a little put out.

'All I mean is, he's a reasonable guy,' Arbuckle hastened to assure him.

Daisy, the sinking feeling in her stomach reaching rock-bottom, decided it was time to learn the worst. 'But what was the Commissioner reasonable about?' she demanded.

Arbuckle beamed at her, triumphant. 'Why, first he agreed to send a man over to advise young J. Edgar, and then he agreed that Detective Chief Inspector Fletcher is the best man for the job.'

'But we're only just married!' Daisy wailed, seizing Alec's arm and hanging on tight. Alec put his hand over hers and opened his mouth, but Gloria got in first.

'Poppa, how could you!'

'Now, now, honey, let your old poppa finish. I'm mighty sorry, Mrs Fletcher – I should've started at the other end. You're going too, see, all expenses paid.'

'Oh, but I couldn't possibly accept . . .'

'It's not me that's paying, not but what I would, and be happy to. I owe you big, you and Fletcher, and don't you think I'll ever forget it. While you're in the States, I surely hope – we hope, don't we, honey? – you'll be our guests at my little country place.'

'Gee, sure thing, Poppa. That's a swell idea.'

'We'll all sail together on the SS *Talavera.* But there're others than me glad to pay your fare, Mrs Fletcher. Yes siree, I've been talking to your editors, here in Lunnon and over in Manhattan. Here's a cable from N'York and a letter from the Lunnon guy. You'll see both of 'em want articles about the voyage and your impressions of America.'

Daisy was speechless, thrilled certainly, yet nettled at being manipulated. While she scanned the two messages, Alec turned to Crane.

'I was promised two weeks' leave, sir,' he said flatly.

The Superintendent's face remained bland, but he had a twinkle in his eye. 'Keep your hair on,' he said. 'You get a nice week's sea cruise each way, courtesy of HM Government; and what's more, it's a bonus. The *Talavera* leaves Liverpool on the Wednesday after you're due back on duty.'

'Ah.' Alec remained cautious. 'What about this invitation to stay with Arbuckle?'

'Your return voyage is booked. If you finish in Washington before the time's up, what you do next is up to you.' Drawing Alec a little aside, Crane lowered his voice. 'I'll tell you this in confidence. Arbuckle has a certain amount of influence over here, and we can't ignore a request from the American Government. However, what persuaded the AC to let you go for so long is the prospect of six weeks without Mrs Fletcher getting herself mixed up in any investigations.'

'My mother . . .? Oh, Daisy!'

Crane chuckled. 'Anything she does in America is out of *our* jurisdiction; and whatever happens there, *you* will at least have peace on board ship.'

'Yes,' Alec said hopefully, 'she can't possibly get into trouble aboard.'

# CHAPTER 2

Her back to the rail. Daisy watched the sun setting beyond the superfluous masts and the green-painted funnels with the white W of the Wellington Line. Pink-tinted gulls wheeled overhead, screeching.

'Red sky at night, sailors' delight,' said Belinda in a tearful voice. 'I'm g-glad you'll have nice weather.'

'So you see, darling, we shan't sink.' Daisy pressed the little hand clasped in hers. 'We'll be back in six weeks, safe and sound.'

'Six weeks is an awfully long time. That's nearly to Christmas.'

'That's right. We'll have to do our Christmas shopping in America. Just think of all the unusual presents we'll bring home, Bel!'

'That will be nice,' Belinda said politely, but without interest. 'Only, what if Gran makes me get rid of Nana while you and Daddy are gone?'

Daisy glanced over to where Alec and Mrs Fletcher Senior sat on a bench, talking earnestly. 'Darling, I'm sure the puppy is one of the things your daddy's discussing with your grandmother.'

Alec had sorted out financial business with his mother

before leaving London, but had postponed other matters until the last possible moment. Nana, a frisky, slipper-chewing mongrel whose advent into her orderly household Mrs Fletcher rightly blamed on Daisy, was only one of the ticklish matters he was now having to tackle.

After a blissful week in the Channel Islands, the St John's Wood half of the honeymoon had been difficult. Though Daisy had abjured any desire to change anything (for the present, at least), far less to take over the housekeeping, Mrs Fletcher remained resentful and suspicious. Daisy could only hope her six-week absence would give her mother-in-law time to accustom herself to Alec's remarriage.

In fact, the trip to America was heaven-sent – except for poor Belinda.

Daisy had no further opportunity to reassure the child, as Mr Arbuckle came up to them, already changed into shipboard garb of a greenish Harris tweed plus-four suit. He raised his matching flat cap, then chucked Belinda under the chin and gave her a ten-shilling note.

'Gosh, thank you ever so . . . I mean, frightfully much!'

'It's no use to me at home, honey,' he said jovially, but his anxious gaze was on the after gang-plank, where passengers were still boarding. 'I'm expecting another friend, Mrs Fletcher,' he went on. 'I sure hope he hasn't piked off at the last minute.'

'Piked – oh, hopped it? Why should he?'

'Waal, it's like this, see. Jethro Gotobed's one smart cookie, a real go-getter. He's a farmhand's son who made his first million by the age of forty, but sixty-and-never-been-married is a tough age. Where women are concerned, he's a babe-in-arms. He's got himself involved with a . . .'

Arbuckle glanced at Belinda, who looked back with innocent interest.

'Is his name really Go-to-bed?' she asked.

'Sure is, honey. I asked the self-same question when we were introduced.'

'An old and venerable name, I believe,' said Daisy. 'Goodness knows what the first Gotobed did to earn it.'

Under cover of Belinda's giggles, Arbuckle whispered to Daisy behind his hand, with a significant nod, 'A chorus girl. Seemed to me he'd be a darn sight better off without her, if you catch my drift, so I invited him to visit. I know you and Fletcher are still honeymooners, but I thought maybe you wouldn't mind lending a hand to take his mind off her, give him a gay old time. But he's not here. I guess she's got her hooks into him deeper than . . . No, there he is!'

'Where?' Daisy turned to look down at the bustling quay. Forward, derricks were still swinging cargo aboard, for the *Talavera* was a freighter as well as carrying about two hundred passengers, no steerage, all cabin class. Aft milled a couple of dozen of those passengers and twice as many friends and relatives come to bid them farewell. 'Which is Mr Gotobed?'

'Just setting foot on the gang-plank. The guy in the . . . Waal, I'll be . . . !' Arbuckle groaned. 'Son of a gun, if he hasn't brought the harpy with him!'

A tallish woman clung with a crimson-gloved hand to the arm of a short but burly man. He wore a grey, caped ulster and an old-fashioned cap with peaks front and back and ear flaps now tied up with a little bow on top of his head. Her lush curves, emphasized by a figure-hugging, blush pink costume, defied the current no-bosom, no-bottom mode. Daisy, whose constant fight with her own curves was a losing battle, admired her blatant disregard for the dictates of fashion.

The voluptuous harpy turned her head to glance up, laughing, into Gotobed's ruddy face. The setting sun struck a red gleam from a clasp attaching a bunch of long, pink feathers to her crimson cloche hat.

Belinda had climbed on to the lowest rail and was watching the embarking passengers with great interest. 'Is that lady really a harpist? A lady came to play the harp at school once. I liked it. Do you think I could learn it one day, instead of the piano, when I'm big enough, M-Mummy?'

She still stumbled a hit over the unaccustomed word – her own mother had died of influenza when she was four. Daisy was beginning to grow used to being called Mrs Fletcher, or sometimes Mrs Alec, but 'Mummy' gave her a queer, warmish feeling inside.

'I expect so, darling.'

'Belinda, get down at once.' Mrs Fletcher Senior's scandalized voice came from close behind. 'Only naughty *boys* climb on railings. You will fall.'

Giving Daisy a sideways, conspiratorial look, Belinda lowered one skinny, black-stockinged leg. Daisy put an arm around her waist.

'Don't worry, I'll hold her.'

Her mother-in-law frowned. 'Come along now, child. We have a train to catch.'

Jumping down, Belinda flung her arms around Daisy for a quick hug, then ran to Alec. He stooped and she clung to him.

Mrs Fletcher Senior gave her granddaughter an impatient look. In her Victorian view of the world, not only must girls be young ladies, though boys were permitted to be boys, but open displays of affection were frowned upon. (Daisy had subversive intentions on both fronts.)

She turned back to Daisy and said unconvincingly, 'I'm sure I hope you have a pleasant journey.'

Belinda's hand in his, Alec accompanied the two to the companion-way to the lower deck and handed his mother down. As they disappeared, Daisy tactfully stayed behind with Arbuckle.

'Little pitchers have big ears,' he said. 'If only Wanda Fairchild really was a lady harpist, not a cheap little gold-digger! This is going to be darn awkward.'

'Perhaps she has just come to see him off. Or . . .' Daisy paused as Phillip, his usually pleasantly vacuous face grim, hurried up towing a resigned Gloria in sable-trimmed scarlet.

'Poppa, was that the woman you told us about coming aboard with Mr Gotobed?'

'Sure was, honey.'

'I'm sorry, sir,' said Phillip, 'knowing Gotobed's a chum of yours, but I can't let Gloria associate with his . . . his . . .'

'Floozy.' Arbuckle shook his head. 'I wouldn't let her myself, son, and Miss Dalrymple – Mrs Fletcher – can't be expected to get acquainted with that type of person. But it's going to be mighty ticklish if the poor old simp tries to introduce her around.'

'Assuming they have separate cabins,' said Daisy, with a flash of sympathy for the reviled Miss Fairchild, 'and that he introduces her as a friend, we can't possibly cut her. Or there's always the possibility that your invitation, Mr Arbuckle, expedited . . .'

Again she was interrupted. A boy in ship's uniform loped by, calling, 'All ashore that's going ashore, please! All ashore that's going ashore.'

Arbuckle turned back to the rail. 'Okay, let's see if she goes ashore.'

Along with most of the passengers, they all leaned against the rail, watching the gang-plank. A few dilatory souls were still boarding, against the flow of departing well-wishers. Among the latter, Daisy picked out Mrs Fletcher's old-fashioned, low-crowned black hat with the curled-up brim and Belinda's navy blue school hat. Bel looked up and madly waved a hankie. Daisy madly waved back.

Nowhere was Miss Fairchild's smart, pink cloche visible. Arbuckle hung further and further over the top rail until Gloria grabbed him by the sleeve and hauled him back.

'No sign,' he said, disconsolately.

'Now, Poppa, you know they call out "All ashore" at least half a dozen times and then blow the whistle.'

'That's so, honey. But even if she stays on board, maybe we still have a chance to save him from her clutches. For a start, I'll have a word with the Purser and see that she's seated at a different table from the rest of us and doesn't get a deckchair near us. I've already fixed it so we're all together.'

He started to turn away, already feeling for his wallet.

Daisy put her hand on his arm. 'Hold on a bit, Mr Arbuckle. It would be too fearfully awkward if you tried to separate them and they . . .'

'Mr Arbuckle? Davis, sir, Second Engineer. You requested . . .'

'Ah yes!' Cheering up, Arbuckle turned to Phillip. 'Son, I've fixed for you to take a tour of the engine room. They switched quite recently from coal- to oil-burning engines, I'm told. I thought you'd like to watch as they start things running.'

'I say, sir, what a ripping idea! Lead on, Davis.'

'I'm coming too,' said Gloria.

'Now, honey, the engine room's no place for a lady.'

'That's all right, sir,' Phillip said firmly, linking Gloria's arm through his. 'I'll take care of her.'

'Well!' Daisy stared after them. After all the times Phillip had insisted that writing for money was not at all the thing for a lady, here he was actually encouraging his wife to take an interest in matters mechanical.

'I tend to forget she's married now, not just my little girl,' Arbuckle said apologetically. 'Ah, here comes Fletcher. He's bound to have some good ideas on how to deal with the situation.'

As Arbuckle explained matters to Alec, he and Daisy kept their eyes on the gang-plank. They were taken by surprise when a jovial voice, pure Yorkshire in intonation, came from behind.

'Arbuckle!'

'Gotobed!' Arbuckle swung round. 'I saw you coming up the gang-plank. I'd recognize that monstrosity on your head a mile off.'

Turning, Daisy saw the man in the grey overcoat with its unfashionable cape and the red-and-green-plaid, fore-and-aft cap. He certainly wasn't dressed like a millionaire.

Beside him, her arm linked possessively through his, stood the woman in pink.

Close to, the setting sun full on her face, her heavy maquillage failed to hide the fact that she was a good ten years older than Daisy had expected. Her best feature was her wide, dark eyes. Daisy was not good at judging clothes, but the costume appeared to be expensively tailored. Could the large, rather flashy rosette brooch holding the feathers in her hat be composed of real rubies?

'All ashore that's going ashore!'

'Hadn't you better . . .' Arbuckle started.

Gotobed laughed, his broad, ruddy face bright. 'Oh, she's not going ashore. My dear, this is my Yankee friend, Caleb P. Arbuckle. Arbuckle, meet Mrs Gotobed.'

As Arbuckle gaped, aghast, Mrs Gotobed simpered. 'Charmed, I'm sure,' she said, in a husky contralto with a careful refinement far more painful to the discerning ear than any undisguised provincial accent. With a frankly curious, slightly myopic stare at Daisy, she added, 'This must be your charming daughter, Mr Arbuckle, that I've heard so much about from Mr Gotobed.'

Since Arbuckle was still apparently speechless, Daisy stepped into the breech. 'No, as a matter of fact, I'm a friend of Mr Arbuckle and the Petries – Daisy Dal – Daisy Fletcher, and this is my husband, Alec. How do you do?'

'How do you do?' Alec echoed politely, raising his hat.

'Very well, thank you, and ever so pleased to meet any friend of Mr Arbuckle's, aren't we, Dickie? That's what I call Mr Gotobed,' Mrs Gotobed said confidentially. 'Richard's his middle name, see. Jethro's his first, but *such* a mouthful. I mean, what can you make of it? 'Jethie' just sounds like you're lisping.'

'It does, rather,' Daisy agreed, avoiding Alec's eye lest she giggle. 'How do you do, Mr Gotobed?' She held out her hand.

He shook it heartily. With a doting glance at his wife, he explained, in a voice from which practically all Yorkshire influence had vanished, 'We got married just a couple of days ago, Mrs Fletcher. It's been quite a rush, what with getting Wanda put on my passport and all.'

'Mr Gotobed swept me off my feet, wouldn't take no for an answer. We'll wait till you get back from America, I says, but he wouldn't have it, would you, Dickie-bird?'

'I couldn't risk losing you to some other lucky man,' Gotobed said simply.

The requisite congratulations were forthcoming, Arbuckle speaking them as if they puckered his mouth like pure vinegar. Daisy thought his dismay excessive.

She didn't suppose Mrs Gotobed to be madly in love with her elderly husband, but she appeared to be mildly fond of him. There seemed no reason why she should not cheer his declining years – not that he looked likely to decline in the near future. Arbuckle said the Yorkshireman had never married before, so there were no children to be done out of his millions.

'But where are Mr and Mrs Petrie?' Gotobed asked. 'Wanda is eager to meet them.'

'Oh yes, I'm ever so keen. Mr Gotobed's told me all about them. Mr Petrie's the son of a lord, isn't he? An Honourable?'

Arbuckle glanced at Daisy and opened his mouth. Daisy frowned at him fiercely. She didn't want Wanda Gotobed, or anyone else on board, sucking up to her because she, too, had an Honorable before her name. Alec was likewise incognito. Perfectly ordinary, law-abiding people tended to get shifty-eyed if they discovered there was a Scotland Yard detective among them.

'Gloria and Phillip have gone to take a look at the ship's engines,' Arbuckle told the Gotobeds. 'And I guess you'll be wanting to take a look at your stateroom – cabin, as you Britishers call it.'

'Mr Gotobed's taken a de luxe suite for us, not just a cabin. My maid's down there unpacking. He made me bring a maid, you know. He says you just can't rely on the stewardesses.'

'I expect they're frightfully overworked today, poor things,' said Daisy, who had unpacked and put away her own and Alec's things. The years since her father's death had accustomed her to doing for herself. She didn't want a stranger pawing through her belongings.

Mrs Gotobed gave her an unexpectedly sharp look. 'Yes, I s'pose they are busy,' she quickly agreed, 'poor things. Dickie-bird, let's go and take a peek at our suite.'

'Right you are, love. Arbuckle, Mr and Mrs Fletcher, I hope you and the Petries will join us there before dinner and drink a toast to my lovely bride.'

They all accepted Daisy trying to sound enthusiastic enough to make up for Arbuckle's lack of enthusiasm. The newlyweds departed.

At that moment, the *Talavera*'s steam whistle let go with an ear-shattering blast. Daisy jumped.

'Last warning for those going ashore,' said Arbuckle gloomily, staring after them. 'Which she's not. Wanda

Gotobed. What a name! You'd think that alone would be enough to make him forget about marrying her. Must be all the old goat's thinking about, though, because why else . . .'

Alec coughed.

Arbuckle blushed. 'Pardon me, Mrs Fletcher. This business has me in such a tizzy, I'm forgetting my manners. No offence, I hope!'

'No offence,' Daisy assured him. 'But I don't believe it's as bad as you fear. She may be . . . well, common, but if he's the son of a farm labourer, that very likely suits him better than a wife who might look down on him. And you say he has plenty of money. The worst she can do now is help him spend it. I expect he'll enjoy the process.'

# CHAPTER 3

The Gotobeds' sitting room was three times the size of Daisy and Alec's tourist-class cabin. On the walls hung large paintings of the *Talavera*'s sister ships, *Vitoria* and *Waterloo.* The furniture was in the style of Sheraton or Hepplewhite (Daisy was vague as to which was which), gleaming with polish and silk brocade. Matching curtains hung at the portholes, which were disguised as casement windows, presumably so that the occupants could pretend they were not at sea.

Under one of these windows stood a table large enough to seat four in reasonable comfort. A tray of champagne glasses and a silver ice-bucket with the wired neck of a magnum protruding promised oil to smooth the social waters.

Alec and Daisy were the first guests to arrive.

'Welcome to our home away from home,' Gotobed greeted them expansively. 'Fletcher, mebbe you'd like to tackle the champagne bottle? I've niver opened one in my life. Beer I was brought up on and beer's my tipple, though I confess to an occasional whisky and water.'

'A man after my own heart,' said Alec, grinning. 'I've never opened champagne either, but Great Scott, how difficult can it be? Absolute idiots do it all the time. Let's have a dekko.'

The two men moved over to the table. Alec tore off the foil and, examining the wiring beneath, they discussed the best way to attack it.

'Have a seat, do,' Mrs Gotobed invited Daisy. With a careless gesture, she waved at the room. 'Not bad, eh?'

Daisy detected tension beneath the assumption of nonchalance. The poor woman must feel like a dandelion in a bed of dahlias. Well, perhaps not quite, not with the peroxided, marcelled hair, that fringed, beaded, rose silk evening frock – probably straight from Paris, as was her perfume – and the long rope of pearls which Daisy suspected of being genuine.

Still, Mrs Gotobed was not altogether at ease. Daisy sympathized, remembering how odd she had felt just after her wedding, although she had been amongst friends and relatives.

'Very nice,' she said, glancing around the room again.

The white walls, picked out in gilt, the blue-and-gold brocade and blue-and-white carpet were in the best of interior decorator taste. Daisy preferred the comfortably eclectic decor of Fairacres, where every style from Jacobean onwards had melded over the centuries into its own particular charm, happily unaltered by Edgar and Geraldine. Possibly Mrs Gotobed preferred something gaudier.

'Very elegant,' Daisy assured her. 'I hope your sleeping cabin is comfortable.'

'Oh yes,' said Mrs Gotobed archly. 'Mr Gotobed insisted on me taking forty winks before you came, after such a busy day as we had. I had to chase him out so's I could get ready in time. He doesn't understand yet how long it takes a girl to make the best of herself, even with Baines to help.'

She paused, apparently awaiting a compliment on her appearance, but Daisy's sympathy did not extend quite so far. It had taken her just fifteen minutes, in the cramped little cabin with pipes running across the ceiling, to wash, dress, and powder her nose. She had been feeling quite smart in a new, black georgette frock, dressed up with a cerise chiffon scarf held with a diamanté brooch, until she saw Wanda Gotobed's Paris model.

'It's such a beautiful evening, Alec and I stayed up on deck. It was interesting watching the tugs pull and push the ship out into the channel. Then we met the *Talavera*'s sister ship, *Salamanca*, coming in. I expect you heard the whistles blowing again? They greet each other with a W for Wellington in Morse code, short-long-long. All the *Salamanca*'s passengers were at the rails waving to us.'

Supremely uninterested, Mrs Gotobed complained, 'I don't see why British ships have foreign names. You'd think they'd want to give them good English names.'

'I suppose, since it's the Wellington Line, they thought it a good idea to name them after Wellington's victories.' History at Daisy's school had consisted of long lists of English kings and battles, that she remembered, with dates, that she forgot. 'I wonder if there's a *Ciudad Rodrigo*.'

'But even the big liners of the other lines, like the *Mauretania*, they have funny-sounding names. I'd've rather sailed on . . . Dickie, someone's knocking.'

'Come in, come in!' called Gotobed, striding to open wide the door. 'Ah, Mrs Petrie, come and meet my wife.

You know the Fletchers, don't you? Arbuckle, happen you or Petrie can help us. Fletcher and I are afraid to open the champagne for fear of sending the cork ricocheting around the room, to the danger of the ladies.' He laughed heartily.

'Phillip's your man,' said Arbuckle.

'Aye, o' course, the technical wizard. Just the lad we need.'

Daisy went over to Alec while the introductions were performed, but she observed the participants. Phillip was, as ever, the courteous English gentleman. Gloria, usually outgoing in the American manner, was reserved. Arbuckle looked on with the impassivity of a good butler.

Phillip came to join Alec and Daisy at the table. 'Have to make the best of a bad job,' he said in a low voice, dealing efficiently with the champagne's wire headdress. 'No good getting into a stew over spilt milk.'

'No,' Daisy agreed, 'nor locking the stable door after the cows have come home.'

He gave her a slightly puzzled look, then concentrated on easing out the cork.

*Pop!*

'Ooh, I do love bubbly!' Mrs Gotobed cried. 'I was afraid we wouldn't be able to get it on this ship. As I was just saying to Mrs Fletcher, I wanted to go on one of the big, fast liners, but Mr Gotobed simply wouldn't hear of it. 'Not on your life,' says he, 'not when my friend Arbuckle's booked on the *Talavera*.'

Though this was uttered in a tone as much playful as complaining, Arbuckle didn't take it kindly.

'I prefer smaller ships,' he grunted. 'For one thing, if I must be one of a crowd, I'd rather it was a small crowd.

And then, I saw the *Vaterland*'s arrival and departure from New York on her maiden voyage.'

Phillip looked round from pouring the champagne. 'It must have been quite a spectacle.'

'It was the largest vessel in the world when it was built, wasn't it, sir?' Alec asked, handing round glasses. 'I remember something about its having trouble leaving New York.'

'Trouble! It was darn near disaster. The Germans enlarged her in the building just so as to beat Cunard's *Aquitania*, with no regard for common sense or engineering principles. The noospapers were full of her expected arrival, with the *New York World* calling her a 'sea monster' in huge headlines. Thousands gathered in Hoboken to watch. Waal, she steamed up the Hudson and came abreast her pier. Then a string of barges cut across her bows.' Arbuckle's pause was a masterpiece of the raconteur's art.

Sipping her champagne, Daisy watched Mrs Gotobed's face. At first bored, she was quickly caught up in the story.

Arbuckle continued. 'The pilot ordered the engines cut. The wind and tide and current were all against her, and she started moving broadside downstream. Being so long, she had no room to manoeuvre. They didn't dare restart the engines. More and more tugs joined in – twenty-five in the end, I heard – and they finally managed to stop her just before she went aground on a mudbank.'

'Cripes!' exclaimed Mrs Gotobed. 'And it was worse when it left New York?'

'Much worse.' Arbuckle actually smiled at her. 'She backed out of her berth much too fast, zipped across the river, and got stuck in the mud between two piers on the other side. The engines were reversed at high speed to try to get her off. A couple of small ships docked nearby were sucked from their moorings, hawsers snapping, then flung back against the piers and badly damaged.'

'Cripes!'

'At the same time, the wash of those great engines swamped a coal barge. The captain of that managed to jump to the nearest pier, but the engineer of a nearby tug was d'rowned.'

'Good heavens!' said Daisy.

'Did the *Vaterland* get out of the mud?' asked Mrs Gotobed, agog.

'Yes siree, she pulled out, turned, and steamed off downriver, calm as you please. She was just too big to notice the difficulties of anything smaller. But you wouldn't get me travelling on anything that size, let alone investing in 'em.'

'I'd give something to see her engines,' said Phillip. 'More champers, anyone?' He refilled glasses.

'I can fix it for you to take a look, son,' promised his father-in-law. 'She's sailed under the American flag since the war as *Leviathan.* She's not doing too well, I guess. Prohibition is in effect on board all US ships. I'm as patriotic as the next man, but you won't catch me sailing in her.' He hoisted his glass. 'Here's to my good pal, Jethro Gotobed, and his blooming bride. May they have many happy years together.'

As Fletchers and Petries joined the toast, Gotobed looked delighted, his wife relieved. Daisy thought 'blooming' was an unfortunate choice of adjective. She was not sure whether the American realized its significance in

English slang, but as neither of the principals took it amiss, all was well.

Arbuckle seemed to have resigned himself to his friend's *faux pas*, a changed attitude which was bound to make the voyage much pleasanter.

The *Talavera*'s comparatively small complement of passengers meant that first, tourist, and third classes all shared the same public facilities.

'Real democratic,' Arbuckle observed to Daisy as they entered the extravagantly named Grand Salon, 'but you won't mind that. They clear away the tables after dinner for concerts and dancing and such. I fixed with the Purser to seat us at the doctor's table. He's an interesting guy.'

'The doctor!' pouted Mrs Gotobed. 'We paid for a suite; don't we get to sit with the Captain?'

'We were invited to the Captain's table eastbound,' Gloria told her. 'He hardly said a word. Gee, most evenings he didn't even turn up to dinner. The crossing was kind of rough, and he had to be on the bridge.'

'Cripes, I'm glad we've got fine weather. I dunno if I'm a good sailor or not and I don't want to find out!'

No one pointed out to her that they were still in the Irish Sea, with three thousand miles of Atlantic to cross.

'Where ignorance is bliss . . .' Daisy whispered to Alec.

'I wouldn't mind being ignorant. I'm in the same boat. I don't know if I'm a good sailor and I'd rather not have to find out.'

'I was all right on a roughish Channel crossing when I was a child,' Daisy said doubtfully.

'Don't anticipate trouble, darling. And don't listen to the story the blooming bride is presently recounting.'

Mrs Gotobed had embarked on an all too vivid description of the revolting symptoms suffered by a dear friend on a ferry from Ireland. Daisy, normally the least high-nosed scion of the nobility, decided there was common and then there was common, and Mrs Gotobed was really too, too frightfully vulgar.

Gotobed's gentle hints failed of their purpose. Fortunately, the Chief Steward came over to take them to their table.

Dr Amboyne was already there, standing behind his chair as he waited to see what the Purser had thrown to his lot. His weatherbeaten face broke into a smile as he saw Arbuckle approaching. They shook hands.

'You remember my girl, Gloria?' Arbuckle introduced the rest of his party.

In turn, Dr Amboyne presented them to the passenger already seated on his right. Miss Oliphant was a lady of middle years, somewhere between forty-five and sixty – her round, pink, chinless face was smooth, though her hair, worn in a coronet of braids, was pure silver.

Her brown eyes bright as a sparrow's, she said cheerfully, in the precise accents of a schoolmistress, 'Oh dear, you are all travelling together? I am quite the interloper!'

'Not at all, not at all,' Gotobed assured her. 'It's for us to do our best not to overwhelm you.'

'I am not easily overwhelmed,' she retorted.

He laughed as he pulled out the chair opposite her for his wife. 'Good for you, Miss Oliphant.'

Daisy noticed that his Yorkshire vowels, having reappeared in the intimate setting of his own suite, had once more vanished. Intrigued, she wondered whether the phenomenon was due to a conscious decision or if he had merely, among friends, relaxed his vigilance over his speech. Arbuckle described him as a canny old bird – a smart cookie – in all but his relations with women, so probably he knew exactly what he was doing.

The remaining empty seat was taken by Arbuckle's secretary, a dark, silent, self-effacing man who appeared to be coming down with a heavy cold. Menu cards were studied and discussed. A steward came to take their orders, including Gotobed's for more champagne.

As soon as he left, Mrs Gotobed took up the story of her friend's travails where she had left off. This time, she did not get far.

'The symptoms of *mal de mer* are indeed most distressing,' Miss Oliphant interrupted firmly. Daisy was convinced she had been a schoolmistress. 'However, certain herbal remedies are remarkably effective. I am a herbalist by profession. Once, and in some societies still, many might consider me a witch.'

Mrs Gotobed gaped at her. So did Gloria, who had been talking quietly with Phillip and had only caught the last few words.

'Here, I say . . .' Phillip blurted out.

Miss Oliphant smiled at him kindly. 'I do not deal in spells, Mr Petrie. Besides, I see you and Mrs Petrie have no need of love potions.'

Phillip and Gloria both blushed. Everyone else laughed, except Gotobed, who looked thoughtful. Perhaps he wondered whether Miss Oliphant might be persuaded to provide a love potion for his blooming bride, Daisy thought. She noticed that Dr Amboyne's laugh was rather forced.

So did the witch. 'I do not mean to set up in competition with you, Doctor,' she assured him. 'I am more of a theoretician than a practitioner. I am going to America to study herbs used by the Indian tribes in hopes of discovering some of genuine utility.'

She and Amboyne continued to discuss medicine over the hors d'oeuvres.

Alec asked Phillip about the engines, whose steady throb underlay life on board, felt as much as heard. Phillip and Gloria were both full of enthusiasm, the former for the technical wonders, the latter for the sheer splendour of the huge, shining machinery.

'Shall we see if we can take a tour?' Alec asked Daisy.

'Yes, let's, darling.' She sighed. 'This soup is divine, but after a seven-course dinner every day, I shall have to let out all my clothes when we reach New York.'

'We'll dance all night,' Gloria proposed. 'We get an extra hour at midnight westbound, remember. And we'll play deck tennis every morning.'

Silently, Daisy groaned.

The dancing started that evening, as soon as the dinner tables had been cleared away and a small dais erected at one end of the Grand Salon. Here a three-piece band, piano, violin, and cello, and a tenor singer settled among a forest of potted palms to play foxtrots, tangos, Charlestons, and, for the old-fashioned, waltzes.

Daisy was not keen on dancing. She was certain she had

two left feet, though she could just about manage a waltz, which she had been taught at school. Her war work, in the office of one of the military hospitals near home, had enabled her to avoid what was left of the London social season (to her mother's despair). Throughout their courtship she had successfully evaded displaying her ineptitude to Alec.

Now she could see no escape.

At least her humiliation was postponed – a waltz, 'Dearest One,' had just begun when they re-entered the Grand Salon. Alec swept her masterfully into his arms and whirled her around the floor. So firm was his lead that she had no time for doubts.

Intoxicated with the motion, not to mention four glasses of champagne, she gasped, 'Darling, I didn't know you were such a marvellous dancer!'

Sadness flashed across his face. He and Joan must have loved dancing, Daisy thought. It vanished in a second and he grinned down at her.

'I'm a marvellous waltzer,' he corrected her. 'I'm none so bad at the polka, two-step, and valeta, and I've been known to trip my light fantastic way through a schottische. But I've never tried a foxtrot, let alone a tango.'

'We could sit them out,' Daisy suggested hopefully.

'Consider the alternatives, love. You can abstain from seven courses at dinner, not to mention breakfast, elevenses, lunch, afternoon tea, and, I gather, a midnight snack to keep us happy. You can run around the deck several dozen times daily to work off your overindulgence. Or you can spend your time in New York with a needle and thread.'

'Beast!' Daisy groaned.

A one-step was next. Alec swore it was easy, and a sceptical Daisy discovered even she could do it. A foxtrot followed, to the tune 'Melody Girl'.

'We'll sit and watch for a bit before we tackle it,' Alec suggested. Daisy was not about to argue.

They found a pair of free chairs. Many of the older couples were sitting out the dance at the small tables left around the perimeter, but among those on the floor were the Gotobeds, moving smoothly together in fine style. Gloria and Phillip were also worth watching.

A group of men heading for the nearby Smoking Room blocked their view. With them was a reed-thin girl with a very short, fair bob, very long, dark lashes, very red lips, and a very high hemline, higher even than last year's extreme fashion.

'But, darling,' she was complaining in a high, languid voice, 'I simply must have a cigarette, and some old stick's bound to rag if I smoke in here.'

'Judas Priest, don't be a bore, Birdie,' said the man she addressed. He was tall, thin, sleek, and, despite his American accent, dressed in the best of English gentlemen's tailoring. 'You can't go with us, so can it.'

'Why not? I play poker as well as you do, Chester.'

'It's gentlemen only, baby. Ever hear of smoking-room stories? If you wanna smoke that bad, go up on deck.'

A dull flush mounted her cheeks beneath the white powder. 'On my own?'

'Take your momma. Tell her I said,' he jeered, and moved on with his friends.

She took two hesitant steps after them, then was intercepted by a ship's officer with the face of a kind and intelligent monkey. 'I don't believe you'd enjoy it in there, Lady Brenda,' he said tactfully. 'May I send for your wrap and escort you up on deck? It's remarkably warm for the time of year.'

Hearing him, the American turned back to say, 'Go ahead.'

'Well, I will then,' said Lady Brenda sulkily. 'It'll serve you right if I . . .'

'Oh, you won't, you won't,' he stated with calm certainty, and followed the others through the door.

'I could slaughter you,' she hissed, fists clenched, then turned with a sweet smile to the officer. 'Thank you, Mr Harvey, I'll accept your offer.'

As they went off, Daisy returned her attention to the dancers. To her astonishment, she saw Arbuckle prancing away with Miss Oliphant.

'Alec, look, the witch!'

'If she can do it, so can we. As far as I can see, everyone does different steps anyway. As long as we keep time, more or less, we shouldn't make absolute asses of ourselves.'

Not absolute, perhaps, but Alec's lack of certainty left Daisy floundering, though she did her best to follow his lead. Fortunately several other couples had tentatively joined in without much idea of what they were doing.

At the end, the pianist stood up and announced, 'There will be a foxtrot lesson in here tomorrow after lunch.' Everyone laughed.

Daisy flapped her hand at her hot face. 'What a pity fans are out of fashion!'

'Shall we go out and look at the stars?' Alec suggested.

Up on the boat deck, they found several people strolling about or leaning against the rail. Some were bundled up in coats and hats against the autumnal nip in the air, some just in evening dress, presumably warmed by dancing or drinking.

Daisy and Alec found a semi-private spot between two adjoining lifeboat davits. A near full moon shone down from the star-filled sky, painting a path across the smooth, black swells. Daisy didn't get much chance to admire the scene, though; and in spite of a chilly breeze from the east, which ruffled her shingled hair, she remained remarkably warm for the time of year.

Eventually she disentangled herself and said, 'Darling, must we really dance all night?'

'I can think of more enticing activities,' Alec admitted, pulling her back into his arms for another kiss. 'Let's go down, love. We can always get up early and walk a mile or two before breakfast.'

As they emerged from their nook, another couple preceded them towards the companion-way. Their silhouettes, against the light by the steps, were easily recognizable, one by her knee-length skirt, the other by his uniform.

'Did you hear what she said?' Daisy asked softly. 'About slaughtering that American chap?'

'Silly child!'

'He was a brute. Don't you think it sounded as if he had some sort of hold over her? I wouldn't blame her for poisoning his pottage.'

'Great Scott, Daisy, please! We've been given an extra week of honeymoon. Let's just enjoy it without attempting to solve other people's problems or, heaven forbid, falling over any bodies.'

'Darling, I *am* enjoying it,' said Daisy.

# CHAPTER 4

The Fletchers did not get up early. By the time they appeared on deck, the *Talavera* had passed the Fastnet lighthouse and was ploughing through great Atlantic rollers. The south coast of Ireland was fading on the starboard bow. The weather remained unusually benign for mid-October, but Dr Amboyne, taking the air, reported that quite a few passengers had failed to emerge from their cabins that morning.

'It always happens as soon as we move from the Bristol Channel into the Atlantic,' he said with a heartless grin. 'Some can't take even this calm. There's really nothing I can do for them except advise tea and toast and fresh air. Not many take my advice.'

'Miss Oliphant said she has a remedy,' Daisy reminded him.

The doctor laughed. 'I'm not about to recommend witch-craft to my patients! The Captain would have me in irons.'

Pluming themselves on their immunity to sickness, Daisy and Alec continued their brisk stroll along the boat deck, circling the central massif of the bridge, funnels, masts, skylights, and mysterious machinery. The sun was warm, but it was after all an October morning so most deckchairs were set out on the enclosed promenade deck below. There were plenty of other obstacles to walkers, however, in the shape of ventilation ducts and game players.

They passed Arbuckle, Gotobed, and Miss Oliphant – in purple bloomers – playing shuffle-board.

'The blooming bride's probably still doing her face,' Daisy observed.

'Cat. She may feel games are beneath her dignity. People who feel inferior have to stand on their dignity.'

'It raises them in their own estimation, if no one else's,' Daisy quipped. 'No, that was beastly of me. I must try to be nice to her. I wish I liked her.'

'You can't like everyone, love.'

'Why do I feel I shall very shortly dislike Phillip extremely?' she asked, as that gentleman hallooed and waved them over to where he and Gloria were playing deck tennis against another couple.

'Daisy, Fletcher, we'll take you on next!'

'Phil, you know perfectly well I'm hopeless at games.'

'Gee, Daisy, that doesn't matter,' Gloria assured her earnestly. 'It's only for fun.'

'As long as you don't chuck too many quoits overboard,' Phillip teased.

With deep misgivings, Daisy allowed herself to be persuaded. On their next circuit, she and Alec stopped to play. The best that could be said of her game was that not a single quoit was actually lost, but she enjoyed it anyway.

A second game with Phillip partnering her and Gloria playing with Alec was more evenly matched. At the end, quite a few spectators were there to applaud, including

Arbuckle and Gotobed. Turning over the court to a waiting group, Phillip picked up his discarded jacket and offered his cigarette case to Alec.

'No, no,' interjected Arbuckle, 'have a Havana.' He opened his cigar case.

Alec shook his head. 'Thank you.' With identical gestures, he and Gotobed felt in their pockets and produced pipes and tobacco pouches, Alec's embroidered by Belinda with a wobbly 'A.F.' Phillip took a cigar.

Daisy was not going to wait around for clouds of tobacco smoke. Besides, she was dripping. (Her nanny's maxim: 'Horses sweat, gentlemen perspire, ladies merely glow,' had clearly not been intended to apply to deck tennis.)

'I'm going to change, darling,' she said.

'Me too,' said Gloria, who really was glowing, her golden curls slightly tousled but prettier than ever. 'Daisy, have you figured out what you're wearing for the Fancy Dress Ball?'

'No,' Daisy admitted. 'What about you?'

Together they went down the forward companion-way to the open area of the promenade deck, in the bows, where more deck games were in progress around the cargo hatch. On each side was a door into the enclosed area, the glassed-in promenade encircling the public rooms. Here they parted, Gloria to the port door and thence down the port companion-way to the Arbuckle suite, Daisy taking the starboard door and the stairs just within.

As Daisy moved from the door to the companion-way, she caught sight of Mrs Gotobed some way along the promenade, sitting in one of the slatted, wooden deck chairs. She was talking earnestly with the men in the chairs on either side of her.

The one facing Daisy was large and dark, good looking in a rather flashy way. She rather thought she had seen him with the young American poker player, Chester, going into the Smoking Room. The other was unmemorable, smaller, wiry, with thinning, mousy hair. Both sat stiffly, leaning slightly towards Wanda Gotobed, giving an impression of nervousness.

Hot and sticky, Daisy had no intention of going to speak to the blooming bride. She was about to turn to go down the stairs when Mrs Gotobed raised one hand and touched the smaller man's cheek.

Daisy must have made some involuntary gesture which caught the other man's attention, for he stared straight at her. He said something which made Mrs Gotobed look round and speak sharply. Both men at once rose and, with slight bows, hurried away.

Mrs Gotobed waved to Daisy, an unmistakable summons.

Reluctantly, Daisy went over to her. 'I was on my way to change,' she said. 'We've been playing a rather energetic game of deck tennis.'

'Oh, games! So undignified. Mrs Fletcher, I suppose you've heard I was on the stage?'

'Well, yes.'

'I wasn't a fancy actress or anything, not a star, but I did have my fans,' she said coyly. 'That was a couple of them, just a couple of stage door Johnnies, like they say. They recognized me and had the blooming cheek to come and introduce themselves, would you believe?'

'How . . . er . . . flattering.'

'Well, if you want the truth, it was, and no mistake. Ever so disappointed they was when I told 'em I'm a married woman now and they wasn't to hang about. So I talked to them for just a minute, just to cheer 'em up a bit, like. Only Mr Gotobed doesn't care to be reminded of what I was, so be a sport and don't tell, eh?'

'I wouldn't dream of carrying tales,' said Daisy, trying not to sound indignant. 'Now if you'll excuse me, I really must go and change.'

If Mrs Gotobed wanted to flirt with her admirers, it was none of Daisy's business, though it didn't make her like the woman any better. She just hoped Mr Gotobed would not find out, since she did rather like him.

They all met at the group of deckchairs reserved by Mr Arbuckle, forward, where they would catch the afternoon sun as long as possible. Here the deck stewards served hot bouillon, Bath Olivers and digestive biscuits. It was very pleasant with the sun shining through the glass, the vast Atlantic spread glittering before them. They were still close enough to land for a few seagulls to sail alongside the ship, peering in hopefully. Gloria persuaded a steward to open a window so that she could throw them crumbs. Swooping, they caught them in mid-air, to her delight.

The *Talavera*'s gentle pitch as she cut through the swells was cradle-like, soporific. Daisy started to drift off, only to be rudely awoken by the noon whistle.

Arbuckle jumped up. 'Time for the mileage pool,' he said. 'I'm not a gambling man in the general way, but I wouldn't miss this for the world.'

'Oh aye, it's like putting a fiver each way on the Derby,' Gotobed agreed. 'Almost a patriotic duty.' He and his wife went off with Arbuckle to find out whether the distance the ship had sailed from Liverpool matched any of the numbers they had acquired in the auction pool last evening.

As half the take would go to seamen's charities, the others had each put a shilling in one of the lesser pools. Each drew a single digit to match against the last digit of the mileage. One of the stewards came round the promenade deck to report the result.

In spite of the one-in-ten odds, none of the four had won. However, a few minutes later Miss Oliphant came up to them, glowing with delight at her winnings of seventeen and sixpence.

They congratulated her and invited her to join them. She was a 'nice old bird', as Phillip later remarked to Daisy. Arbuckle and the Gotobeds returned.

'Nowt doing today,' Gotobed reported.

'If you was to ask me,' said the blooming bride resentfully, 'that American Riddman rigged it with the stewards. I ought to've won, if he hadn't got hold of my number.'

'You sold it to him, lass,' Gotobed reminded her with a smile. 'And I seem to remember you were right pleased with the price he paid.'

After glowering at him momentarily, she switched on a blinding smile and squeezed his arm. 'That's right, love; and after all, it was you bought the ticket for me in the first place. So kind he is to his little Wanda!' She mouthed a kiss at him, then turned her glower on Miss Oliphant. 'Hey, that's my chair!'

'I'm so sorry,' said the witch, flustered by the attack, and floundering as she tried to stand at the same time as retrieving her handbag from beneath the chair.

Alec sprang up to lend her his arm, and Phillip knelt down to fish for her bag.

'Don't go, ma'am,' said Arbuckle. 'We can easily get ahold of another seat.'

'No, no, I really must go and tidy myself for lunch.'

'Me too,' said Daisy, trying – as were all the rest – not to look at Gotobed's red face. As she and Miss Oliphant walked towards the ladies' room, Daisy apologized. 'My fault. I should have offered you my chair, or Mr Arbuckle's.'

'My dear, how could you have guessed that Mrs Gotobed was so ferociously attached to that particular seat?'

'I couldn't, of course. After all, I only met her yesterday. But I'm afraid she seems to be rather on the look out for slights.'

'Only natural in her position,' said the witch forgivingly. 'Lavender, I think, to lift her spirits and calm her nerves. Perhaps even St John's Wort. It must be difficult for her, married to a gentleman so superior to her.'

'Oh, but she's not,' Daisy protested. 'That is, Mr Gotobed has lots of money now, but his antecedents are no better than hers.'

'One cannot help but notice the influence of Yorkshire in his speech. However, I referred to his manners, not his birth.'

'Only the most inveterate snob could hold his birth against him,' Daisy agreed. 'From all I've seen, he's thoroughly *nice*.'

'So I have observed. I do not believe him a weakling, however, except in having married a . . . No, I must not cast invidious aspersions! But if I were her, I should take great care how I behaved in his presence.'

'He's no doormat,' Daisy agreed, 'or he couldn't have made his millions. You're right, he worships the ground she treads; but it wouldn't surprise me if he put his foot down if she carries on carrying on.'

Mrs Gotobed was quite subdued at lunch, so perhaps her husband had put his foot down. In fact, Alec told Daisy later that he had whisked her off willy-nilly to their suite on the specious excuse of changing his tie before lunch. She even invited Daisy and Gloria to call her Wanda, forcing them to reciprocate.

After lunch, Alec and Daisy attended the dancing lesson, the teacher adding the tango to the curriculum. Alec emerged confident of having mastered the foxtrot. Daisy hoped she'd be able to follow his lead.

She breathed a sigh of relief when he said apologetically, 'I'm not sure I'm prepared to attempt the tango in public, not among experts like the Petries and the Gotobeds.'

'Let's not,' Daisy said fervently.

Next on the programme came the lifeboat drill. Wanda didn't turn up.

'She said she wouldn't be seen dead in one of these hulking great things,' Gotobed explained, as they tried on the clumsy life jackets under the direction of the second mate, Mr Harvey. 'Leastways, she wouldn't be seen in one unless the alternative was imminent death.'

'There are always a few who don't come,' sighed Harvey. 'Ladies who'd rather risk their lives than don anything so unfashionable, and men who refuse to be told what to do.'

'That's why Chester wouldn't leave his blasted poker game.' Lady Brenda, who had created a fuss at the next boat station until she was transferred to Harvey's boat, batted her eyelashes at him. '*I'll* do anything you tell me,' she cooed, 'but may I take it off now? It's frightfully uncomfortable.'

With great solicitude, he helped her undo the straps. If Wanda had bothered to attend, she could have learnt a lesson about making the best of the most unpromising occasion.

Later that afternoon, Wanda did unbend sufficiently to join Gotobed and Arbuckle in a decorous game of shuffle-board, at which she proved surprisingly adept.

'Not so surprising,' Gloria said when Daisy commented, as they watched. 'Dancing in a chorus line, you'd have to make every move real precise, so your muscles and reflexes would get trained. I guess she'd be good at deck tennis, too, but I doubt she'll play. It might mess up her hairdo.'

Daisy giggled, but said, 'We really must try to be more charitable to the blooming bride. We have the rest of the voyage to get through, and then you'll be entertaining her at the other end, won't you?'

'Yes, Poppa invited Mr Gotobed to stay before he married, of course; but he can't very well take back the invitation, let alone exclude Wanda. You're right, Daisy, I'll try to like her. Come and have a game of tennis now. You'll get better with practice.'

'Not me! I've always been hopeless at sports, though I liked bicycling and climbing trees. Besides, what with playing this morning and dancing and everything, I'm going to be so stiff by tomorrow I shan't be able to move.'

'What you need's a bit of gentle exercise to loosen up those muscles,' said Gloria ruthlessly. 'Come on, I'll coach you so when we play tomorrow you'll dazzle them all.'

'A hot bath, followed by poplar-bark salve,' came a murmur from behind.

'Miss Oliphant!'

'Sorry,' said the witch. 'I do endeavour not to push my remedies, and I promised Dr Amboyne . . .'

'You're not competing with him,' Daisy said, 'since I wouldn't go to him anyway, not for stiffness. Your prescription sounds much pleasanter than Gloria's, though it doesn't seem likely that the shop sells poplar salve.'

'I can let you have some,' offered Miss Oliphant hesitantly.

'Spiffing! Gloria, if the salve works, you can coach me tomorrow, I promise: but it really is time I did a bit of work before I forget my first impressions of the voyage. Lead the way, Miss Oliphant. I'll stagger along after you.'

In a third-class cabin shared with three strangers, the witch showed Daisy her medicine chest, a plain but well polished teak box with a brass lock. It was lined with green plush, with dozens of blue glass vials and jars, neatly labelled, resting each in its own niche. Some of the labels were bright red, Daisy noted, perhaps those of dangerous herbs like foxglove which had both therapeutic and deadly qualities.

No wonder herbalists had been regarded as witches with mysterious powers for good and evil. She wouldn't want to get on the wrong side of someone with that sort of knowledge.

Luckily, Miss Oliphant was a good witch. She refused payment for the salve, saying, 'You will not need a great deal. Rub a little into the stiff muscles and please return the rest.'

'Of course. Thank you so much; it's very kind of you.'

Daisy left the jar in her cabin and went to the writing room. One wall, or bulkhead as it was called by those in the know, was devoted to the ship's library. This was kept in glass-fronted cabinets, not because of its value – it consisted of all the books passengers had brought to read on board and not considered worth keeping – but to stop the volumes flying about in rough seas.

The several writing desks, like the swivel chairs in front of them, were securely fastened to the deck. Like school desks, they had holes to hold sunken inkwells, with the addition of hinged caps to stop ink sploshing about in a storm. At one of the desks, Alec was already intent on the stacks of information his superiors at the Met considered necessary to his job in Washington.

Daisy glanced around. All those reading and writing seemed to be minding their own business, so she kissed the back of Alec's neck, where the crisp, dark hair she loved turned into tiny, curly wisps. He jumped.

'Darling, I couldn't resist. How is it going?'

'Ghastly. Great Scott, they expect me to be a diplomat and a bureaucrat crossed with a don, not a policeman!'

'What a frightful miscegenation! But I know you can handle it, darling. You'll show Mr Arbuckle's J. Edgar Whatsit what's what. I'll leave you in peace – I've got to get deck tennis and lifeboat drills and dancing lessons down on paper, and the auction pool Mr Gotobed explained to me. Not to mention fellow passengers!'

'I wonder if I ought to warn them?' Alec mused.

'Don't you dare! They won't be half so amusing if they know they might turn up in a magazine article. Names changed to protect the guilty, of course.'

'I hope so. The AC would have a fit if you were sued for libel.'

They both stayed there for a couple of hours. Daisy did not have to go in search of tea. A steward brought it around, complete with triangular, crustless cucumber and gentleman's relish sandwiches, assorted biscuits, and those decorative *petits fours* which look so much better than they taste, as Daisy told herself firmly.

In due time, she went down to bag the bathroom they shared with three other cabins. Whether it was the poplar-bark salve or simply the hot seawater, she felt much less stiff after her bath. She returned to the cabin feeling able to face an evening of dancing.

Under Lucy's critical eye, Daisy had bought two new evening frocks for the trip. Both were simple, so that their appearance could be altered with a coloured scarf or a length of the newly fashionable coloured glass beads.

The black she had worn last night. Tonight she put on the dark blue silk charmeuse, the shade of the sky when the first stars come out. It consisted of a thigh-length tunic over a straight underskirt to just above the ankles, more flattering to her figure, according to Lucy, than anything with a belt around the hips.

Alec came in just as she put a long string of azure blue beads over her head.

'Just the colour of your eyes,' he said approvingly, kissing the tip of her nose. 'You look stunning, love. Every man there will want to dance with you.'

'Oh, gosh, I do hope not!'

'Don't sound so panic-stricken. We'll tell them we're still honeymooning.'

Daisy breathed a sigh of relief.

After dinner, they waltzed together to 'Swanee River Moon', watched a tango, then tackled a foxtrot while the tenor warbled some sort of twaddle with a chorus beginning, 'Stealing, stealing with your eyes appealing . . .' Daisy didn't think she utterly disgraced Alec, but in spite of his strong lead, she was so tense she was exhausted by the end.

Alec grinned at her as she sank into a chair. 'They're playing Schubert and Dvorak tomorrow afternoon,' he said. 'You'll enjoy that.'

'As long as I don't have to dance to it!'

'All you need is practise, darling.'

'I feel such an absolute ass.'

'We must practise in private. There's nowhere on board, but when we get ashore . . . In the meantime, suppose we go "stealing" away to see what the moon's doing tonight?'

Up on the boat deck, it was a little warmer than the night before. The almost balmy breeze came from the southwest, rather than the east, sending wispy clouds drifting across a haloed moon.

'"Wrapped in a gauzy veil",' said Daisy, who knew her English literature if she knew nothing else, 'but it never looks to me "like a dying lady, lean and pale". More of a "Goddess excellently bright".'

'Mmmm,' said Alec, putting a stop to Ben Jonson and Percy Bysshe Shelley alike in the most agreeable manner possible.

For some minutes Daisy was too busy to contemplate the moon or attend to her surroundings. Low voices, the scrape of a match nearby, footsteps coming and going barely impinged upon her consciousness, but she was jerked back to awareness by a sudden, wordless yell, followed by a splash.

'Man overboard!' someone bawled, and others took up the cry.

Alec sprang into action. Grabbing the nearest lifebelt, he hung over the rail, peering down at the water. 'There!' He flung the belt. 'Damn, he's gone down again!'

Heart in mouth, Daisy leant beside him as a second lifebelt spun down. In the moonlight, the bow wake was a white frill, losing definition as it spread. The water just below them was a dark, heaving mass, glimmering as it swelled and receded, with the white circles of the lifebelts floating swiftly backwards as the ship steamed on. Daisy and Alec ran aft, along with an agitated group, trying to keep up with the receding circles.

Between the rings, something broke the surface. Arms reached upward, flailing, begging for help.

'The belt!' shouted several voices. 'Grab the belt!'

As the drowning man floundered towards the nearest lifebelt, Daisy discovered she was holding her breath. Suddenly she realized that the throb of the engines, the constant, unheeded heartbeat of the *Talavera*, had ceased.

'Fast reflexes on the bridge,' Alec commented.

'I think he's got it,' someone said. 'Yes, he's got it!'

'Hang on!'

'Hold hard, fella, we'll get you out of there.' That was surely Harvey, the second mate – and a dozen seamen had materialized on deck. 'Here, men, this boat. Lower away, now! Ladies and gentlemen, out of the way, if you please.'

They moved back, crowded to the rail a little further along. Someone was sobbing. Daisy clung to Alec, weak with shock and still tentative relief. Creaking, the davit swung the lifeboat out over the side and began to lower it.

'Lights!' called Harvey impatiently.

'How the dickens did he come to fall?' a man wondered aloud.

'I saw it,' a hysterical voice responded. 'He was pushed!'

# CHAPTER 5

Electric lights sprang to life, drowning the shifting moonlight. Their faces white in the glare, the group at the rail stared at each other.

The sobs emanated from Lady Brenda. 'I saw, I tell you,' she insisted, covering her blotched face with her hands. 'Don't look at me like that. I saw, I saw!'

On realizing who had made the startling announcement, most of the spectators turned back to the rail. Alec's arm, which had tensed beneath Daisy's hand, relaxed.

'Little fool,' he murmured, 'just trying to be the centre of attention.'

'Maybe,' said Daisy, 'but whether she saw something, or imagined it, or made it up, she's had a shock. If she feels like me, she's all quavery inside. Mr Harvey's busy, that beastly man she was with isn't here, and she doesn't seem to be with anyone else.'

'Great Scott, Daisy,' Alec groaned, 'must you invariably find some lame duck to take under your wing?'

'I'll just help her over the stile,' she promised, wrinkling her nose at him. 'I hate to miss the rescue, but I'd better take her below. You watch and tell me all about it.'

With a sigh, Alec gave in. 'All right, but don't go putting

any more ideas into her head. And tell her not to broadcast her story any further. She might start a panic.'

Daisy went over to the girl and put her arm round her shaking shoulders. 'Lady Brenda, you don't know me from Adam – or Eve, rather, but won't you let me help? My name's Daisy Dal – Daisy Fletcher. It was a beastly shock when he fell in, wasn't it? I'm all shaky. We'll both feel the better for sitting down with a cup of tea.'

Lady Brenda raised red-rimmed eyes. 'You don't believe me, do you?'

'I have an open mind on the subject. We'll talk about it, if you like; but if you're certain of what you saw, you should tell the Captain.'

'Oh no! Ron – Mr Harvey – says Captain Dane is a frightful Tartar.'

'Well, tell Mr Harvey then,' Daisy said pragmatically, 'but I wouldn't go shouting it to the world if I were you. Come on, let's go below now. It's turned freezing out here.'

She urged the girl towards the aft companion-way. As the ship lost way, the rocking motion became more pronounced. Descending the steep, ladder-like stair to the promenade deck, they hung on tight to the rail.

Through the glass, they could see passengers inside thronging to the port side, where the man had gone overboard. The news had spread quickly. Quite a few people came out on to the open stern deck. Most rushed to the port rail, but several made a dash for the starboard side, where they leaned over, heaving. The increased motion had discommoded quite a few previously contented stomachs.

'I can't go to our cabin,' wailed Lady Brenda. 'Mumsie's been seasick since we left the Mersey.'

'We'll go to the ladies' lounge.' Daisy glared at a man pushing through the door until he stepped aside and held it open for them. 'I doubt many . . .'

'Say, Mrs Fletcher!' Arbuckle hailed her. 'Were you out there? Did you see what happened? They say some guy was pushed overboard.'

Daisy frowned at him, squeezed Lady Brenda's arm warningly, and said in her firmest tone, 'Someone fell over the rail. I expect he'd had a few cocktails too many. Alec threw him a lifebelt and he managed to catch hold of it. If you hurry, you'll see the poor chap hauled aboard.'

'Too much to drink, eh?' The look Arbuckle gave her suggested he didn't swallow her story but was willing to go along. 'Must be a fellow-countryman. With our danged Prohibition, people don't learn to hold their liquor like they used to. You want to go rubberneck, Miss Oliphant?'

The witch was just behind him. 'I believe not.' Thoughtfully, she regarded Lady Brenda's pale face. 'But don't let me keep you, my dear sir. I dare say Mrs Fletcher will not mind describing the scene above, which will be quite enough excitement for me.'

'Okay, ma'am. See you later then.'

'My dear Mrs Fletcher,' said Miss Oliphant, 'you have had a nasty shock, I'm afraid. Our good doctor would prescribe brandy, I suspect, but I cannot advise it. Be guided by me, and let me procure you some camomile and lemon balm tea. Both of you.'

'Oh yes, thank you, or anything hot.' Daisy supposed she must look as shaky as Lady Brenda, who was shivering convulsively though they were now out of the wind. 'We'll go to the ladies' lounge.'

'Ask the stewardess for blankets and hotwater bottles, child, and tell her to boil water for a tisane.'

Miss Oliphant hurried off down the companion-way to the cabin deck. Daisy, her arm around Lady Brenda's waist, started for the lounge. As they approached the wide double doors to the Grand Salon, she heard a waltz beginning. A moment later, Phillip and Gloria came out.

'Daisy, I say, is it true . . . ? Here, I say, old sport, you look rotten!'

'Thanks a lot, Phil!' Daisy pulled herself together. After all, the unfortunate man overboard was being rescued. It wasn't nearly as bad as falling over dead bodies – well, finding them lying about – which she had an unfortunate habit of doing. 'I'm all right, but Lady Brenda's feeling pretty ghastly. Give her a hand to the ladies' lounge, will you?'

'Oh, Daisy, did you see the guy fall in?' asked Gloria, as Phillip, ever the gentleman, took over the job of supporting the drooping girl. 'Golly gee, that must have given you quite a fright.'

'Be an angel, Gloria, and don't let's talk about it just now. I'm worried about Lady Brenda.'

'Let me help. Is there anything I can do?'

'Yes, darling.' Daisy took over Lady Brenda again at the door to the lounge. 'Ask the stewardess for blankets and hotwater bottles while I get her settled.'

The ladies' lounge was decorated in ivory and half a dozen shades of pink, all lace and flounces, so twee as to be sickening. However, it did have comfortable chairs and a couple of chaises longues; and as Daisy had suspected, it was nearly empty at that hour. Lady Brenda was draped on a chaise and the attendant bustled about swathing her in rugs and hotwater bottles.

Daisy sank into a nearby chair, and Gloria perched on the edge of another, all agog. Though exhausted, Daisy had got over the worst of the shock. Now she wanted to question Lady Brenda about just what she thought she had seen, but it couldn't be done with so many ears close by.

She was on the point of advising Gloria to find Phillip and hurry to see the end of the rescue, when it dawned on her that there might be no happy ending. The man might have lost his grip on the belt before the rowers reached him. Much better if Gloria stayed where she was, even if the interrogation of Lady Brenda must be postponed.

In any case the girl was still in no state to answer questions. She lay slumped against the cushions. As far as one could tell through the smeared powder, rouge, and eye makeup, her face was white as a sheet.

'She looks pretty bad,' Gloria whispered. 'Shouldn't we send for Dr Amboyne?'

'He'll be busy with the chap who fell in. Miss Oliphant – ah, here she is.'

The witch came in, with two of her blue glass jars in her hand. Daisy noted the red label on one. She was too worried about Lady Brenda's condition to quibble. She couldn't imagine any reason why Miss Oliphant might have it in for the girl, and so precise a person would surely not make a mistake about dosage.

Besides, if Lady Brenda became ill after drinking the tea, the culprit would be obvious. Miss Oliphant was not such a fool.

The stewardess, who had at hand all the necessary apparatus for making tea or coffee, had water boiling. In no time the herbs were steeping. The steam coming from the teapot's spout smelled more like new-mown hay than lemons, more appropriate for horses than invalids, Daisy thought. However, she accepted a cup, glad to see that Miss Oliphant was also going to drink some of the medicinal brew.

'A sedative,' the witch said, smiling, 'but very mild, and I happen to like the flavour.'

Gloria sniffed the scented steam, her nose wrinkling. 'Gee, you mustn't waste any on me,' she said tactfully. 'I wasn't out there when it happened. Let me help Lady Brenda with hers. Here, honey, let's just sit you up a bit. There, that's dandy. Take care now, it's hot.'

As Lady Brenda reached for the cup and saucer with a tremulous hand, adorned with a large, diamond engagement ring, the familiar throb of the ship's engines started up again.

'Oh,' she cried, 'they must have got him aboard! Don't you think so, Mrs Fletcher? Now *he'll* be able to tell them what happened.'

Daisy caught the slight stress on 'he', and wondered whether the brainless, 'bright young thing' was sharper than she appeared. At least she had realized the sense in not parading her unverifiable story.

Miss Oliphant took a sip of the tisane, so Daisy tried hers. It tasted just as it smelled. Mentally holding her nose, she drank some more. At least it was hot and wet.

The *Talavera*'s roll was easing as she got under way, cutting through the waves instead of wallowing. Daisy finished her tea and was about to excuse herself to go and find out what had happened when the door to the lavatories opened and from the inner room tottered Wanda Gotobed.

'Has this bloody ship stopped see-sawing?' she demanded.

'Yes, madam,' the stewardess assured her. 'It's always a bit uncomfy when they cut the engines at sea.'

'Uncomfy! Why the hell did we stop? I've been sick as a dog, and all that stupid woman in there can say is fresh air helps some people and no one ever died of it.'

'Ginger or mint,' Miss Oliphant murmured to Daisy as the stewardess defended her colleague, 'but I don't suppose Mrs Gotobed would accept anything from me. In any case, it is best taken before symptoms arise.'

'Come and sit down, Wanda,' Daisy invited. 'I'm sure you'll feel better shortly.'

'Oh, it's you, Daisy. Have you been sick, too? I can't see why they'd want to stop the engines in the middle of the sea, unless they broke down. Don't tell me the bloody engines broke down?'

'No,' Gloria broke in, 'a man fell overboard and they had to stop the ship to fish him out.'

Looking horrified, Wanda gasped, 'Fish him . . . ? No, don't tell me, Gloria. I'm not feeling strong enough for . . . Gawd, it wasn't . . . it wasn't my hubby, was it? Break it to me gently!'

'We don't know who it was,' Daisy said, 'but there's no reason to suppose it was Mr Gotobed. Was he up on the boat deck?'

'He went up to smoke his pipe. He says the Smoking Room stinks. I came in here to powder my nose; then I started spewing up my guts and . . . Oh, Gawd, Daisy, what if it's him?'

'I'm sure it isn't,' Daisy said soothingly, but she did not recall seeing Gotobed among those who had gathered at the rail on the boat deck. 'I'll go and see what I can find out.'

'Me too,' said Gloria, jumping up.

Daisy glanced at the heavy-eyed girl on the chaise longue. 'I don't think Lady Brenda should be left alone.' Especially alone with the appalling Wanda.

'I shall be happy to keep Lady Brenda company,' offered Miss Oliphant. 'Another cup of tea cannot hurt her and might help.'

Daisy leant over Lady Brenda. 'Just take it easy,' she said. 'Don't try to talk.'

Nodding, the girl touched Daisy's arm. 'I'm feeling much better. Thank you!'

'I'll be back. Wanda, you don't look at all well. Why don't you go to your suite and lie down? I'm sure you're worrying for nothing, but if . . . if there's bad news, I'll come and tell you, I promise.'

'Blimey, no. I'm that wobbly, I'd never make it. 'Sides, I wouldn't want to be alone at a time like this.'

She certainly would not be alone in the lounge. A number of women had entered since the *Talavera* had resumed her voyage. Two or three, pallid-faced, staggered out of the inner room and sank into chairs. Others came in from the promenade, chattering about all the excitement.

'Unconscious or dead, they say,' Daisy overheard as she and Gloria made for the door.

'But who *is* he?'

'No one seems to know.'

Almost certainly not Gotobed then. Someone would have recognized the occupant of one of the only two suites aboard, possessor of a glamorous wife much younger than himself, and therefore indubitable target of gossip.

'Alec will know if anyone does,' said Gloria.

'Not necessarily. He's incognito, remember.'

'I bet he's found out by now.'

They went out to the promenade. At once four figures converged upon them: Alec, Phillip, Arbuckle – and Gotobed.

'Mr Gotobed, thank heaven!' Daisy exclaimed. 'Wanda has been unwell, and . . .'

'She's ill?' cried the anxious husband.

'No, not really, just suffering from the effects of the increased rocking when the ship stopped.' The men, even Wanda's adoring spouse, all took on the smug look of those immune to seasickness. 'But she's feeling pretty rotten, and she's got into a bit of a state. She says you went up to the boat deck, and she's taken it into her head it was you who fell overboard.'

'I was only up there a few minutes. Then I went back to the Grand Salon to wait for her. I must go to her!'

'You can't go in there,' said five voices in unison.

'Ladies only, sir!' added Phillip, horrified.

'Wanda's just fine.' Gloria put in. 'Miss Oliphant's looking after her and Lady Brenda, probably gotten her to drink a dose of lemon balm by now.'

'Miss Oliphant?' said Gotobed doubtfully. 'She's an admirable lady, but I don't know . . .'

'I'll go and tell Wanda you're safe and sound,' Daisy proposed, 'and bring her out to you.'

Wanda burst into floods of dramatic tears at the news. At least, she sobbed noisily into her handkerchief. Daisy could not help wondering if they were stage tears. The blooming bride might well be slightly disappointed at the survival of her rich, elderly husband.

Chiding herself for uncharitableness, Daisy patted Wanda's shoulder. 'Pull yourself together,' she urged. 'Mr Gotobed is worried about you.'

'Not half as worried as I was about him. It's the relief, that's what.'

'I know, but he's waiting for you. Do come along.'

The sobbing ceased. 'I must look a real fright. I must powder my nose,' said Wanda, and, handkerchief to face, hurried into the inner room.

Daisy turned to Lady Brenda and found her fast asleep. 'The lemon balm really worked,' she said to Miss Oliphant. 'At least, I'm not at all sleepy – but on the other hand, I don't feel jumpy from shock any more.'

Miss Oliphant smiled. 'That is probably because you are a strong-minded young woman, but perhaps the tisane helped. I am delighted to hear that the unfortunate person who fell overboard was not Mr Gotobed. Have you discovered who it was?'

'No, I didn't have a chance to ask Alec if he had found out. I only wish it may turn out to be the beastly bully Lady Brenda appears to be engaged to. But if her mother is incapacitated, perhaps I ought to let him know she isn't well?'

'I think not, my dear. As she fell asleep, Lady Brenda murmured a few words which I understood as "Don't tell Chester".'

'That's the chap. I wish I knew . . . but as Alec says, it's none of my business. We can't leave her here though. I'll have to get a steward to carry her to her cabin.'

'She can walk,' said Miss Oliphant quite sharply. 'It was not a narcotic that I gave her. She will be the better, however, for sleeping a little longer.'

'Right-oh. If you don't mind staying with her, I'll deal with Wanda first.' Strong-minded or not, Daisy began to wonder why on earth she had taken on responsibility for two weak-minded females. 'Or I'm sure Gloria would take over.'

'Mrs Petrie is an obliging child, but I assure you, I am perfectly happy here.' She took a book from her handbag.

As she opened it, Daisy glimpsed the title: *Poisonous Plants of North America.* Assuredly, it would be unwise to get on the wrong side of the witch!

Daisy went to collect Wanda. She found her seated before the wide looking glass, concentrating earnestly on outlining her mouth with crimson lip-rouge.

Seeing Daisy's reflection, she said defensively, 'Mr Gotobed likes me to look smart. When you get to be my age, you'll understand how important it is to always make the best of yourself. Not that I'm *that* much older than you.'

Daisy hastily powdered her own nose, noting that her hatless hours on deck had already brought out a new crop of freckles. She had given up her fruitless efforts to conceal the little mole by her mouth when Alec told her a face-patch in that position was known as 'the Kissing' in the eighteenth century – he had studied the Georgian period at Manchester University.

She delivered Wanda to Gotobed. Tenderly solicitous, he bore her off to their suite to recover from her tribulations.

'Now,' said Arbuckle, 'I went along with Mrs Fletcher and I've been telling all and sundry how it was liquor that did the damage. But l heard differently, and I wanna know what's what.'

'Not here,' said Alec.

'Okay, come along to my suite then.'

'I ought to get Lady Brenda to her cabin first,' said Daisy wearily.

'We'll see to that, won't we, Phil?' said Gloria.

'What? Oh, right-ho, if you say so, Glow-worm.'

'Bless you, darling.' Daisy kissed Gloria's cheek. She was beginning to think that Phillip could not possibly have done better for himself.

As they followed Arbuckle to the suite, Alec said to Daisy, 'I assume you have already found out exactly what Lady Brenda claims to have seen.'

'No, actually.'

'Then I'm astonished that you left her in other hands,' he teased.

'I'm tired, darling. Besides, by the time she got over being too upset, she was too sleepy to answer questions. The witch's potion really seemed to work.'

'You let Miss Oliphant administer a potion? Suppose she'd been in league with the thrower overboard and wanted to silence the only witness?'

'You don't believe in the thrower overboard,' Daisy pointed out. 'Anyway, she couldn't very well poison her so publicly, and she and I both drank the tisane, too. I'll talk to Lady Brenda tomorrow.'

'By which time,' Alec said with satisfaction, 'she'll have thought better of her story, if she made it up; or she'll realize she can't be sure of what she saw in that shifting moonlight. Too much to drink is a much more likely explanation.'

'We shall see,' said Daisy.

Arbuckle's suite was even more spacious than the Gotobeds', having two sleeping cabins and a commensurately larger sitting room. The paintings on the walls were of the *Salamanca* and the *Ciudad Rodrigo.* Otherwise, the furnishings and colour scheme were just the same.

'Nightcap?' offered Arbuckle. 'I guess you won't want Scotch whisky, Mrs Fletcher. How's about some malted milk? My little girl always has a cup at bedtime. Ovaltine it's called in England.'

'Thanks, I'll wait till Gloria comes. Alec, do you know who it was, the man overboard?'

'No. I waited till they brought him up, but no one there recognized him.'

'He . . . he didn't drown, did he?'

'No, love, but he wasn't capable of speech. Harvey rushed him below to the sickbay.'

'What's this about someone pushing him in?' Arbuckle asked.

Alec sipped his whisky while Daisy told Arbuckle about Lady Brenda's hysterical outburst up on the boat deck.

'I don't imagine there's anything in it,' said Alec. 'With the clouds sliding across the moon, every shadow seemed to move. Lady Brenda is not a reliable witness in any case. A decidedly flighty young thing.'

'Her story oughta be investigated though,' said Arbuckle.

'Well, it's not my pigeon, thank heaven,' Alec pointed out. Arbuckle frowned.

# CHAPTER 6

'He's gone and told the Captain I'm a Met detective!' Alec groaned, closing the cabin door. He waved the sheet of paper handed him by the messenger. 'Captain Dane wants to see me after breakfast.'

'Mr Arbuckle gave you away?' Daisy swung round from the tiny mirror above the washstand, where she was brushing her hair. 'What a rotten thing to do! Now I'll be cut out of things altogether.'

'I doubt it, love. I shall tell Dane firmly that I'm sure it's a storm in a teacup. So you'll be able to investigate away as much as you like.'

'You only say that because you don't think there's anything to investigate,' Daisy said resignedly. 'Right-oh, I'm ready. And I'm starving.'

As they walked along the passages and up the stairs to the dining room, it became obvious that the *Talavera* was pitching more than she had the day before. The motion was even a bit more than when the engines had stopped, though not enough to require the use of the handrails on the corridor bulkheads. Up in the enclosed promenade, a small boy with a toy motor car was having a wonderful time letting it race downhill in one direction as the bows went up, and the other when the stern rose.

It was no surprise not to see Wanda in the dining room. She had earlier announced that she was 'banting' and never ate breakfast, but this morning she was no doubt prostrate, as Gotobed confirmed.

'T'poor lass doesn't want anyone but her maid by her,' he said, sounding very Yorkshire in his distress, which did not, however, appear to affect his hearty appetite. 'As if I'd care a jot that she's looking peaky.'

'I fear Mrs Gotobed was unwilling to try the remedy I suggested last night,' said Miss Oliphant.

'Aye, well, happen she'll have changed her mind by now. I'll pass on t'offer again, and thank you kindly.'

Dr Amboyne was the only other person missing from their table, presumably not suffering from seasickness. Other tables had more gaps, Daisy noted, though some were probably first-class passengers breakfasting in their cabins. A majority of the passengers were present and eating with various degrees of heartiness.

After the exertions of the previous day, Daisy had an excellent appetite, but Alec had lost his. In fact, served with a poached egg, he stared at it with loathing and requested its immediate removal.

'I'm not very hungry,' he said. 'Tea and toast will do me.'

Daisy looked at him with concern. 'Darling, you're not . . .'

'I'm perfectly all right,' he snapped, 'just not very hungry.'

He toyed with a piece of toast for a couple of minutes, until Arbuckle's kippers, a taste he had developed in England, were served. The smell wafted down the table, and Alec rose abruptly.

'I might as well go and see the Captain right away,' he said. 'Get it over with.' He hurried out.

'I'll try to persuade Alec to give your potion a chance, Miss Oliphant,' said Daisy, 'but he'll have to admit, first, that he's seasick.'

As long as Alec kept moving, he was all right. As he mounted the forward companion-way to the boatdeck, he repeated to himself that he just was not hungry. A Chief Detective Inspector of Scotland Yard could not possibly suffer from seasickness like any ordinary passenger. After all, he had not been sick on the boat to Jersey. Admittedly the Channel had been unusually calm both ways – like a millpond, the boatman had claimed.

Crossing to the bridge, he stood at the door for a moment, wondering whether to knock or walk straight in. The bridge was something of a holy of holies, he gathered, like the Commissioner's office at the Yard.

But standing and waiting was not a good idea. He was definitely just a touch queasy. All that rich food, he thought; he simply wasn't used to it.

The door opened. Mr Harvey's monkey-face smiled a welcome.

'Chief Inspector Fletcher? Come in, Captain Dane is expecting you.'

His mind on his middle, Alec was not his usual observant self. He was aware of a vast sweep of sea and gun-metal sky beyond the curved window, the gleaming wheel with its protruding spokes, and the man at it, who did not glance round at his entrance. He recognized the Captain in the large man, besprinkled with gold braid, who took a pace forward to meet him.

'Good of you to come, Chief Inspector,' Captain Dane grunted. He wore a beard and moustache reminiscent of the Kaiser, an impression which bellicose eyes of a pale, chilly blue did nothing to dispel. 'Mr Harvey here's come to me with a lot of stuff and nonsense about skulduggery regarding the fool who fell overboard last night. A cock-and-bull story if ever I heard one! There will have to be some sort of investigation, I suppose, as it seems to have spread among the passengers – among them this fellow Arbuckle, who informed me of your profession.'

'I'm inclined to agree with you, sir, that it's nonsense.'

'Of course it is,' Dane said angrily. 'Murders do not take place on my ship. Sort it out with Harvey. I've a storm ahead to keep my eye on.'

A storm ahead? Alec's stomach lurched.

'If you'll come into the chartroom, sir,' Harvey invited, 'we shan't be in the way.'

At least he couldn't see the sea from the chartroom. There was not much floor space, but what there was Alec utilized to pace, in the process backing Harvey into a corner.

'Tell me,' he growled.

'I understand you were on deck when it happened, sir. I expect you heard Lady Brenda cry out? I didn't, or at least I didn't hear what she said, being already occupied in lowering the boat.'

'Yes, I heard her claim that she had seen the man pushed.' Alec did his best to concentrate, to take his mind off his own woes. 'By the way, I assume he has been identified by now?'

'A Mr Denton, a tourist-class passenger travelling with his wife. Dr Amboyne says he's in pretty poor shape, I'm afraid.'

'I'm sorry. But Lady Brenda was hysterical, you know. I think we can discount what she said last night.'

'I know she was overwrought, but she's not hysterical this morning. She sent me a note quite early.' He flushed. 'We've become quite friendly, as it happens. I went to meet her, and she told me she was absolutely certain she saw someone push Denton over the rail. I know she was in a good position to see what happened. You see, we . . . we were together on deck last night.' His colour deepened.

'As you were there, you know that the moonlight was fitful and the only electric light was a not very bright one by the companion-way. I'm sure Lady Brenda believes what she says,' Alec lied, 'but it seems to me probable that she imagined the whole thing or perhaps misinterpreted something she actually saw.'

'Maybe.' Harvey looked troubled.

'There is another difficulty with her story. I should like to discuss it with you, but you must give me your word not to mention it to Lady Brenda until I have seen her.'

'You have my word,' the second mate said stiffly.

'Thank you. What's her surname, by the way?'

'Ferris. Her mother's Lady Wilmington.'

Alec nodded. 'Now tell me, how easy would it be to push a man over the rail?'

'Not easy,' Harvey conceded. 'It's about waist-high to the average man. You might catch a tall man off balance with a good shove, but Denton's on the short side.'

'That's what I thought, watching you bring him up. Unless he was knocked out and pushed before he fell to the deck, the chances of his going over seem to me pretty slim. And we can assume he wasn't unconscious, since he squawked.'

'A blow might have dazed him just enough to make it easy to push him over.'

'Possibly. Dr Amboyne will be able to tell me if there's any contusion. Lady Brenda hasn't mentioned a blow to the head?'

'No. You know, sir, the best way to do it would be to grab him around the legs and heave.'

'Exactly,' Alec agreed cordially. 'And I don't want you putting that idea into the girl's head. If that is what she describes to me, then of course I shall have to take a more serious view of the matter.'

'You will talk to her then, sir?'

Alec sighed. 'Since Captain Dane has asked me to investigate, yes. I'll have to see Denton as well, of course. Victims of unanticipated violence not uncommonly forget the details of the attack, but at least he should be able to tell me whether he has any enemies who might be on the *Talavera*. I'd hate to think we have a homicidal maniac aboard.'

'Ye gods, yes!' Harvey exclaimed, paling. 'Don't even suggest the possibility to the Captain!'

While Alec was concentrating on the interview with Harvey, his stomach seemed to have adjusted somewhat to the ship's motion. He passed back through the bridge with barely a qualm, acknowledging Dane's glare with a noncommittal 'I'll see what I can do, sir.'

He crossed the deck with his eyes averted from the swaying horizon, so he did not see Daisy until she said, 'What's going on, darling?'

'Captain Dane doesn't credit the girl's story any more than I do, but he can't ignore it, of course. I'm elected to investigate, thanks to Arbuckle.'

'I suppose millionaires get used to doing things their own way. What's first? Do you want me to take notes?'

'Great Scott, no! This isn't an official enquiry. Here, hang on to the rail going down, Daisy,' he put in as they reached the companion-way, 'or you'll take a tumble. First of all, I'm going down to the sickbay to have a word with Denton, the chap who fell over. I'll be surprised if he doesn't clear up the whole business by admitting he was tiddly and turned giddy.'

'Probably,' Daisy admitted regretfully.

'I believe you'd prefer mayhem!'

'Oh, Alec, not really. I'm delighted that Denton didn't drown.'

'Yes, thank heaven. At worst it was attempted murder, not murder. Not that I think for a moment it was either.'

'But a drunken accident is simply too dull, too prosaic for words,' Daisy mourned.

She wrinkled her adorable nose at him, so he pulled her into the lee of a ventilation shaft and kissed her. Since she responded with her usual enthusiasm, several minutes passed before they went inside.

This morning there was no squabbling over the port side deckchairs. Not only was there no sun to make it preferred over starboard, but the number of passengers seeking seats had diminished considerably. Reminded of the reason for the reduction, Alec felt his inner qualms return.

There had been no deck stewards setting up games on the boat deck, he realized. Quite a few hardy souls were setting out for their usual tramps around the ship's circumference, but today more of them were down here on the promenade deck than up above in the fresh air.

'I left Phillip and Gloria trying to convince the third officer that the sea isn't too rough for deck tennis,' said Daisy. 'Failing that, they're hoping for a tug-o'-war. I'm coming with you.'

Alec didn't feel up to a probably fruitless effort to dissuade her. They went down to the cabin deck and along to the doctor's quarters amidships.

Here at the comparatively still centre, the pivot of all the complex motion, Alec perked up again.

Below the sign on the door that read DOCTOR was another saying ENTER, so they went in, into a small waiting room. A desk faced them, with what appeared to be an appointment book lying open on it, but no one behind it. On one side was a door labelled SURGERY, opposite another labelled SICKBAY. The kind of chairs meant to discourage lingering stood stiffly along the walls.

On one of them sat a large, robust woman in a flower-print frock, with grey hair in a bun, rosy cheeks, and red eyes.

'The doctor's busy,' she said in a strained voice with a marked East Anglian accent. 'Nurse, too, in there.' She pointed at the sickbay. A sob escaped her.

'Mrs Denton?' Daisy rushed to her side, and put an arm around her massive shoulders.

Nodding, Mrs Denton groped for her handkerchief, a sodden mass in her lap. With an inaudible sigh, Alec took out his and handed it over. The case – if case it turned out to be – was full of weeping women.

He was wondering whether to knock on the sickbay door or leave a message on the desk for the doctor, when the door opened and Amboyne came out. His face lined with weariness, he went over to Mrs Denton and said heartily, 'We'll pull him through, never fear. You really must get some rest, or you won't be able to take care of him when you're needed.'

'Do let me help you to your cabin,' said Daisy. 'You'll feel much better for a cup of tea, I'm sure, and perhaps something to eat.'

'Oh, I couldn't,' mumbled Mrs Denton, but she lumbered off with Daisy.

There she went again. Alec thought resignedly, weaseling herself into the middle of things as usual. In no time she would probably have the woman confiding that her husband was a confirmed drunkard prone to dizzy spells. Trust Daisy!

'Bless her,' said Amboyne. 'What can I do for you, Fletcher? Not seasick, I assume. Those patients rarely make it to my surgery, and there's not much help I can give them anyway, poor devils.'

'I am not seasick,' Alec said, more loudly and firmly than he had intended. 'In fact, I'm not a patient. Much against my will, I've been unmasked as a policeman, and Captain Dane wants me to find out just what happened to Mr Denton. I've one or two questions to put to you; then I must speak to him.'

'Impossible, I'm afraid.'

'I promise I shan't . . .'

'I mean impossible. I'm not just being cautious. Denton is comatose. He has developed pneumonia, and whatever I may have said to his wife, I'm not at all certain I can pull him through.'

# CHAPTER 7

Daisy got the cabin number from Mrs Denton and steered the weeping woman along the corridors, feeling rather like a tug tackling the *Vaterland.* On the way, she collared a steward and ordered tea and sandwiches to be brought to the cabin.

Hearing the number, he protested, 'But that's in tourist. We don't –'

'This time you do,' Daisy informed him, attempting to infuse her blue eyes with some of Alec's grey-eyed iciness or at least her mother's hauteur. 'Doctor's orders.'

'Yes, madam. Right away.'

The cabin was more or less a replica of the Fletchers', with nowhere to sit but the berths or a couple of fold-down seats.

'At least it's private,' said Daisy, as Mrs Denton flopped down on one of the berths.

'Oh yes, ma'am. Our Danny wouldn't hear of me and Pa going third. That's not much better than steerage, he said. We'd've had to go in sep'rate cabins, him with men and me with women I didn't know.'

'You mustn't call me ma'am. Alec and I are tourist class, too.'

'But you talk posh; I can tell you're a lady. We're just plain Suffolk farm folk.'

'Is Danny your son?'

That was the right question. Mrs Denton's mind was taken off her husband's plight to dwell on the excellencies of their youngest. Having emigrated to America and made good, he had paid his parents' fares to visit him.

'He wanted us to give the farm to his brother and go and live there,' said Mrs Denton, 'but me and Pa, we're stuck in our ways, I reckon. Time enough for Albert to get the farm when we die. 'Sides, there's Albert's kids, and Betty and Molly married with kids and living in the village just by. We wouldn't feel right leaving 'em all.'

A Suffolk farmer – what enemies could he possibly have? There might be local people he had offended, Daisy supposed, but surely fisticuffs outside the village pub on a Saturday night were more likely than following him aboard the *Talavera* to murder him.

Albert, eager to inherit before his time? Presumably he had been left in charge of the farm during his father's absence, and he had a wife and children, so he could hardly depart for several weeks without being missed. In any case, if Danny had had to pay the Dentons' fares, it didn't sound as if Albert was likely to be able to afford a ticket.

While Daisy pondered, Mrs Denton had gone on to enumerate her swarms of grandchildren, with names, ages, and salient characteristics. Unfortunately, Albert's youngest's chief delight was following his grandpa around the farm 'helping'.

'He's only five, but he does what he can.' Mrs Denton's

broad face crumpled. 'And now, lor' knows if he'll ever see his grandpa alive again!'

A knock at the door saved Daisy. Tea and sandwiches arrived. Mrs Denton accepted a cup of tea and drank thirstily but waved away the sandwiches.

'I couldn't, not while Pa's lying there . . .'

Daisy put the plate on the berth beside her; and as she went on talking, the sandwiches gradually disappeared.

'Never had a day's illness afore, my Bert, saving little accidents like you get on a farm. Healthy as a horse, the doctor said, when he went in to get his hand stitched up a month or two back.'

'Then I'm sure he will recover nicely.'

'Oh no, ma'am. The doctor – this ship's doctor – he says Bert breathed in water into his lungs, and that and the cold's gave him new-monier. How come he fell in, that's what I want to know. We was in the Grand Saloon watching the dancing and he had a pint of mild, that's all.'

'Just one pint?' Daisy asked.

'Just one. He's not a tippler, my Albert, not like some I could name.'

'And then he went up to the boat deck?'

'Aye. "I fancies a pipe, Ma," says he, "and a spot o' fresh air. Coming up with me?" says he. "Not me," says I, "'tis mid-October, not midsummer. You wrap up, go get your coat and hat on," I told him. 'Course at home he's out in all weather, but sea air, it's not like at home, is it?'

'Bracing,' Daisy suggested.

'That's it, bracing. Everyone knows you can't trust it. It must've made him come over dizzy, mustn't it? And if I'd gone along like he wanted me to, maybe I'd've been able to catch him!'

'And maybe you'd have been pulled over, too.'

'What'll I do without him?' Big fat tears dribbled down her plump cheeks, but a vast yawn took her by surprise. 'Beg pardon, ma'am. I was up all night, you see.'

'Then you must lie down now to keep your strength up, as Dr Amboyne advised. I'm sure he will send word if there's any change. Shall I help you get ready for bed?' Daisy offered bravely.

'Oh no, thank you. You've been that kind, but I'm used to doing for meself. I didn't think I'd be able to sleep a wink, but . . .' She yawned again.

'You will let me know if there's any way I can help, won't you? Here, I'll write down my name and cabin number.' Daisy tore the sheet from the notebook she carried at all times. 'You can always send a steward to find me.'

Mrs Denton looked alarmed at the thought of ordering one of those grand beings to do her will, but she nodded, and Daisy left her yawning.

Yawns being contagious, she yawned herself as she set out to look for Alec. Not that she felt in the least sleepy. She was dying to hear what he had found out from Denton, though the more she considered, the less probable it seemed that a Suffolk yeoman farmer should be the target of murder. Of course it had been an accident.

She stuck her head into the doctor's waiting room, but no one was there. Alec might have been in the sickbay still, but she doubted he would spend so long with a man as ill as Denton must be. She went on up to the promenade deck.

Arbuckle and Gotobed were ensconced in their deckchairs. As Daisy approached, she gathered that they were arguing over whether shipping or aviation was the best investment for the future.

'There will always be a place for ships, any road,' Gotobed conceded, 'for large and bulk cargoes, and for pleasure cruises. But for people travelling long distances, the day of the aeroplane is coming, mark my words.'

'Not much! You're never going to find that many people willing to take their lives in their hands in one of those crates. Say, Mrs Fletcher, how'd you feel about going up in an airplane?'

'Alec has promised to take me up one day,' said Daisy, smiling at his surprise. 'He was a pilot in the Royal Flying Corps during the war. Have you seen him, by the way?'

'Not since breakfast, which he left in an almighty hurry,' said Arbuckle, and Gotobed shook his head. They both had that smug expression of the non-seasick.

Daisy gave Arbuckle a severe look. 'He went to see the Captain. I've talked to him since then.'

'You must think I'm a regular blab-mouth,' said Arbuckle penitently. 'Spilling the beans to the Captain about Fletcher, I mean. But there seems to be some question about what happened last night, and there's no one I'd rather trust to clear it up.'

'It doesn't look as if there's anything in it. I wonder where he's got to?'

Taking her leave, Daisy heard the argument resume behind her.

'And what's more, airplanes are always on the fritz. You'd never keep to a schedule.'

'Now that's where America's behind Europe! We've already got passenger air service companies running scheduled flights between big cities. I've flown from London to Paris myself and on to Berlin.'

'Is that so?' said Arbuckle, as Daisy passed beyond earshot.

She knew Alec wanted to talk to Lady Brenda. The writing room seemed a good place for a quiet interview, so she headed that way. Then she saw the girl, huddled in a deckchair with a plaid rug over her knees. She was alone and looked thoroughly miserable.

'May I join you, Lady Brenda?' Daisy asked.

'Oh yes, please do, Mrs Fletcher,' said Lady Brenda eagerly, 'but please drop the title. Call me Birdie. Everyone does.'

'Right-oh, and I'm Daisy.'

'I want to thank you for last night, Daisy.'

'Gosh, that was nothing. I'm glad Miss Oliphant was able to help you. Did you sleep well?'

'Marvellously. Better than in a long time. Chester said I was beginning to look like an old hag, with bags under my eyes. Chester's livid – he says I have to apologize,' she added resentfully.

'Apologize? Whatever for?'

'For getting all "het up", in his words, and spreading rumours.'

'Then you didn't see Mr Denton pushed over?' Daisy tried not to sound regretful. 'Have you already told my husband?'

'Mr Fletcher? No, why? I don't believe I have met him.'

'Maybe not,' Daisy said vaguely. 'Why on earth did you make up a story like that, Birdie?'

'But I didn't! Chester thinks I was just trying to make myself interesting, bid I wasn't, truly. I saw someone creep up to him – Mr Denton, you said?'

'Yes. Creep? Bent double?'

'No, just walking slowly and cautiously. At least, that's the impression I got, as if he didn't want to be heard. And then . . .' Brenda looked sick at the memory.

'He pushed?'

'Not exactly. He suddenly bent down. I thought he must have spotted some money someone dropped and wanted to bag it without being noticed. Then he gave a sort of heave and the other man practically flew over the rail. That's when I screamed.'

'Gosh. I don't blame you!' Daisy was puzzled. After talking to Mrs Denton, she had pretty much given up on the attempted murder theory, but Brenda was much more convincing this morning.

No doubt Alec would point out that she had had all night to think up improvements to her story. He would trot out that favourite quotation of his from *Mikado*: 'Merely corroborative detail intended to lend artistic verisimilitude to an otherwise bald and unconvincing narrative.'

'It was simply frightful.' Brenda shuddered. 'I'm so glad they fished him out. But you won't tell anyone else, will you? Ron – Mr Harvey – asked me to keep it to myself so as not to start a panic on the ship. And *please* don't tell Chester I told you. He's got a fearful temper.'

'Of course not. Is he your brother?' Daisy asked disingenuously.

'My fiancé. I hate him!' she said, in a low voice but with startling vehemence.

'Then why?'

'Money. My father died less than a year after my grandfather, and the death duties were simply *crushing*. Mumsie squeezed enough out of my brother – not that it's his fault, poor pet – to take me up to London for a husband-hunt. I don't suppose you went through all that. I'm not saying I didn't have fun, all the parties, dancing till dawn and then piling into someone's car and motoring to Maidenhead to go on the river, silly stuff like that.'

'And then you met . . . What's his surname?'

'Riddman.'

'Riddman?' Daisy had a vague memory of having heard the name recently, but could not remember in what context.

'Chester F. Riddman III, "the Third" meaning old money by American standards. His great-grandfather bought the patent of the safety pin from the inventor, for a hundred dollars, and made millions. Chester's grandfather decided it was time the family added a spot of blue blood, so he sent Chester to Europe to find a titled bride. And he found me.'

'But he can't have forced you to get engaged.'

'Oh no, I liked him right from the first. And I thought he liked me.' Brenda sounded bewildered. 'We had a lot of fun together, doing all sorts of crazy things. I was thrilled when he asked me to marry him and so was Mumsie. Not that she approved of all our larks, but she liked the look of the money. So we got engaged, and that was fun, too. We had a ripping engagement party at the Ritz, and all my friends were frightfully envious.'

'Then what went wrong?'

'We'd been going to a gambling club, a swish place, lashings of good champagne, not a dive, but it was madly exciting because it could have been raided by the police at any moment. We – Oh, hello, Miss Oliphant.'

'Good morning, my dear,' said the witch, with a kindly smile. 'I hope you feel better this morning?'

'Much. Won't you sit down? It was frightfully kind of you to take such good care of me last night. I was an absolute ninny making such a fuss, but it was a fearful shock seeing Mr Denton fall overboard.'

'It was most fortunate that you did, or he might not have been rescued so promptly, if at all.'

Brenda brightened. 'That's true, isn't it? But I shouldn't have let my imagination run away with me.' She cast a look of appeal at Daisy. 'The moonlight was very deceptive, wasn't it?'

'Frightfully,' said Daisy, then caught herself up. It was rather *infra dig*, she had decided, for the wife of a Detective Chief Inspector to go around saying 'frightfully'. 'Clouds kept dashing across the face of the moon,' she explained to Miss Oliphant, 'so shadows moved, or at least seemed to.'

She was no nearer coming to a conclusion as to whether Brenda's story was true. For once she would be glad to let Alec make up his own mind without trying to influence him.

With Miss Oliphant sitting on Brenda's other side, Daisy was not going to hear any more about Chester Riddman. She was about to excuse herself to resume her search for Alec when a young deck steward brought elevenses, the usual bouillon and biscuits.

'Not many customers this morning,' he said with a cheeky wink, 'and it'll get rougher before it gets smoother.'

'I say, don't frighten the ladies,' said Phillip severely, coming up behind him with Gloria.

'I seem to be quite all right,' Daisy said cautiously.

'So far,' observed the steward, not quite sotto voce. 'Another biscuit, madam?'

Daisy took two, just in case Phillip and Gloria inveigled her into any vigorous games. They joined the group, and the others were treated to a tug-by-tug description of the tug-o'-war.

'I busted three nails,' said Gloria ruefully, spreading her hands, 'and chipped the polish. I better go make an appointment at the beauty parlour for a manicure.'

'I'll come with you,' Brenda said. 'I must get my hair done. The salt air is simply murder.'

They went off together, and then Miss Oliphant went to look for a library book, leaving Daisy and Phillip together.

'Have you seen Alec?' she asked. 'I don't know where he's got to.'

'Seasick, isn't he?' Phillip said with a heartless grin. 'He left breakfast in quite a hurry. I expect he's in your cabin in bed.'

Daisy was indignant. 'He's done lots since breakfast. The Captain asked him to investigate Mr Denton's falling overboard.'

'How do you like being married to a 'tec, old bean?'

'He hasn't done any detecting since we've been married, except this business, and it doesn't look as if there's anything in it.'

'I suppose you're mixed up in his fishy business, as usual. Dash it, Daisy, why don't you keep your nose out of things?'

'You're a fine one to talk! It's not so long since you begged me to sort out your own fishy business.'

Phillip had the grace to look abashed. 'That was for Gloria,' he said doggedly in extenuation. 'And . . .'

'And Alec had to join in and pull your hot potatoes out of the fire for you. He nearly got into frightful trouble over that.'

'Yes, but that's his job. He really ought to stop you meddling in his cases.'

'He can't,' she said with considerable satisfaction, 'though actually it's just as often I who involve him. I just seem to land in the middle of things.'

'At least you'll stop this writing tommy-rot now you're married.'

'Not likely!' Daisy exclaimed. 'Even if I wanted to, or Alec wanted me to, which he doesn't, your own poppa-in-law's responsible for my present job of work. *You* introduced him to me.'

'Americans,' Phillip muttered, 'they don't quite cotton on to what's expected of a lady.'

'I didn't notice you trying to stop Gloria going with you to inspect the engines. Don't let's quarrel, old dear. I really must go and find Alec. I'll try the cabin first,' she conceded.

'Right-ho. Dashed fond of you still, you know, old bean,' Phillip said anxiously, giving her a hand to rise from the low deckchair. 'Just feel I ought to put in a word since Gervaise can't.'

Daisy patted his cheek. 'I know, Phillip. But I never did anything Gervaise told me to; and to do him justice, he rarely tried to make me. Toodle-oo.'

'Pip-pip. See you at lunch.'

Making her way down the companion-way, Daisy realized that the *Talavera* was tossing about noticeably more than earlier. The handrails along the passages came in useful now and then to steady her steps. At one point, she didn't grab on quite quick enough and found herself on the opposite side of the corridor. The heaves and bucks were fairly regular though, once one caught their rhythm. It was rather like dancing.

She found Alec not in but on his berth, curled up and hugging his stomach. He groaned as she entered, but he did not open his eyes.

Daisy was glad to see that the white china basin on the floor between the berths was empty. No doubt it was a wife's duty to hold his head, make soothing noises, and empty slops, but the longer she could postpone it the better. It was entirely by choice that she had worked in a hospital office, not on the wards as a VAD nurses' aide, in the last years of the war.

'Poor darling.' Sitting down on the other berth, the one they had both squeezed into every night so far, she noticed the spray constantly spattering the porthole. She regarded Alec's greenish pallor with sympathy – and a touch of smugness, she had to admit to herself.

'Go away and let me die in peace.'

'No one ever died of seasickness.'

'Maybe not, but just now I'd like to.'

'Buck up, darling,' Daisy said bracingly. 'I've got lots of news.'

'There's nothing wrong with my ears, and I can hear just as well lying down. With my eyes shut.'

'Right-oh, but first tell me what Denton told you. Everything I've discovered may be irrelevant.'

'He's too ill to speak. He wasn't hit on the head, Amboyne says, but he's unconscious, lucky devil.'

'Oh dear! The Dentons first, then. Mrs Denton says they're ordinary farm people, from Suffolk. A younger son emigrated and made enough money to pay their fare for a visit to America. The older son is in charge of the farm while they're gone. He'll inherit it when Denton dies, but I can't see him sneaking away to sea to bump his father off, let alone hiring someone to do it, can you?'

Alec groaned.

'According to Mrs Denton, her husband is not a big drinker and is healthy as a horse – or was till last night. Not subject to dizzy spells, but she suspects the effect of the sea air, which everyone knows is treacherous.'

'It's not the air; it's the water,' Alec muttered.

'Denton only had one pint of beer last night,' Daisy continued, 'before he went up to the boat deck to smoke his pipe. I didn't like to ask if he's the quarrelsome sort, who might have made enemies. Even if he is, I simply cannot believe a village squabble could lead to an elaborate plan for murder at sea. And the odds against anyone he knows being on board by chance must be astronomical.'

'Nautical, at any rate.'

'If you're making bad jokes, you must be feeling a bit better, darling. I'm sure a breath of fresh air, however treacherous, would do you good.'

Alec merely grunted, but at least his eyes were open now.

Guessing that listening to her kept his mind off his troubles, Daisy quickly went on. 'On the other hand, I bet everyone in the Dentons' village knows all about their trip, what ship they're sailing on, how long they'll be away, the lot. You're a townsman, but that's how it is in the country. So if someone did dislike him enough to plot to kill him . . .'

'Highly improbable.'

'You really believe the whole thing is a storm in a teacup?'

'Don't talk to me about storms!'

'Sorry, darling. Well, since you've squashed my only conjecture arising from what Mrs Denton told me, I'll go on to Brenda.'

'Dash it, Daisy, you didn't question Lady Brenda!' He sat up and swung his legs off the berth. 'I wanted to talk to her before anyone put any ideas into her head.'

'I didn't mean to. I was looking for you and she was sitting in a deckchair looking so miserable I couldn't just go past.'

Alec sighed. 'No, knowing you, I suppose you couldn't. All right, what did she have to say?'

'I didn't exactly question her either, nor put ideas into her head. She was dying to talk. Chester Riddman, who's her fiancé, told her to apologize for making a fuss and spreading rumours.'

'I thought so!'

'Wait! So I asked her why she'd made up such a story, and she said she hadn't. She saw a man sneak up on

Denton. He bent down and she thought he'd stooped to pick something up – perhaps he'd noticed something valuable which he didn't want to be seen snabbling. But then he heaved and Denton flew over the rail. Well, toppled, anyway.'

'Merely corrob –'

'– orative detail intended to lend verisimilitude . . . I knew you'd say that.'

'All the same,' said Alec thoughtfully, 'it's exactly the scenario I'd envisioned.'

'I suppose it would be pretty difficult to send someone over with just a shove.'

'Yes, but I wouldn't have thought she was bright enough to work it out for herself.'

'She's not really thick,' Daisy protested, 'just rather silly.'

'I wonder whether Harvey is sufficiently infatuated to suggest it to her in spite of my prohibition.'

'Harvey? The second officer? I thought he was just doing his duty by a prominent and pestiferous passenger.'

'Up on the boat deck in the moonlight?'

'I wouldn't put it past Brenda to drag him there. She may not be thick, but she's pretty silly.'

'I dare say, but I doubt it took much dragging. *She* may only be trying to score off Riddman. Harvey's smitten.'

Daisy frowned. 'All the same, why would Harvey explain to her the best way to chuck a man overboard? Just so that she wouldn't look quite such an utter ass?'

'It's weak,' Alec admitted, 'but possible. I'll have to ask him. Sorry, love, for a minute it did seem that Lady Brenda's story might have something in it.'

'It still might. You don't think she's in danger, do you, if she really did see something?'

'Hardly. Since she broadcast the news to the world immediately, there's no reason to shut her up.'

'No, of course. Then we come back to why on earth anyone would . . . Oh, Alec, what if it was a mistake? Suppose Harvey mistook Denton for Riddman and decided to dispose of the competition?'

'What an imagination you have, love!'

'No, seriously, darling. You're the one who said he's madly in love with Brenda. I get the impression Riddman has some sort of hold over her, and she claims to hate him. It would explain her hysterics if she suddenly realized the wrong man went over.'

'Great Scott, Daisy, are you inventing complications just to get me up and moving? I suppose now I'll have to investigate the possibility of a Suffolk small farmer being mistaken for an American playboy. I wonder what Denton was wearing?'

'You didn't ask Harvey? He must know as he hauled him out. And Riddman's probably in the Smoking Room. You can look for him after lunch.'

'Urgh,' uttered Alec, reaching for the basin. 'Go away!'

Wishing she had not mentioned smoking or lunch, Daisy fled.

# CHAPTER 8

Banished from Alec's side, Daisy felt rather at loose ends. She wondered what she could do that would help him without irritating him.

Or perhaps irritation was an efficacious remedy against seasickness. At least she might try to get a physical description of Mr Denton to see if he could possibly have been mistaken for Riddman. The latter, she recalled, was tall and thin. His darkish hair had been sleeked back, and he was very well dressed – unlikely to be true of Denton. But if Denton had put on an overcoat and hat, as instructed by his wife, the pomaded hair and perfect evening togs would be hidden, so to speak.

Denton had gone up to smoke his pipe. Did Riddman ever smoke a pipe? He looked more the cigarette or cigar type. Brenda would know, of course, but if there was anything in the theory at all, she was probably involved. Alec would be simply livid if Daisy put her on the *qui vive.*

The first thing was to establish whether Denton was tall and thin.

Mrs Denton should be sleeping. Daisy didn't want to ask the steward she had had to put in his place. Dr Amboyne was the man to approach. She knew him, and he knew Alec was supposed to be investigating, semi-officially.

In the waiting room, a fair, plump woman in nurse's uniform, crackling with starch, was putting sticking plaster on the forehead of the small boy who had been having such fun with his toy car. Daisy sat down and waited patiently.

'You want to be careful in these seas, Mrs Beale,' the nurse said to the child's mother. 'Don't take Bennie out on the open deck. Little kiddies lose their balance that easy, and we don't want him sliding over the edge, do we?'

'It's criminal,' said Mrs Beak fiercely in a rather adenoidal voice, 'the way there's that great gap below the bottom rail. Why, anyone might slide through.'

'Well, we haven't lost anyone that way yet.'

'I'm going to get my husband to write to the steamship company. They ought to put in a solid barrier.'

'Oh, they can't do that. They have to be able to sluice down the deck, and then think what'd happen when the seas come over.' The nurse laughed merrily. 'My heavens, you'd have water sloshing back and forth with no way out, and then sometimes when the waves are big we get fishes and octopuses, even sharks landing on the deck. Wouldn't want them barricaded in, would you?'

Mrs Beale gaped at her, appalled. 'Waves come over the promenade deck?'

'Not often,' the nurse disclaimed hastily.

'Gosh, Mummy, I hope a octopus comes and I can catch it and keep it for a pet!'

'You are not going out on deck unless there's a dead calm, young man. And don't say "gosh". Thank Nurse nicely and come along now.'

They left, and the nurse turned to Daisy.

'Do you really get sea creatures landing on deck?' Daisy asked.

'Oh yes, madam. Not that often though. I wanted to make sure Mrs Beale doesn't take the little one out. You never can tell what some mothers'll do, 'specially when they're used to a nanny, but I didn't reckon on the young limb wanting to take home an octopussy for a pet.' She laughed again. 'Fancy that! I hope I haven't put ideas into his head. Now what can I do for you, madam? Surgery's closed and Doctor's not in.'

'I just wanted to ask after Mr Denton. I was in here earlier with my husband, and I met Mrs Denton.'

'You'll be the lady took her to her cabin?' The nurse nodded approvingly. 'Doctor told me about you, and he said Captain Dane asked your hubby to find out how Mr Denton came to fall. Mrs Fletcher, is it?'

'That's right. Unfortunately, Alec's been laid low by seasickness. Would you mind if I asked you one or two questions?'

'Right you are. I'll just pop in and see how he's doing. Doctor's catching a spot of shut-eye having been up all night, so I don't leave him alone for more than a minute or two when there's something needs doing in here. I'll be right back.'

She popped and returned, shaking her head.

'Not good?' said Daisy.

'His breathing's something awful, poor lamb. I hope he's not going to slip away. That's why I went to sea instead of hospital or private work, we hardly ever have people pass on, which is what I don't care about with nursing, to tell the truth. What did you want to know, madam?'

'Mostly just whether he's tall or short, fat or thin. Alec's trying to work out exactly how he could have fallen over the rail.'

'It is odd, isn't it? He's on the short side, sort of stocky if you know what I mean, not a big man but quite strong I should have thought. After all, he's a farmer and it's a hard life. My uncle's a farmer.'

If Denton was short, that just about put paid to Daisy's theory. He could not have been mistaken for the tall, thin American. On the other hand, it made it less likely that he could have fallen without a boost. 'What was he wearing when they brought him in?' she asked, in case the information might turn out to be useful anyway.

'Oh, we weren't here, me and the doctor, not right away. By the time they fetched us both, Mr Harvey'd stripped Mr Denton's wet stuff off and had it taken away. All sailors know it's the wet and cold that's worst, you see; it can kill you even if you haven't inhaled water, like poor Mr Denton did. It's a wonder they got him out quick enough that he didn't drown. Like I told Mrs Denton, it's Fate, that's what it is, and he's not meant to go yet. "You hold that thought, dearie," I told her.'

'I'm sure it's a comfort to her,' Daisy said sincerely. She had known too many nurses, in that wartime hospital, who always prophesied the worst. 'Thank you so much for your help.'

'Is that all? Well, that wasn't hard, I must say. What does Mr Fletcher think happened then; was it just an accident or did the young lady really see – Oh, bother!' she exclaimed as a passenger came in and deprived her of her gossip, to Daisy's relief. 'Can I help you, sir?'

'Nurse, my wife's most frightfully ill. You simply must do something!'

'Seasick? Dry toast or plain biscuits and fresh air.'

'I insist on seeing the doctor.'

'Dr Amboyne won't tell you any different, sir, and that's the truth. He was up all night with a patient, and you won't catch me waking him, not for seasickness.'

The passenger started to argue. Daisy slipped out with a farewell wave, wondering whether she could coax Alec to eat some dry toast and go up on deck. Perhaps he'd be willing to give Miss Oliphant's remedies a chance, too.

She would try after lunch, she decided, or else she might find herself missing the meal to share his spartan rations.

In the meantime – she glanced at her wristwatch, a present from Alec – it was too late to get any work done, even if she had not left her notes in the cabin. She might as well see if she could find out what Denton had been wearing. It just might be significant. Alec was always saying any detail could prove vital.

Since Denton was short and sturdy, Lady Brenda could not possibly have mistaken him for Riddman. She was no longer a suspect, so Daisy could ask her about the clothes. Clinging to the handrail, she went up to the promenade deck.

Arbuckle, Phillip, and Gloria were on their reserved deckchairs, Arbuckle with his head bowed over some number-covered papers on his lap. Miss Oliphant was with them. Daisy asked Gloria if she knew where Brenda was.

'She's having her hair done. They gave her an appointment right away because so many people are laid low.'

'Has Mr Gotobed succumbed?'

'No, he went to see how Wanda's doing.'

'Alec's feeling pretty rotten.' She glared at Phillip when he snickered. 'Miss Oliphant, if I persuade him to take it, can you spare some of whatever it is you recommend?'

'Of course, my dear, though I must remind you that, as I said, it is better taken before the onset of symptoms. Still, I have plenty of mint tea, a mixture of peppermint and spearmint, and if that does not help, enough ginger for one or two people. Should either relieve Mr Fletcher, however, I must ask you not to trumpet my fame abroad. I have not sufficient for everyone aboard.'

'I bet they have ginger in the galleys, though,' said Gloria. 'Is yours the same as cooking ginger?'

'The grated root is to be preferred to the powdered form. I should not wish anyone who failed to be helped by the powder to discount therefore the efficacy of all herbal remedies.'

'Maybe they have some roots,' said Phillip, unfolding his lanky length from the chair. 'I'll go and find out.'

'We can ask the steward at lunch, honey.'

'Just showing willing, dash it, so that Daisy stops scowling at me.'

'Thanks, old dear,' said Daisy, laughing. 'But before we go upsetting the cooks, let's hope Alec agrees to try the mint tea and that it works.'

A steward came round, booming on his portable gong. They all stood up to go to the dining room, all except Arbuckle. Daisy realized he had been unusually silent. His long face was wan.

'Poppa?'

'I'm not that hungry, honey. You go ahead.'

Phillip and Daisy exchanged meaningful glances.

'Mint tea?' the witch suggested hesitantly.

Arbuckle shuddered, making shooing gestures. 'I'll be just fine. I have some work to do.'

They left him. In the dining room, they discovered, wooden bars had been raised along the edges of the table to stop things sliding off. 'Fiddles, we call 'em,' said the steward, handing out menus.

Dr Amboyne did not come in, so the table was half empty, but Gotobed appeared as they were studying the bill of fare. He sat down next to Daisy, and she asked politely after Wanda.

'Ee, lass, she's none so grand. Any road, that's what her maid telt me. She won't see me,' he said gloomily.

'I expect she knows she looks as wretched as she feels.'

'Aye. Well, there's nowt more I can do, for she doesn't care to try Miss Oliphant's simples.'

'And she won't let you help her up for some fresh air, I suppose.'

'So Baines says, and happen Wanda's right to refuse. I was up a bit ago. There's a rough, blustery wind blowing, and spray everywhere – reminds me o' walking on the fells wi' me da when I were a lad. It's not right, but, for a delicate lass used to town ways. She were on the London stage, you know.' He sighed. 'She were that excited about sailing to America, but mebbe it wasn't such a grand notion after all.'

Daisy was far too well brought up to ask if he was also having second thoughts about having married Wanda, but that did not stop her wondering. 'It was fine the first two days,' she pointed out, 'and I dare say it won't stay rough all the way across. She'll enjoy seeing America, anyway.'

'Aye, that she will.' Gotobed cheered up, in the process losing much of the Yorkshire influence in his speech. 'I'm greatly looking forward to it myself. You and Fletcher are off to Washington, I gather?'

The others joined in the conversation, with Gloria frequently applied to as the fount of all knowledge. Daisy asked Miss Oliphant what her plans were.

The witch, with the aid of a small legacy, intended to tour small towns in the long-settled eastern states, where she hoped to find people who remembered old herbal remedies. 'Then, if my funds stretch so far,' she said, 'I shall visit Indian reservations to learn what I can about native medicine. Witch hazel is an example, widely used now, of course. I am sure there must be other plants whose medicinal properties are little known.'

Gotobed was fascinated. He had thought of America chiefly in terms of its industrial might, with a special interest in steel as used to construct skyscrapers.

'Wanda was a little vague about what she wanted to see and do,' he said. 'T'lass has niver been abroad. As I expect you others know, she was a singer and dancer in the theatre, Miss Oliphant, with no opportunity for travel. I thowt we might cross the country by train, see the Mississippi and the Rocky Mountains and whatever other natural wonders can be visited. She'll like that.'

Daisy blinked. She was prepared to bet natural wonders were not what had attracted Wanda to America, if, indeed, there was any attraction other than marriage to Gotobed.

'I expect Mrs Gotobed would enjoy visiting Hollywood, in the state of California,' suggested Miss Oliphant. 'I understand that is where many cinematographic films are made.'

'Now there's a grand idea! But I'm very taken with this plan of yours to visit the Indians. Suppose I hire a motor car, and the three of us go jaunting off to the reservations together?'

Dismay flashed across Miss Oliphant's face. 'That would be delightful,' she said tactfully, a fib if ever Daisy had heard one, 'but perhaps you had better consult Mrs Gotobed before making new plans and wait and see how your existing arrangements work out.'

'We've nothing settled yet, save a visit to Arbuckle's place. I've all the time in the world, for I'm semi-retired, and what business I need to do can be done by cable for a few months.'

'Miss Oliphant, why don't you come and visit, too?' Gloria said impulsively. 'I'm sure Poppa would be happy to have you.'

'Why, that is very kind of you, my dear! It is true I have no definite plans. Perhaps a few days . . . But I should not wish to impose . . .'

'Do say yes,' Gotobed urged heartily. 'It'll give you a chance to find your feet. Arbuckle won't mind; he's a hospitable sort of bloke.'

'He certainly is,' Daisy confirmed. After all, her commissions from her editors and Alec's invitation to Washington all stemmed from Arbuckle's determination to have them go to stay at his 'little country place'.

'If Mr Arbuckle chooses to repeat the invitation,' said

Miss Oliphant, a trifle flushed, 'when he is feeling quite well again, then I shall be happy to accept.'

'Jolly good,' said Phillip.

The steward brought their sweets, balancing his full tray with ease as he crossed the room. However, instead of circling the table as usual to place each dish before its orderer, he plunked the tray down at the end and passed out the bowls and plates. 'Don't want to give anyone an earful,' he explained cheerfully. 'There's a bit of a blow on.'

Savouring her *poire belle Hélène*, Daisy glanced around the Grand Salon. Their table was typical – about half the passengers had not turned up for lunch. The Purser and Chief Engineer headed their tables, but none of the sailing officers were present.

Lady Brenda was there, with Chester Riddman beside her, looking morose. Her new hairdo did not appear to have improved his temper. Daisy decided to try to catch her after lunch to ask what Denton had been wearing.

Their coffee came, sloshing about in the heavy-based mugs which had been substituted for cups and saucers. The steward offered liqueurs 'on the house', at the Purser's behest, as a tribute to those still on their feet.

'By Jove,' said Phillip, grinning, 'if there's anything in what Miss Oliphant says, we'd better have *crème de menthe* all round to help us stay on our feet!'

'I am not at all certain that the alcohol does not nullify any benefit from the mint,' the witch said dryly. 'However, none of you appears to need it.'

'Touch wood,' said Daisy, suiting action to the word. She laughed. 'All the same, I'll have some. What about you, Miss Oliphant?'

'I shall take a glass of Crabbe's Green Ginger Wine, if you have it, Steward. It is an excellent cordial, and who knows but that it may help in our present situation.'

Phillip and Gloria opted for *crème de menthe*, while Gotobed joined Miss Oliphant in requesting ginger wine.

'My mam used to make ginger beer,' he reminisced. 'There was always a crock brewing in the larder. She used to give it us for the collywobbles, from scrounging green apples like as not.'

'There you are,' said Miss Oliphant triumphantly. 'Your mother was a herbalist in her way.'

Gotobed laughed. 'So she was, think on! I'm a healthy man, but gin I fall ill, I'll come to you afore I trouble our good doctor.'

When they left the Grand Salon, Lady Brenda and Riddman were just receiving their coffee, so Daisy resigned herself to losing track of her quarry again.

Gotobed walked beside her. 'Mrs Fletcher,' he said, in perfect King's English, 'I hate to trouble you, but might I ask you to drop in to see Wanda? I understand why she doesn't want to see me, or rather, doesn't want me to see her, but I'm troubled in my mind as to whether her maid is doing all that can be done for her comfort.'

'Of course I'll go. She may refuse to see me, too, but if not I'll try to persuade her at least to try some mint tea. Or ginger beer might go down better.'

'Very likely.' He lowered his voice, a touch of Yorkshire creeping in again. 'I'm afraid she's taken agin Miss O. I dare say it wouldn't do for the three of us to do a bit of travelling together. A great shame. Miss O. is an interesting lady.'

'Isn't she,' Daisy agreed.

'If you want to find me afterwards, I shall very likely be up on deck, smoking a pipe. You won't want to go out, but you can send a deck steward to fetch me.'

'Right-oh.'

They reached the door, where Miss Oliphant was waiting. 'Mrs Fletcher, if you would like to come with me now, I shall give you some mint for your husband,' she offered.

'Yes, please.' Daisy smiled at Gotobed, and she and the witch started towards the companion-way. 'Mr Gotobed has asked me to pop in to see Wanda. He's afraid the maid may not be taking proper care of her. Would you mind if I managed to persuade her to drink some mint tea, too?'

'Not at all. I have plenty. He is a dear man,' she added, so low Daisy only just made out the words and was not sure whether she was intended to hear or not. 'That creature does not deserve him.'

Wanda had not hidden her dislike of Miss Oliphant. Obviously, the feeling was reciprocated.

Daisy did not enter Miss Oliphant's cabin, as one of the women sharing it was laid low in her bunk. However, though she did not see them this time, she recalled with unease the red labels on certain of the array of vials and jars in the teak chest. Had the envelope the witch handed to her not contained enough crushed leaves for both patients, Daisy would have thought twice before giving any to Wanda.

# CHAPTER 9

With the envelope of mint leaves tucked in her handbag, Daisy decided to dash up to the promenade deck to see if she could catch Brenda before ministering to Alec and Wanda. She was in luck. The girl was just coming out of the Grand Salon, alone and disconsolate.

She brightened when she saw Daisy. 'Hullo! You're not busy, are you? There's nothing to do.'

Daisy thought of Wanda to be checked on, Alec to be coaxed from his bed, the neglected work which justified her presence aboard, the concert she wanted to attend later that afternoon. But she also wanted to talk to Brenda. It seemed unlikely that Denton's clothes were relevant, but they might be a vital detail. One simply could not be sure.

'Not just now,' she said. 'Where's Mr Riddman. Birdie? I saw him with you at lunch.'

'He's gone to the Smoking Room to smoke one of his beastly cigars.'

'Does he ever smoke a pipe?'

'No, Americans don't much. Chester says only fuddy-duddy old college professors smoke pipes. He's in a putrid mood,' she went on as they strolled aft past rows of deserted deckchairs, balancing automatically as the ship rolled and pitched. 'He lost pots of money yesterday afternoon.'

'At poker?'

'Mostly, and he paid a fortune for a number in the mileage pool, which didn't win. He was sure he'd win back last night what he'd lost earlier, but one of the chaps he's been playing with didn't turn up, and the other one he'd lost, too – was so nervy he couldn't sit still. So they only played a couple of hands. Chester won both of them, but he's still down by a lot and both men told him they weren't going to play this afternoon.'

'They sound to me like a pair of sharps trying to whet his appetite.'

'Oh no, he knows they're honest. At least, one of them found his wallet lying on the quay and brought it back to him, and he hasn't tried to cash his cheques with the Purser. He said he'd hold them till we get to New York if Chester didn't win the money back. And the other one loses as often as Chester does. Besides, Chester doesn't need his appetite whetted. He spends all his time in his cabin playing, never thinks about anything else.'

'Is that what you were going to tell me earlier,' Daisy asked, 'that Chester's become a gambler?'

Brenda nodded, tears in her eyes. 'At first it was fun. We played chemmy and roulette. He staked me, and we won a bit and lost a bit, never much. Then he started playing poker. He'd played at Yale, only not with the high-rollers – that's what they call people who make big bets – because his grandfather's against gambling and kept him on a tight rein.'

'I suppose he had plenty of money available in England as he was travelling?'

'Yes, and he kept losing, and he was more and more worried about what his grandfather would say, and less and less interested in me, and he kept hoping his luck would change.'

'The slippery slope,' said Daisy. 'Can't you just give him the push? I mean, I know your family needs the money, but money isn't everything.'

Dropping on to the nearest chair, Brenda pulled out a handkerchief and sniffled into it. 'I tried. One night when he was being particularly beastly, I gave him back his ring. He just grabbed my hand, and pushed the ring back on to my finger, and told me not to be silly because his grandfather would be simply livid with him if he went back without me and he was in enough hot water over the money already. I told Mumsie, and she was simply livid with *me.* She said we couldn't afford to look a gift horse in the mouth; I simply had to stick with it.'

'Oh dear,' Daisy murmured, unheard.

'And next day Chester came round and said he'd reconsidered and I was right, we shouldn't get married, and Mumsie threatened him with a breach-of-promise suit!'

'Oh Lord, so there you are, stuck in the middle. How frightful! Your mother's serious?'

'I think so. She was when we came aboard, but I haven't been able to talk to her since we left Liverpool. All she can think about is her poor tum.'

'So she doesn't know about . . .' Daisy paused invitingly.

'About Ron Harvey? No.' Brenda suddenly took an extraordinary interest in her fingernails. 'There's nothing to know.'

'You were up on the boat deck with him last night when . . .'

'Don't remind me. I can still see it when I close my eyes.'

'What, as if it was a film in a cinema?' Daisy infused her voice with scepticism. 'With all the details? I bet you can't even remember what Denton was wearing.'

'An overcoat and one of those old-fashioned hats,' Brenda said promptly. 'The kind Daddy used to wear for shooting. His hat must have fallen off when he fell, but I'm sure Ron will confirm the overcoat.'

'I dare say he'd back you up.'

'You mean he'd lie for me? He wouldn't. He's honest, sometimes devastatingly. You really think he cares enough to . . . ? But he hasn't any money!'

This Daisy met with silence.

'You don't know what it's like,' Brenda burst out, half indignant, half wretched, 'growing up on a big estate with lots of servants and everything you want, and then suddenly the money's all gone.'

'Oh yes I do,' Daisy retorted. 'That's exactly what happened to me. My brother was killed in the war, my father died of 'flu, and my cousin inherited the title and the estate.' She ignored Brenda's gasp. 'Instead of doing the London season, I went out and found a job.'

'I didn't know your father was titled!'

'He was Viscount Dalrymple. But I met and married a wonderful man who happens to be middle class and to work for his living. And of whom, I must add, my mother strongly disapproves. Are you in love with Mr Harvey?'

'I . . . I'm not sure. I've only known him a couple of days,' Brenda protested plaintively.

'It is early days,' Daisy conceded. 'Though I knew right away that Alec was something special.'

'Ron is something special. But I don't want to be poor!'

'I'm sure the second mate of a ship like this earns enough to feed a family.' And maybe he already had a family to feed, Daisy thought in alarm. Everyone had heard of sailors with a wife in every port. Too frightful if she encouraged Brenda into the arms of a bigamist! 'Oh well, sorry, Birdie, it's none of my business. I'm afraid I'm going to have to desert you. I promised to look in on Mrs Gotobed.'

'Do you know where Mr and Mrs Petrie are?'

'Probably trying to persuade one of the deck stewards to set up some strenuous game.'

'Oh. Oh well, maybe it would be fun,' said Brenda dubiously. 'I'll see if I can find them.'

Alec was right, Daisy acknowledged penitently as she went back below. She was a fearful meddler. Just because her situation had certain parallels with Brenda's, it did not follow that a happy ending on the same lines was possible. Whatever Harvey's marital status, his and Brenda's present feelings could well be no more than a brief infatuation, one of those fabled shipboard romances.

On the other hand, very likely Chester Riddman was also going through a temporary aberration, from which would emerge the charming and fun-loving man Brenda had wanted to marry. Alternatively, his grandfather might cut him off with the proverbial shilling – or American equivalent – because of his gambling, in which case Lady Wilmington would surely veto the wedding.

At least, Daisy told herself with a sigh, perhaps she had

made Brenda think twice about whining over her fate while doing nothing to change it.

Unenthusiastically, she knocked on the door of the Gotobeds' sitting room. The maid opened it. A dumpy, pudgy-faced woman of about forty, Baines was dressed in black, with mousy hair pulled back into an unbecoming bun. Daisy wondered if Wanda had chosen her deliberately for her lack of feminine attractions.

On top of her everyday plainness, the maid looked exhausted. She blinked at Daisy, squinching her eyes. 'Yes?'

'I'm Mrs Fletcher. I've come to see Mrs Gotobed.'

'Oh, but she won't . . .'

'Perhaps you'd like to lie down for half an hour,' Daisy suggested, 'while I sit with her?'

Baines seized her chance. 'Thank you, madam!' she exclaimed, already in motion.

Daisy stepped in, feeling a bit awkward at not having been announced. She went to tap on the half-open bedroom door.

'Go away, Dickie!' Wanda said pettishly. 'I'm not fit to be seen.'

'It's Daisy, Daisy Fletcher.' She advanced into the gloomy room. The brocade curtains were drawn at the fake windows. A multicoloured glow from the Tiffany bedside lamp gleamed on a vast array of gilt – solid gold? – topped bottles and jars on the dressing table. It dimly illuminated the huddled figure curled in a pose of misery on the double bed. 'Mr Gotobed asked me to make sure your maid is taking good care of you. He's worried about you.'

'Poor Dickie-bird. I'm not being much of a bride to him, am I? But I can't bear for him to see me not looking my best.'

'I should think you could quite safely let him come in here,' Daisy said dryly, sitting down on a chaise longue as she had not yet been asked to leave. 'What little I can see of you looks more like the Pied Piper than anything else.'

'What's he, when he's at home?'

'The Pied Piper? A character in a poem, sort of like a pantomime Harlequin.'

'Oh, him. It's the light. They're ever so expensive, that kind.'

'You could always turn it off and let him come and hold your hand for a while.'

Wanda groaned. 'Well, if you want the truth, he makes me feel worse. He's so bloody healthy, I can't stand it, feeling so poorly like I do.'

'I'm sorry you're having such a hard time of it. Miss Oliphant has sent one of her remedies for you, if you'd like to try it.'

'That quack! Anyone can see what *she's* up to.'

'Up to?'

'On the catch for Mr Arbuckle, isn't she?'

'Surely not!' Daisy exclaimed, startled.

'An old maid like that? What else'd she waste her money crossing the sea for? You can tell she hasn't got any to spare. Take my word for it, Daisy, I know what I'm talking about. Me, I can spot 'em a mile off.'

Being one yourself, Daisy thought unkindly. She didn't believe it of the witch though. 'All the same,' she said, 'it can't hurt to try her mint tea.'

'Not bloody likely! I bet she'd like to poison me so there're two millionaires free.'

'I'd have thought one was enough for any woman.'

Wanda was oblivious to irony. 'Give her a choice, wouldn't it? Not that she's got a hope, looking like what she does. Still, you better warn Gloria to watch out or her inheritance'll go down the drain.'

'I don't believe Miss Oliphant is looking for a husband,' Daisy declared, 'and supposing Mr Arbuckle did take a liking to her and she agreed to marry him, I don't believe he'd cut Gloria out of his will. I sincerely hope you won't pass on such bosh to Gloria. Or anyone else, for that matter. Now, if you won't try the mint tea, is there anything else I can do for you? Is Baines taking good care of you?'

'I suppose so,' Wanda said grudgingly. 'Nothing she does makes me feel any better.'

'There doesn't seem to be much one can do.'

'It's helped you coming and talking to me though. It's ever so kind of you, reelly. Gives a girl something else to think about than her insides. That reminds me, Dickie said you saw that man falling overboard last night. Tell me about it, do.'

Daisy disliked the avid curiosity in her voice, but she had to find something to talk about until Baines returned, so she described what she had seen.

'I didn't stay to watch them pull him out. I was coping with the hysterical girl, remember.' She did not report the hysterical girl's story. 'Alec said they lowered the lifeboat pretty smartly and pulled the chap in easily enough.'

'Did he say how he came to fall?'

'No; he was half drowned and he's still too ill to talk. He must have had a dizzy spell, I suppose.'

'I bet that's it.' Wanda sounded relieved, as if she had imagined there might be a madman on the loose, chucking people overboard right, left, and centre or – starboard, port, and amidships. 'Poor bloke. Is he going to be all right?'

'It's still touch and go, I gather.' Daisy was glad to hear the latch of the outer door click. 'Well, I'd better be on my way. Alec has succumbed, too. I must go and soothe his fevered brow, or at least attempt to pour some mint tea into him. Cheerio, Wanda. I hope you feel better soon.'

And that was a fib, she reflected. The longer Wanda was incapacitated, the happier everyone else was, except, presumably, her adoring husband.

Wanda's only response was a groan.

Alec greeted Daisy with a groan. Having taken the precaution of stopping at their steward's pantry for hot water and Marie biscuits, she presented him with a *fait accompli*.

'I've brought you mint tea. It smells delicious.' She set the tray on the little fold-down table between the berths, pleased with herself for carrying it safely.

'No thanks.'

'Darling, you simply can't go on lying here feeling sorry for yourself when there may be a murderer aboard. Sit up.'

'Bully.' But he sat up, though he stayed hunched over, hugging his knees to his chest.

Daisy poured half a mugful, the most that was safe with the ship behaving like a rocking horse in two directions. 'Here, eat a biscuit while the tea cools a bit.'

'Ugh!'

'Right-oh, tea first, then biscuit, then the fresh air treatment. Alec, Denton was wearing an overcoat and hat, so it was impossible to tell whether he was in evening dress, but all the same, no one could possibly have mistaken him for Riddman. One's tall and thin and smokes cigars, and the other's shortish and sturdy and smokes a pipe.'

'Not Harvey then, thank heaven. I hate to think what Captain Dane would have said if I'd told him to clap his second officer in irons. But if Denton's short, it makes it all the less likely that he should fall over the rail without assistance.'

Pondering, he relaxed his death grip on his knees. Daisy put the cup into his hand and he sipped automatically. Since the taste did not cause him to fling mug and contents across the cabin with a cry of disgust, Daisy ventured to pour some tea into the second mug she had brought. After all, Miss Oliphant had said it was better for warding off sickness than curing it. One might as well make sure.

'It is delicious,' she said in surprise.

'Huh? Oh, not bad. Daisy, the whole thing seems inexplicable, but it strikes me that as Denton holds the only key, he may be in danger.' He nibbled the biscuit she put into his free hand.

'The nurse said she's never away from him for more than a couple of minutes.'

'That's all well and good while he's so ill. But when he starts to recover, as we must hope he will if we're ever to get to the bottom of this . . .'

'Not to mention for his wife's sake, and his family's, and his own!'

Alec smiled at her, holding out his empty mug. 'That goes without saying. I want you to arrange for a trustworthy member of the crew to he with him at all times.'

'Darling, they'll never do it on my say-so, not in a million years!' She watched him thirstily drink another half cup of tea and crunch a second biscuit. 'You'll just have to come up and give the order yourself.'

'I'll write a note to Harvey.' He set the cup on the tray and swung his feet to the floor.

'No, you jolly well won't. Here, put your jacket on while I get our coats. We're going out.'

'Daisy, I . . .'

'For the honour of New Scotland Yard!'

'There's a ringing slogan.' He gave her a crooked grin, stood up, and staggered. 'I'm going to have to keep moving or I shall disgrace the Yard, myself, and you. Come along.'

He shrugged into his jacket as he strode along the corridor, weaving in response to the ship's sway. Trying not to giggle at his gait, Daisy trotted after, burdened with their winter coats. At the companion-way he ran upwards, his hand on the rail, and Daisy freed one hand from the coats to hang on.

She was glad she had. Halfway up, the rhythm of the pitch and roll was interrupted by a sudden plunge in an entirely new direction. Dropping the coats, Daisy grabbed the rail with her other hand and hung on with both.

'Alec, wait!'

He turned back. 'Sorry, love. Come to grief?'

'The ship did a peculiar wiggle, sort of like doing the tango. I can only cope with a waltz.'

'It's been wiggling peculiarly for quite some time. Don't remind me.' He started to stoop to pick up the coats, but straightened abruptly, sweat on his pale forehead. 'I don't think I'd better bend down, and I really must keep moving.'

'It's all right, I can manage. Just slow down a bit, darling.'

'I'm trying to leave my stomach behind. I'll take my coat; yours too if you like.'

Daisy gave him his but kept her own over her arm as they started upwards again. 'Where are we going?'

'The bridge. There's no need for you to come though.'

'I'd quite like some fresh air, if it's not pouring. I left my hat below.'

Reaching the promenade deck, Daisy was relieved to find that the *Talavera* had settled back into her steady waltz. The windows were streaming with water, whether spray or rain she couldn't tell. Practically all of the deckchairs had been folded, stacked, and roped to iron rings on the bulkhead, though a few hardy passengers still sat out in the draughty promenade, wrapped in rugs.

Daisy and Alec put on their coats and ventured out into a damp, blustery, grey world. Air and water were inextricably mixed, the horizon invisible in an all-encompassing blur of leaden clouds and leaden waves. Not a soul was out on the open forward deck.

Alec took Daisy's arm, both steadying himself and bracing her as they battled the buffeting wind to the central companion-way. The climb up the steep steps was a matter of hauling oneself up with both hands.

Up on the boat deck, the south-west wind gusted more fiercely. Sheet metal boomed and the wire guys on the masts twanged. The *Talavera* was no longer merely a tilting floor but a live creature, meeting the challenge of the ocean with a steady purposefulness.

'If I'd worn a hat, I'd have lost it in no time,' Daisy bawled, exhilarated.

'It's drier up here,' Alec bawled back. 'Not much spray comes so high.'

'I think it's raining a bit. Mizzling.' She stuck out her tongue. Her lips were salty but the drops touching her tongue were not. 'I must look like a drowned rat!'

He grinned. 'Not yet. Let's see if Captain Dane will allow you on to his sacrosanct bridge.'

Several determined exercisers were marching around the deck, some in full suits of oilskins, some in Burberries, macs, or overcoats, and tweed caps which only a miracle could possibly keep on their heads. As Alec and Daisy crossed to the bridge, the miracle blinked and a cap went cartwheeling between two lifeboats and over the side. Its owner rushed to peer after it, as if he hoped there was some chance of retrieving it.

Alec banged on the bridge door, and they were both invited in. Captain Dane was taking a watch below, leaving the first officer in charge. He agreed to station a man to sit with Denton.

'But I hope it doesn't mean you now think it was attempted murder, sir,' he said. 'If so, the Captain won't be happy, I can tell you.'

'No, I still doubt it. but it's an elementary precaution I ought to have seen to sooner. I suppose I ought to report my findings so far to Captain Dane when he's next available.'

'I'd wait till he sends for you, if I were you. He doesn't really want to hear any more about it unless he's forced to.' He glanced at Daisy's damp hair. 'Let me lend you a couple of sou'westers before you step outside again.'

Settling the yellow oilskin hat on her head as the door closed behind them, Daisy exclaimed indignantly, '*Your* findings!'

'For the honour of Scotland Yard. If I end up having to write a report on this business for the Super, I'll give you full credit.'

'Better not. The AC might burst a blood vessel.'

With the sou'wester folded back so that she could see out, the strap tightened under her chin, Daisy felt quite waterproof and ready to accompany Alec for a turn about the deck.

'I do feel better in the fresh air,' he admitted. 'The trouble is, now I dread going below.'

'We'll keep walking till you get your sealegs,' Daisy said optimistically.

They strolled aft along the port side, crossed to starboard, and started back. Here the superstructure protected them from some of the wind. Two or three people stood leaning against the railing. Daisy recognized the nearest, a familiar figure in his caped overcoat and fore-and-aft cap, with the ear-flaps down now. His back to them, Gotobed appeared to be sheltering his pipe in cupped hands.

As they approached, he turned, saw them, and waved. Daisy veered towards him, but Alec held her back.

'Just wave,' he said into her ear. 'I don't think I can cope with pipe smoke.'

'Stay to windward, darling. Or do I mean leeward? I want to tell him about my visit to Wanda.'

In the brief delay, a tall man who had been walking towards them went up to Gotobed, cigarette in hand, and said something. He was pretty well bundled up in a beige raincoat, blue muffler, and soft hat jammed down on to his head, but Daisy thought he looked like one of Wanda's admirers. Both men turned towards the rail, backs to the wind, Gotobed reaching into his coat pocket.

As he withdrew his hand, a cross-wave hit the *Talavera.* She plunged skittishly: 'Tango-ing again,' squeaked Daisy as she lost her balance and scampered involuntarily forward, putting out both hands to catch the rail. Concentrating on not crashing into it, she caught a glimpse of Alec lurching past her, hand to mouth, while Gotobed and the other man did a sort of dance step around each other.

And then the stage-door Johnnie spun round, slumped doubled up over the rail, and toppled over.

# CHAPTER 10

Appalled, Daisy saw the man plummet down the ship's side and plunge head first into the turbulent water. A moment later, a lifebelt landed beside him.

'Man overboard!' Daisy shouted, but even if her voice had overcome the wind's reverberation, no sailors were in sight.

Alec was fully occupied in leaning over the rail, his shoulders heaving, so Gotobed must have thrown the belt. His broad face a mask of horrified shock, he watched it recede as the *Talavera* steamed on.

'Have you seen him surface?' Daisy asked hurriedly.

'Not yet. He were shot!'

Daisy looked around. No man with a gun, but the two men who had been standing at the rail nearer the bows were running towards them. As far as she could see, no one was heading for the bridge.

'I'll stop the ship.' She pelted forward, burst into the tranquil bridge without knocking, and panted out, 'Man overboard!'

From the first mate down, everyone gaped at her. Even the man at the wheel turned his head and gasped, ''Strewth, not another 'un!'

The first mate quickly recovered his mental equilibrium. 'Does he have a lifebelt?' he snapped.

'One was thrown, but he hadn't come up when I left.' How long? she thought desperately. It had seemed like forever, but . . . 'A minute, not more than two.'

'Where did he fall?'

'Left rear. I mean, port aft.'

He flashed her a smile as he barked out orders which sent men running. Scanning the ocean, he reached for a speaking tube, but he addressed the helmsman. 'Can you hold her if we lose all way?'

'Not agin one o' they cross-seas, sir.'

'He'll be beyond the screws' turbulence by now.' More orders flew.

Daisy felt the engines slow beneath her feet until their vibration was barely perceptible. Having set the rescue attempt in motion, she was superfluous. One of the orders she had understood was to wake the Captain, and she decided she'd rather be gone when he arrived. She slipped out. Aft, toiling sailors under the third mate's command were already swinging a lifeboat over the ship's side.

Alec still leant against the rail, hanging on to it in a white-knuckled grip. He was in need of distraction. What better to distract him than Gotobed's extraordinary report that the man overboard had been shot?

Gotobed and the other men had all left. Through blowing spume, Daisy saw a group which was probably them down on the promenade deck at the stern-rail. She thought she saw Gotobed's distinctive hat among them, and she hoped he had got over the shock enough not to be blurting out his story to all and sundry, *à la Brenda*.

Joining Alec, she said, 'Darling, I have something to tell you. Let's walk.'

He turned his head, his eyes the same dull, leaden grey as sea and sky, focussed inward. 'I daren't leave the side.'

'You feel better walking; you said so yourself. We shan't be far from the side, and we'll stay to leeward.' She had sorted out leeward and windward in her mind since last using the term. 'This is important. Come along.'

'What is it now?' he grunted irritably, yielding to her tug on his arm.

She gave him a critical look. 'I take it you saw the man fall overboard?'

'I'm not blind.'

'No, but your attention was definitely elsewhere. The thing is, Gotobed said he was shot.'

'Shot! Great Scott, what next? I'm no more deaf than I'm blind, and I heard no shot. Did you?'

'No, but it's frightfully noisy out here.'

'And I dare say the marksman could have used a silencer. But if the shot was inaudible, Gotobed couldn't hear it either. And speaking of marksmen, how the deuce could anyone shoot straight on this corkscrewing deck? Another case of hysteria!'

'No, but, darling, can you imagine anyone less hysterical than Gotobed? Though admittedly he was in a state of shock. So was I.'

'There's your answer then. Between shock and the din, you misheard him.'

'I suppose I might have. Could he have said the chap was dotty? Maybe he threw himself over in a fit of madness?'

'I don't know, and frankly, just now I can't bring myself to care. I'm going to lie down.'

Disconsolate, Daisy watched Alec hurry down the forward companion-way and disappear. She turned back, heading for the group of men at the stern. Alec might not care at present, but *someone* ought to find out what Gotobed had really said, and why.

A second lifeboat was being lowered. On her way aft, Daisy stopped to see the first boat splash down. A ship's boy was shouting something at its crew through a megaphone. The sailors below cast off the chains and started heaving on the oars. Daisy presumed the boy had given the third officer instructions as to which way to steer, but they must be pretty near guesswork. The chances of finding the missing man seemed minimal, even if he had surfaced and caught the belt.

Contemplating the frail cockleshell as it crawled up the side of a wave, bobbing on the choppy water, Daisy only hoped she would never have to trust her life to one.

She stopped again at the top of the aft companion-way. From there, a stretch of the ship's wide, white wake was visible through the murk. An arc. The *Talavera* was turning. Daisy scanned the trough between the great rollers, but she could not pick out the lifebelt.

It was surely several waves back by now, but she leant forward a little, hanging on to the rail, as if the extra six inches might enable her to see more clearly.

From the corner of her eye, she was suddenly aware of a swell approaching from quite the wrong direction. Before she could react, it hit. The *Talavera* lurched. If Daisy had not already been holding on tight, she would have pitched down the ladder-like steps head first.

Breathing rather fast, her heart thumping, she picked her way carefully down.

Gotobed was no longer with the dozen or so men at the rail. When she reached them, she noticed Chester Riddman. He had on a narrow-cut overcoat in blue, the latest in London fashions for men, and for once he was without his truculent, disgruntled air. In fact, he looked quite as 'het up' – in the American idiomas – as he had accused Brenda of being.

The whole group had crossed to starboard to watch the first lifeboat. Moving in the opposite direction from the *Talavera*, it was already some distance away. As the ship's stern slid down into the trough, the boat disappeared over the crest of the next wave; but before it vanished Daisy saw that the third mate was standing up at the tiller, gazing back.

She and several others looked to see what he was staring at so intently. A sailor had climbed high on the nearest mast and was making hand signals. Perhaps from his vantage point he could see the lifebelt.

'Perhaps they'll find him after all,' someone said.

Lowering her gaze, Daisy saw Gotobed coming down the companion-way. She went to meet him. He looked shaken still and uncharacteristically undecided.

'Mrs Fletcher,' he said in his most formal English, 'I was going to ask you to pay no heed to what I said in the heat of the moment. I had no business burdening a young lady with such a dreadful shock.'

'But?'

'But I have just been to the Captain to report what I saw, and he instructed me to inform Mr Fletcher, who is, he gave me to understand, a police detective.'

'Mr Arbuckle didn't tell you?' Daisy asked. 'He spilled the beans to Captain Dane when Denton fell overboard and Lady Brenda claimed he'd been pushed.'

'I feel a great deal more sympathy now with that young lady. Captain Dane actually told me to take my "imaginings" to Fletcher.'

'I suspect he'd have brushed you off altogether if you'd been a third-class passenger.'

'Ee, lass, happen he would,' Gotobed sighed.

Daisy seized her chance, not sorry to be distracted from the new disaster. 'Mr Gotobed, do you mind if I ask you a question that has been preying on my mind? Sometimes you speak perfect King's English and sometimes broad Yorkshire. I think I've worked out at least partly what brings on the change, but I've been wondering whether it's deliberate or just happens.'

'Sometimes one, sometimes either,' Gotobed said with a smile. 'When I made up my mind I was going to get on in t'world, I reckoned t'first thing to do was learn proper English. I were right chuffed to find I've a gift for it. I also found a great many gentlemen underestimated me when l spoke Yorkshire, so I'd use it in business negotiations, but not in situations where I wanted to be accepted as a gentleman.'

'But then in situations where you feel at home, at ease with friends, you relapse.'

'Ay, that I do, think on! Any road, t'next step were when I started looking into export markets for special steels. French and German come almost as easy to me as good English, and I have some Italian. It's no bad thing to be able to speak to customers in their own lingo.'

A halloo from the mast top made them both look up. The lookout was signalling again to the invisible lifeboats, pointing over to starboard.

'Surely that must mean he's seen the man,' said Daisy hopefully.

'Likely just the lifebelt.' Gotobed had lost his cheerfulness. 'I hope you can advise me, Mrs Fletcher. As I said, Captain Dane wants me to report to your husband, but on my way to the bridge I saw you go to him and it seemed to me he's – not well. In fact, I went round by the port side so as not to embarrass him.'

'He's feeling rotten, poor darling. As a matter of fact,' Daisy went on, no doubt with what Alec called her deceptively guileless look, 'I've been involved with him in several of his cases. Why don't you tell me what happened, and I'll report to him?'

Gotobed hesitated. 'It's not pretty.'

'I'm no shrinking violet.'

He gave her a hard look. 'You didn't get hysterics when the poor beggar fell,' he admitted. 'In fact, you kept your head better than I did, off to the bridge right away for help. I ought to've caught him before he went over, but I were that flabbergasted.'

'It's a pity,' Daisy agreed, 'but you'd just been rocked by that cross-wave, too, which was utterly disorienting. Anyway, it's no good crying over spilt milk. What happened that made you think he'd been shot?'

'You saw him come up to me? He asked for a light for

his cigarette, which was right daft considering t'rain and wind. I were feeling in my pocket for matches, but, when yon big wave hit t'ship and rocked the both on us, I took my eyes off him for a moment, a split second, just. When I looked back, there was a gurt red patch on his shoulder and he was reeling round as if from a blow. I heard no shot, but if 'twere not a bullet as hit him, what it was I cannot guess.'

Forcing herself not to dwell on the impact of a bullet on flesh, Daisy tried to conjure up alternative possibilities. 'He couldn't have brushed against wet paint? Or rust? And perhaps knocked his head against a davit, knocked himself silly?'

'I'd not dare suggest rust to yon Captain,' Gotobed said dryly. 'Nor was the colour rusty. Red paint – I don't recall seeing any.'

'A wet paint sign could easily have blown away.'

'Aye, very true. And he might have knocked his head, though I'd have said he stepped away from the nearest davit towards me.'

'I'd better go and look for rust and red paint anyway. Alec's bound to ask about it when I report to him.'

'I'll come wi' thee, lass.'

Daisy went up the companion-way hand over hand on the railing. She noticed that Gotobed climbed with the vigour of a much younger man. In the transition from farm labourer to millionaire man of business, he had not let himself run to seed, and he retained the countryman's sturdy indifference to the weather.

The weather had changed abruptly, Daisy realized. It had stopped raining, and the wind had veered to the north, a steady blast with icy fingers that scrabbled through the interstices in her green tweed coat and pinched at her ears and nose. She shivered.

At the top, they stopped to look back. The wake was still a long curve.

'We're steaming in a circle,' said Daisy. 'It will play havoc with the mileage pools.' She turned to look towards what she guessed was the centre of the circle. As the *Talavera* crested a wave, she caught a glimpse of one of the lifeboats. 'Maybe they'll find him. But if you're right and he was shot, I shouldn't think the blood would come through his coat so quickly unless an artery was hit.'

'Aye, lass,' Gotobed said heavily. 'I fear he'll have bled to death long since if he didn't drown first. I know what I saw.'

'We'll check for wet paint anyway.'

The davits by which Gotobed and the victim had been standing were plain white, like all the rest, but for the bottom foot or so, which was green. Not a speck of rust was visible, not even around the bolt-heads. Daisy looked for blood on the deck, but either the man's mac had absorbed it all, or any splashes had been washed away by the rain.

She sighed. 'I'd better go down and force Alec to take an interest,' she said. 'If he wants to speak to you, I'll send a steward.'

'I'll be up here, at least until the boats come back.'

Down she went once more. Every cloud, even the cloud of murder, had a silver lining: At this rate, with the amount of exercise she was getting, she'd be able to eat anything put before her without gaining an ounce.

Alec was curled up on his berth again. 'What now?' he groaned.

'Darling, it does look as if the man was shot.' Daisy recounted Gotobed's description of what he had seen. 'No red paint around, let alone wet red paint. I can't see what other explanation there could be, can you?'

'There's a medical condition,' Alec said, frowning, 'some sort of bubble in the wall of a blood vessel, which may burst at any time.'

The concept did not seem to disturb his stomach any further, though it made Daisy feel slightly sick. 'I suppose the shock of feeling it happen might have made him spin around,' she said doubtfully. 'It's an awful coincidence, though, two men falling overboard in such a short time span.'

'It would be even more of a coincidence having two murderers aboard.'

'Maybe there's only one. Not that I can imagine what connection there could be between a Suffolk farmer and a stage-door Johnnie.'

'A *what*? You know who the second victim is?'

'No, not exactly,' Daisy said reluctantly. 'Only, when he was walking towards us, I thought I recognized him as a man I'd seen talking to Wanda. She told me he was one of her admirers when she was on the stage. I promised not to tell anyone, in case Gotobed was upset by the reminder of her antecedents. I'm not sure it was him though. I couldn't see much of his face between his hat and his scarf.'

'A highly speculative identification,' Alec grunted. 'But supposing it was him, you don't know the fellow's name, do you?'

'Haven't the foggiest. Wanda didn't go so far as to introduce him. In fact, he rather sloped off when he saw I'd noticed him with her. It seems to me, darling, that we can't do much until we know who's missing.'

'We!'

'Oh, spiffing, you're going to get up and take over.'

'I'm not stirring until the d . . . blasted ship stops shimmying. It's up to Dane to find out who fell off his blasted ship this time, and you can tell him so from me.'

'Right-oh,' said Daisy, with trepidation. 'I'd better get it over with at once.'

'Not in those words!' Alec called after her.

# CHAPTER 11

Captain Dane was already swollen with indignation because a second idiot had had the temerity to fall off his ship. 'I should have banned passengers from the open decks and steered straight through the storm we avoided. And again we have these hysterical rumours of foul play,' he bellowed, glaring at Daisy as if she had either started the rumours or pushed the men overboard herself. 'Where's Fletcher? I was just about to send for him.'

'I'm afraid he's rather unwell.' Daisy was sure she was going to be blamed for Alec's dereliction of duty, as well as the rest.

But the Captain's thin lips actually quirked. 'Seasick, eh?' he said quite mildly, 'and sent you, ma'am, to make his excuses.'

'Exactly.' Honesty was definitely not the best policy. The question was, would Dane prefer to deal with a put-upon little woman or a reasonably competent person, regardless of her sex? 'I've told him what Mr Gotobed saw . . .'

'Claims to have seen,' roared Captain Dane. '*Claims* to have seen.'

'I don't think Mr Gotobed is over-imaginative,' Daisy protested, dropping any pretense of meekness, 'and he has no conceivable reason to make it up. I myself checked that there was no wet paint the victim might have brushed against.'

'Victim? Victim of his own stupidity!'

'Perhaps. Do you want this second incident investigated or not?'

'Two of the blighters,' groaned the Captain. 'On *my* ship!'

'*Off* your ship.' Immediately recognizing such levity as unsuitable, if not downright hazardous, she hurried on, 'I don't think Alec has an absolute duty to investigate a possible crime just because he's on the spot, but in the absence of any other officer of the law, he may have.'

'On the *Talavera*, *I* am the law!' Captain Dane considered his bellicose statement in a moment of gloomy silence and unwillingly amended it. 'I am the chief officer of the law. There're company regulations and there's maritime law . . . both English and American, if this wretched fellow turns out to be an American citizen.' He groaned again.

'It sounds most frightfully complicated,' Daisy sympathized. 'It seems to me the first thing is to find out who he is.'

'Which will be easier if we fish him out, dead or alive, so may I suggest, ma'am, that you leave me in peace to direct the search.'

Thus dismissed, Daisy decided she was free to go and enjoy the concert in the Grand Salon with a good conscience.

Leaving the bridge, she saw that the group watching the rescue attempt had moved up to the boat deck for a better view – though nothing was presently visible – and had grown to a small crowd. As Daisy crossed to the forward companion-way, the Petries detached themselves from the others and hailed her.

'I say, old bean, is it true another chappie's been chucked overboard?'

'Why ask me, Phil?'

'Because if it's true, Fletcher will be sleuthing it; and if I know you, which I have since you were bawling in your cradle, you're in the thick of it.'

'Alec's flat on his back – well, curled up on his berth – and not sleuthing anything.'

'So's Poppa,' said Gloria sympathetically. 'I guess we're just plain lucky.'

'But I can tell you this: The man who went overboard wasn't pushed. I was there and I couldn't have helped but see. So if that's what people are saying, I hope you'll tell them it's absolute tommy-rot.'

'Sure, won't we, honey? Things could get real nasty if everyone thinks there's a mad killer on board.'

A mad killer on board? Daisy shuddered at the thought as she continued down to the Grand Salon. Yet Alec was right, two unconnected murders on the same voyage would be the wildest of coincidences. A mad killer, or a connection between Denton and the latest victim . . .

There was no sense trying to pursue the latter possibility before they found out who the second man was. Captain Dane obviously wasn't going to do anything about that question until the lifeboats returned, with or without a body.

Daisy turned into the Grand Salon, prepared to give her

mind over to Schubert and Dvorak for the next couple of hours.

The audience was decidedly sparse, but Miss Oliphant was just taking a seat in the third row. Daisy went to join her.

She looked round with a smile. 'Ah, Mrs Fletcher, another lover of good music. We are a minority, I fear.'

'Alec would be here if he wasn't ill.'

'The mint tea did not help? I'm sorry.'

'It did seem to help, but only until a cross-wave spoilt the pattern of motion.'

'I shall give you some ginger after the concert.' Miss Oliphant glanced back at the doors. 'I thought I had persuaded Mr Gotobed to come, but it seems he has run shy. He is not familiar with the works of the masters.'

'I'm sure he would have kept his word if it wasn't for the . . . the accident.'

'He is hurt?' asked the witch in alarm, half starting up.

'No, no, sorry, I shouldn't have put it like that. You haven't heard that another man fell overboard? He was speaking to Mr Gotobed a moment before, so naturally Mr Gotobed is watching anxiously to see if the lifeboats have rescued him.'

'Another! Oh dear, how very shocking.' Miss Oliphant turned with relief to the small stage. 'Ah, here are our musicians.'

Daisy was by no means a knowledgeable judge of musical performance. Her own musical training had progressed little beyond singing hymns in church and a few painful piano lessons, at the last of which her teacher had suggested she might like to try a different instrument.

It was Michael who had introduced her to classical music. That never-to-be-forgotten summer, she had cycled into Worcester to meet him whenever her hospital job allowed, telling her mother she was going to work. The Three Choirs Festival was in abeyance for the war, but there were concerts both in Worcester and in Malvern. They had attended as many as could be crammed into their brief time together.

She had discovered that Alec was a music-lover when she was given tickets to a concert and had boldly invited him to go with her. That murder in the Royal Albert Hall had ensued was not her fault, whatever he had insinuated at the time.

Now she wished he was beside her as the Schubert E flat piano trio, poignant in its apparent simplicity, brought tears to her eyes. He was not only missing the music, he was wasting time they could have spent together, likely to be rare enough in his line of work. After the concert, she would go and pour ginger tea down his throat, by force if she had to.

In the interval, she was reminded of the other reason she wanted Alec on his feet and thinking clearly, when Gotobed came in and sat down beside Miss Oliphant.

'My dear sir,' Miss Oliphant said, 'have you news of the unfortunate person sought by the lifeboats?'

He shook his head gravely. 'They found the lifebelt I threw out, but no sign of the young man. I understand they have given him up for lost.'

The ship's engines had resumed their steady throb, Daisy noted.

It dawned on her that Gotobed was one person who might know who the missing man was. After all, they had spoken together, though briefly. How remiss of her not to have asked and of Alec not to have suggested it.

Fortunately, the omission was easily remedied. 'Mr Gotobed, do you know who he was?'

'Nay, lass, he didn't introduce himself, just asked for a light.' Gotobed frowned. 'I think I've seen him about once or twice wi' yon American, Lady Brenda's young man.'

His words jogged Daisy's memory. That time when she saw Wanda's two admirers, she had recognized one as one of Chester Riddman's companions. Not a 'highly speculative identification', then – she could tell Alec that the second man overboard was almost certainly a stage-door Johnnie. What connection could he possibly have with Denton?

'I took him for a card-sharp,' Gotobed interrupted her train of thought, 'but I dare say I was mistaken.'

'*De mortuis nil nisi bonum*,' said Miss Oliphant in a slightly reproving tone. 'One ought not to speak ill of the dead.'

'Madam, that is the only reason I suggested I might have been mistaken,' Gotobed said, with a rather sharkish grin, which made him look suddenly like a captain of industry instead of a kindly old gentleman.

'Lady Brenda has confided in me that the young man has fallen into bad company,' Miss Oliphant admitted sadly. 'Ah, here come our trio back again. I do hope you will stay to hear them play, Mr Gotobed.'

He stayed, and Daisy observed him beating time on his knee during the lively final movement. At the end, he applauded vigorously, then turned a beaming face to Miss Oliphant. 'Ee, lass,' he began, then blushed and corrected himself. 'I beg your pardon, Miss Oliphant. I was just going to say, it was grand. I'm right glad you talked me into coming.'

Rather pink herself, Miss Oliphant murmured, 'I am very glad you enjoyed it.'

'I'm sorry Wanda missed it. Mrs Fletcher, Baines tells me you were kind enough to visit my poor lass. I've been wanting to ask how you found her.'

'I'd say she's about the same as Alec, uncomfortable and unhappy but not desperately ill. She said Baines was doing all for her that could he done. But she wouldn't take any mint tea, which did seem to do Alec some good.'

'That's a pity, but one can't force it down her throat. Any road, I take it kindly of you, Miss Oliphant, to have offered your remedy.'

'And I'll take it kindly,' said Daisy, 'if you'll spare me a spot of ginger, which I have every intention of forcing down Alec's throat. He simply must pull himself together and get up to find out what's going on.'

Miss Oliphant looked rather surprised. 'What is it you expect Mr Fletcher to discover?' she asked.

Oh blast! Daisy thought. She had momentarily forgotten that the witch did not know Alec was a police detective. In fact, Miss Oliphant didn't even know there was anything for a police detective to detect.

Gotobed came to Daisy's rescue. 'Fletcher will be sorry to find out he's missed the concert. There's the passengers' concert yet to come, of course. Have you a turn prepared, Miss Oliphant?'

'Oh dear me, no! Have you, Mr Gotobed?'

'I've been known to sing "Ilkley Moor" when pressed,' he admitted.

'Then we shall press you, shall we not, Mrs Fletcher?'

'Certainly. The more people we can persuade to perform, the less likely that we shall be coerced into making asses of ourselves.'

They laughed, and Gotobed said something. Daisy did not catch his words because they had reached the door of the Grand Salon and a ship's boy waiting there approached her.

'Mrs Fletcher?'

'Yes?'

He stepped aside, so she followed him. 'Captain Dane's compliments, ma'am. He begs the favour of a word with you on the bridge.'

Daisy thought the Captain was more likely to have bellowed something on the lines of 'Bring me that Fletcher woman!' Likewise, she doubted he had instructed his messenger to hold the summons until the concert ended. It probably had not dawned on him that to haul her out in the middle would be bound to cause just the sort of rumour-mongering he deplored.

She wondered how long he had waited already. A few more minutes could hardly make him much madder, she decided.

'I'll go up in half a tick,' she told the boy, and turned back to Miss Oliphant.

'You would like some ginger,' said the worthy witch at once. 'Shall we go and fetch it now?'

Daisy gratefully accepted.

With the envelope of ginger in her pocket, she headed for the bridge. It was nearly dark outside. The north wind was biting but it had swept away the clouds, and an awe-inspiring multitude of stars besprinkled the indigo sky. Daisy stopped for a moment with the companion-way light behind her, gazing up. She had always thought of the stars as friendly, but now they seemed cold and uncaring. In the middle of a vast, impersonal emptiness, the *Talavera* was a haven of human warmth.

Or would be if there weren't a murderer, possibly two, aboard her. Shivering, Daisy went to knock on the bridge door.

A subdued Captain Dane had aged ten years since she'd seen him just a couple of hours ago. In fact, everyone on the bridge was grim-faced. Dane motioned Daisy to a chair in a corner and dropped into another.

'It goes against the grain to stop searching,' he said, 'but it's useless. My boats thoroughly quartered the area where we might have hoped to find him. It's not like a shipwreck where there's flotsam to hold on to.'

'I heard you found the lifebelt.'

'Aye, and a felt hat nearby. If he'd been anywhere near them . . . and where else could he be?'

'So either he just couldn't swim, or it looks as if Mr Gotobed was right and he was badly injured before he fell in.' Daisy made a mental note to ask the doctor about Alec's theory of some sort of bubble in the artery. 'I take it no one has reported a friend or relative missing?'

'No. That's what I wanted to consult you about, assuming Scotland Yard is still under the weather?' Captain Dane had recovered his spirits sufficiently to put a trace of sarcasm in the query.

'I'm afraid so. But I don't think he – or I – can advise you as to how to find out who he was.'

'It's damned . . . dashed difficult if we don't want to start a panic. I can't send out a general summons to the Grand Salon. Half the passengers are confined to their beds anyway, so it's no good having the dining room stewards check by tables at dinner.'

'Wouldn't the cabin stewards and stewardesses know pretty much who is stuck in bed?'

'Only if they have been asked for assistance. I suppose they will have to go around knocking on doors, unless you have a better idea?' he asked hopefully, as if he expected Scotland Yard's deputy to pull a rabbit from her hat.

'That sounds like the best way to go about it,' Daisy affirmed.

'They aren't going to like it in first.' Dane was once more sunk in gloom. He heaved a sigh. 'Very well, I'll give the orders right away and let you know what we find out.'

With ambulant passengers scattered about the ship, a final answer might not arrive until after dinner. The first order of business was to get Alec moving, Daisy decided, as she once more descended the companion-way from the boat deck. She hung on to the rail as tight as ever. Though for the most part the *Talavera* had resumed a regular, anticipatable pitch and roll, every now and then she gave a sort of uneasy twitch. It was easy to compensate for on the level deck, but to lose one's balance on those steep steps was bound to result in a painful tumble.

Down on the cabin deck, Daisy went along to the doctor's offices. The surgery was officially open, but there were no patients in the waiting room. Dr Amboyne was seated at the desk, talking to the nurse who stood beside him.

He rose when Daisy entered. 'Mrs Fletcher, what can I do for you?'

'I wanted to ask after Mr Denton.'

'He's in bad shape, poor chap. Hasn't come round yet and I'm afraid pleurisy is setting in. There's not a great deal a medical practitioner can do beyond making the patient as comfortable as possible. Mrs Denton's sitting with him now and a crewman Captain Dane sent to keep an eye on him. Do you know anything about that?'

'My husband considered it advisable,' Daisy evaded. 'I'd like to ask you another question if you don't mind. Is there a medical condition which consists of a sort of bubble in the wall of an artery?'

Amboyne raised enquiring eyebrows. 'One might describe an aneurism thus. They occur in veins as well as in arteries.'

'They sometimes burst?'

'They rupture, yes.'

'And then they bleed?'

'In the case of major blood vessels, there is heavy internal bleeding, generally fatal.'

'Oh, only internal?'

'I've never heard of a ruptured aneurism producing sufficient force to rupture the skin. The dermis is an amazingly resilient organ. May I ask the purpose of your questions?'

'Just eliminating an untenable theory,' Daisy said airily.

'With regard to the man who fell overboard today?'

'Yes, actually.'

'I didn't know there was any question of an effusion of blood,' Dr Amboyne said with interest.

'It's a deep, dark secret, and Captain Dane will have *my* blood if it gets out.'

'You may rely upon my professional reticence. *Ours*, eh, Nurse?'

'Of course, Doctor,' said the nurse primly.

Daisy escaped before she let any more cats out of bags.

A stewardess kindly carried the tray of ginger tea from the stewards' station to the cabin. During the handover at the door, the teapot nearly came to grief; but between them they saved it. Daisy managed to set the tray on the bedside table with its contents intact except for a damp spot on the tray-cloth.

Alec was no longer curled on his side in a ball of misery. He sat propped against the pillows from both berths, his knees pulled up under his chin, looking, if not exactly happy, at least more human.

'What's that?' he asked suspiciously. 'It doesn't smell like mint.'

'You missed a wonderful concert, darling.'

'Was it good? I'm glad you went, anyway. I didn't think it would enhance the audience's enjoyment if I had to rush out in the middle.'

'Spiffing. You must be feeling much better if you even contemplated going.'

'A little,' Alec admitted grudgingly. 'Unquiet rather than agitated about the middle. What's in the pot?'

'Ginger tea. Miss Oliphant says it works even better than mint.'

'Ginger? Great Scott! Not for me, thanks.'

'Coward. If you try it, I will too.' Daisy started to pour. 'Remember when you took me to the Cathay? I'd never tried Chinese food before, but you didn't catch me pulling faces and saying, "Not for me, thanks." That was the first time you ever took me out to dinner. Lucy was sure you'd turn up in a lounge suit and take me to a Lyons Corner House. I said I didn't mind if you did.'

'As I recall, we were celebrating your first American commission.' A faraway look in his eye, Alec sipped the tea.

'Yes, and now here we are, married and going to America! How is it?'

'Marriage? Oh, the tea.' He sipped again, cautiously. 'Not bad. Warming. What's the latest on the second victim? I take it he wasn't found or you'd have told me at once.'

'No, though they did find his hat and retrieved the lifebelt Gotobed threw. Captain Dane seemed pretty sure they would have found him if he hadn't sunk. The burst blood vessel theory is out, by the way. I asked Dr Amboyne.'

'Pity. That leaves us with the same three possibilities we faced with Lady Brenda. With Gotobed, hysteria seems inconceivable.'

'It does, doesn't it? Though he admits to having been shocked to the extent of not grabbing the man when he bent over the rail. He's kicking himself for not stopping him falling.'

'It's easy to be wise after the event, but I dare say he'll go on blaming himself for quite a while. You're still referring to "the man". No name yet?'

'Captain Dane has set things in motion to find out who's missing. What's your second possibility, that Gotobed made up the whole story? I can't imagine why on earth he should do such a thing. He has no need to make himself important, and in fact he's keeping mum about it.'

'There could be other motives for making it up.'

'Such as?'

'Um. I can't think of any at the moment,' Alec confessed.

'You haven't been thinking about the case at all, have you?' Daisy accused him. 'You've been lying here thinking about your beastly stomach, while I've been running up and down stairs, getting shouted at by the Captain, racking my brain to work out what information you need.'

'You seem to have done very well,' Alec said soothingly.

'But I'm not a detective! I have no idea about guns, where the shot could have come from if it did, and all that sort of stuff.'

'Nobody expects you to, love. As I said, you've done very well. Tomorrow will be time enough to check where a gun might have been aimed from. I doubt whether any traces of the marksman lasted longer than a few minutes in that wind and rain.'

'You're taking Gotobed's report seriously now?'

'I see no alternative. If we eliminate hysteria and self-aggrandizement, we appear to be left with truth.'

Daisy sighed. 'Yes, which means we have a murderer aboard. Not a pleasant thought.'

'We'll find him. Once we know the victim's identity.'

'Oh, by the way, it looks as if he *was* one of Wanda's admirers. At least, the one I thought he looked like was the one I thought I saw with Chester Riddman, and Mr Gotobed thought he recognized him as someone he had seen with Riddman.'

'Say that again slowly.'

Daisy complied.

'It's a good job you don't write sentences like that.'

'Beast! Gotobed suspects he was a card-sharp.'

'I believe there's one or two on every transatlantic steamer. Often the victims, having ignored all warnings, are too embarrassed to go to the police.'

'Well, this time the card-sharp is the victim,' Daisy pointed out. 'Alec, Brenda told me Chester Riddman has lost a lot of money playing poker, and I saw him with the crowd on deck just after you left.'

'Probably sheer coincidence,' Alec said thoughtfully, 'but I'll bear it in mind. By all reports, Americans can get hold of guns a lot more easily than Englishmen.'

# CHAPTER 12

Time or the ginger tea had settled Alec's stomach to the point where he agreed to accompany Daisy to the library. She hoped to get a little work done before dinner.

'It's a pity I don't write for one of the Sunday rags,' she said wistfully, watching him put on his jacket and force a comb through his thick hair. 'Just think what I could make of all the goings-on on board!'

He regarded her in the looking glass. 'I expect they would buy it even though you're not a regular contributor.'

'Probably.' Daisy shook her head. 'But it's simply not my line.'

'There's bound to be a good bit of publicity when we reach New York,' Alec consoled her. 'People will buy the magazine with your impressions of the voyage just because of the notoriety. All right, let's go, before I lose my nerve.'

'You'll be perfectly all right if you don't think about it.'

'I dare say, but don't expect me to go in to dinner. That would be tempting fate. By the way, when you spoke to Amboyne, I imagine you asked after Denton?'

'He's no better, maybe even worse. Still unconscious.'

'It's not easy,' said Alec in tones of strong disapproval, 'to investigate an attempted murder in which one cannot speak to the victim, and a murder in which the victim's body is unavailable.'

In the library, he settled down with an R. Austin Freeman novel in which the murder or murders would be solved without fail by the inimitable Dr Thorndyke, probably with the aid of dust from the murderer's pockets. Daisy managed to put aside thoughts of murder and bring some order to her notes on the lighter side of shipboard life. Absorbed, she found herself with only ten minutes to change for dinner. She rushed off, leaving Alec steadfastly refusing to contemplate food.

Mr Arbuckle did turn up to dinner, though he limited himself to clear soup and a dry roll. Horrified to learn of the second man overboard, he exacted a promise from Phillip never to let go of Gloria's hand or arm while they were on deck.

'My pleasure, sir,' said Phillip, grinning.

'He never does anyway, Poppa,' Gloria said complacently, 'unless we're playing a game, and they haven't allowed any deck games since this morning. Phil's been teaching me to play pool – snooker, he calls it. It's a mighty interesting game when the slope of the table changes from moment to moment.'

Everyone laughed, even Gotobed, who was out of spirits, not at all his usual lively self.

'It's a hanging table,' Phillip explained, 'so it stays level in calm seas, but it can't cope with what we've been having.'

'I'll have to come and watch you play tomorrow,' said Daisy. 'It might make an amusing paragraph for my article.'

'Yes, do come along, old bean,' Phillip urged. 'You'll have to give it a try. Daisy's not a bad player, Glow-worm.'

'I've beaten you more than once,' Daisy reminded him, adding hastily, 'playing on a level table. Do you play, Miss Oliphant?'

'I never have. In my youth, it was considered a game strictly for gentlemen.'

'I'll teach you,' Phillip offered.

'If you learn on a swinging table, Miss Oliphant,' Arbuckle put in with a chuckle, 'you'll be unbeatable on *terra firma.* I'd sure like to come and cheer you on, but I guess I'd better not risk it. Just the thought of watching . . . no, better not. Gotobed, can I depute you as cheerleader?'

'Aye, I'll be glad to,' he agreed, smiling at Miss Oliphant, 'and mebbe I'll take a hand meself.'

'Ripping, we'll have a tournament,' said Phillip. 'We'll have to work out a system of handicaps, Glow-worm. Will Fletcher play, Daisy?'

'No,' Daisy said firmly. Alec was going to be much too busy for games. 'He's up, but I don't suppose watching a swinging table would be any better for him than for Mr Arbuckle. How is Wanda, Mr Gotobed?'

The words were scarcely out of her mouth when it dawned on her that the first person to ask about the second man overboard should have been Wanda Gotobed. Surely he had introduced himself to her when he approached her to express his admiration. She might have forgotten his name though. Anyway, Captain Dane's cohorts of stewards probably had the answer by now, but if not . . .

She had missed what Gotobed said, but he didn't look happy. 'I'll try to pop in again this evening,' she promised.

The other person to ask, of course, would be the other stage-door Johnnie. Unfortunately, all she could remember about him was that he was unmemorable. On the short side for a man, she thought, certainly smaller than the flashy one. Greying? Perhaps.

Not enough to identify him by, even among the ship's limited population. Daisy turned her full attention to a heavenly apple and almond tart.

'What Alec's missing!' she sighed.

After dinner, she was going to rejoin him when she was stopped by the Purser, Timmins, a tall, stout man whose professional joviality thinly disguised a perpetually anxious nature.

'Mrs Fletcher? May I have a word with you?'

The stewards would report to the Purser, of course. 'Yes,' she said, 'but if you come to the library, my husband is there and you can tell us both at once.'

'If Mr Fletcher is on his feet again, I need not trouble you, ma'am. I understand he is a policeman.'

He wasn't getting rid of Daisy so easily. 'Alec's still not well. I'll be lending him a hand.'

Timmins was accustomed to handling awkward passengers, but in this unprecedented situation he was unsure of his ground. 'I suppose it's for Mr Fletcher to say,' he conceded.

They proceeded to the library together. Alec was a few pages from the end of his book, and he set it aside reluctantly.

'Not bad,' he said. 'At least Freeman doesn't make the police out to be complete idiots, as most detective novelists seem to. We have an identification?' He reached for the pad of ship's notepaper on the table beside him, and took his fountain pen from his pocket.

The Purser cast a significant glance at Daisy, but as Alec failed to shoo her away, he shrugged and said, 'Yes, sir. Captain Dane instructed me to inform you. The only passenger not positively located is a Curtis Pertwee.' He spelt the name.

Alec wrote it down. 'Curtis Pertwee. What, if anything, do we know about him?'

'Not much. He is . . . was in a tourist-class cabin, sharing with another gentleman, a Mr Welford, who is one of our sufferers, confined to his bunk. When the steward knocked and popped his head in to check who was there, Mr Welford almost snapped it off. I suppose you'll want to speak to him, sir?'

'Yes, of course. I need all the information I can get about Pertwee, and his travelling companion is the obvious source.'

'Er, they weren't necessarily travelling together,' said Timmins uncomfortably. 'That is, they didn't necessarily know each other before the voyage or book together. Although at this time of year we generally have a few empty cabins, the company prefers us to double up passengers where possible. It's a matter of economics.'

'One cabin to clean instead of two,' said Daisy, whom living with Lucy had taught that though two cannot live as cheaply as one, they can live much more cheaply together than apart. 'I expect you can shut off some heating ducts, too, and things like that.'

'Exactly, madam, just a few odds and ends of savings. It's

not much but it adds up, and this is a highly competitive business.'

'At any rate,' Alec said impatiently, 'this Welford is as likely as anyone aboard to be able to tell me something of Pertwee.'

'Yes, sir, though he did seem pretty chummy with the young American, Mr Riddman. I suppose there's no harm mentioning it since the fellow's dead: I had some suspicion that Pertwee might be one of the professional, none too scrupulous gamblers we sometimes get aboard. My staff noticed him playing poker with Riddman in the Smoking Room the first night out and going in and out of Riddman's first-class cabin since.'

Daisy gave Alec a look of triumph.

'I'll bear it in mind,' he said.

'However,' Timmins continued, 'he's not a regular, not one of the fellows we watch out for, and I may be maligning him. If you must speak to Riddman, I hope you'll, er, be tactful.'

'He's a Detective Chief Inspector of the Metropolitan Police CID, not a village bobby,' Daisy said indignantly.

'Sorry! It's got us all on edge, two passengers falling overboard. Suppose it's something in the food or the ventilation system that's giving them dizzy turns? That's my department, and I don't mind admitting it's got me worried. The last thing I need on top of that is a first-class passenger blaming me for letting him – so to speak – fall among sharks.'

'It's the shark who drowned,' Alec pointed out. 'If I were you, I'd be more worried about general panic among the passengers. Believe me, I'll do my best to avoid any move which might have that result. Which cabin is the late Pertwee's?'

The Purser gave him the number, and the names of the day and night stewards attendant on that cabin. 'They may know something useful to you, though I don't know quite what it is you're looking for. Still, since Captain Dane wants a police officer to investigate this accident, I'm happy to leave the whole wretched business in your hands.'

Looking more harassed than happy, he shook Alec's hand, bowed to Daisy, and took himself off.

'I'm surprised the Captain hasn't told him it wasn't an accident,' said Daisy.

'*Possibly* was not an accident,' Alec corrected her. 'Dane's playing his cards close to his chest, and I can't say I blame him. The fewer people who know, the less chance of a leakage. I hate to think of the result of panic in a closed community like this, where no one can escape. Well, I'm off to interview Welford. I only hope he doesn't set me off again.'

Standing up, he turned pale and had to put a hand on the table to steady himself. Daisy looked at him in alarm.

'You've had nothing to eat all day. You'll be the next one overboard. Darling, promise you won't go out on deck alone!'

'I've no intention of going out at all,' he said testily, heading for the door, his stride reassuringly resolute.

'But you might change your mind after seeing Welford. I'm coming, too. Don't worry, I shan't insist on invading the cabin of a sick man, but couldn't I talk to the steward while you talk to Welford?'

'I'd rather you tackled Mrs Gotobed, since I can't. Pertwee just may have let drop something helpful when he approached her, and if you can get the name of her second admirer, he might be able to help.'

'Not tonight, darling. I did promise I'd pop in, but she's probably trying to fall asleep, if she's not asleep already. It's not the moment for an interrogation.'

'Go and do your popping then, love, and leave the steward to me.'

'Right-oh,' Daisy sighed, 'but then I'm coming to find you.'

The steward tapped on the cabin door.

A shaky voice called, 'Who's there?'

'This is your steward, sir. A gentleman to see you.'

'Can't see anyone. I'm not well.'

Though Alec was beginning to think he might survive the voyage, the memory of his ordeal was vivid enough to make him feel like a cad for disturbing someone still in the throes. Nonetheless, he said firmly, 'I'm sorry, Mr Welford, but I am under the Captain's orders. There has been an accident. I'm afraid I must insist on speaking to you.'

When no response came, he tried the door. It was locked. He nodded to the steward, who had his pass-key at the ready. A moment later the door swung open.

The cabin was in near darkness, lit only by the light from the passage and the dim night safety bulb on the ceiling, which was not in the passengers' control. Alec automatically reached for the switch by the door, then hesitated. His intrusion was bad enough, without exposing the poor fellow to the full glare of electric light.

He closed the door. After a few seconds his eyes adjusted to the dimness.

The cabin was an inside one, with no porthole, but otherwise the twin of his and Daisy's: two cabin trunks against the bulkhead (his and Daisy's came from the Fairacres attics, courtesy of Edgar, Lord Dalrymple), a washstand, wall hooks for coats and hats, railed shelves over the two berths – and a china basin on the floor between them.

Fortunately, Welford didn't seem to have actually vomited. Alec was not sure he could have coped with that smell. As it was, having more or less found his sealegs, he felt pleasantly superior to the miserable shape huddled in the right-hand berth.

'My name is Fletcher,' he said. 'I most sincerely beg your pardon for intruding. I'm afraid your cabin-mate has suffered an accident, a fatal accident, and Captain Dane has instructed me to find out what I can about him.'

A groan was the only answer.

If Daisy had suffered an accident while Alec was feeling his worst, he liked to think he would have jumped up to do whatever was necessary. However, had his cabin-mate been a stranger assigned at random by the Wellington Line, he doubted he would have been able to summon up much interest in the fellow's fate. He sympathized with Welford but pressed on.

'Were you acquainted with Mr Pertwee before the voyage, sir?'

'No.'

'So you've known him only a few days. That's a pity. Still, any information you can give me is more than I have now. Did he talk about his family?'

'No.'

'His work? His friends or associates at home?'

'No.'

'His purpose in going to America?' Alec persisted.

'No.'

'Not a conversable gentleman. But you must be aware of whom he associated with aboard?'

'No. Just because we shared a cabin, it doesn't mean we had to stick together.' Welford's peevish voice was educated, perhaps minor public school.

'True,' Alec agreed. He shot an arrow at a venture, not really supposing that serious animosity could be generated in so short a time. 'I take it you found you had little in common, then. Perhaps you even found being confined together at such close quarters irksome?'

Welford responded by performing a sort of half dive over the side of the berth, reaching for the basin. Alec fled.

The steward was waiting in the passage. 'Any luck, sir?' he enquired.

Alec shook his head. 'It sounds as if Welford and Pertwee scarcely exchanged a word.'

'That's not so bad, sir. Sometimes them that's put in together get to where they rub each other's nerves something dreadful. They come running to us stewards with complaints about hairs in the washbasin, and lights left on when someone's trying to sleep, and someone else getting up early with a lot of noise when the other chap's trying to sleep. Not much we can do about it 'cepting ask 'em to be more considerate.'

'You haven't had any complaints from those two?'

'Nary a murmur, sir, nor Brittlin hasn't, that's on days. We pass 'em on to each other, see, so's we know what to look out for. I reckon they just ignored each other. I never saw 'em go in or out together, and the Purser always seats people sharing a cabin at different tables, 'less they're a married couple, of course, or ask to be together.'

'I'll have to go through Pertwee's luggage tomorrow,' Alec said. 'His next of kin must be informed of his death as soon as we reach New York.'

'I 'spect the Captain's already sent the company a wireless, sir. They'll be looking for next of kin.'

Unaccustomed to being anywhere he might need it, Alec had temporarily forgotten the existence of wireless telegraphy. He would telegraph the Yard and see what they came up with. If Pertwee was unknown to Records, Tom Tring could have a go at digging out his life history, including any enemies who might have wanted to do away with him.

'I'll still need to go through his things,' he told the steward, 'and I must have a word with Brittlin, was it? May I leave it to you to arrange matters?'

'Right you are, sir,' said the man resignedly.

Who next, Alec thought, the unlucky gambler, Riddman, or Gotobed, whose story he really ought to hear for himself? Or should he go straight to the wireless room? No, it opened off the bridge, and he had more or less promised Daisy not to go outside alone. He did feel pretty groggy. He would wait and see if she had learnt anything new from Wanda and then decide what to do next.

Meanwhile, Daisy called on Wanda. The maid admitted her with a hopeful look, which faded as Daisy said, 'I can only stay a minute. How is Mrs Gotobed?'

'Restless, ma'am,' Baines said tiredly. 'I'll tell her you're here.' She went into the bedroom, returning a moment later to invite Daisy to step in.

This time the room was lit by a standard lamp behind the chaise longue on which Wanda reclined. She dropped a copy of *Vogue* on the floor as Daisy entered. Clad in silk lounging pyjamas in her favourite bright pink, she looked much recovered.

'I'm glad you've come, Daisy,' she said. 'I'm ever so bored.'

'I can only stay a few minutes. Mr Gotobed would be happy to come down to entertain you, I know.'

'Oh no, I'm not well enough.' She put a theatrical hand to her forehead. 'I did make an effort for his sake and get out of bed, but I'm reelly not well. It's the make-up; it makes me look lots better than I feel.'

'Since you've recovered enough to get up though, just tell me, do you recall the names of your two admirers who were talking to you the other day?'

Sitting bolt upright, Wanda demanded in alarm, 'Why?'

'Don't worry, I haven't told your husband about them. It's just that there's been an accident and . . .'

'An accident! What's happened?'

'I'm afraid a man I think was one of those two, a Mr Pertwee, fell overboard and drowned.'

Wanda burst into tears, burying her face in her hands. Astonished, Daisy dug into her evening bag for a handkerchief.

'Here, take this. I'm frightfully sorry. I didn't think it would upset you so.'

'It's the shock,' Wanda sobbed. 'He was . . . he was . . .'

'Don't try to talk now. I'll call your maid.'

'No, no, don't. I'll be all right in a minute, honest.' She raised her head, her face white beneath the smeared cosmetics. 'I – I'm just too soft-hearted for me own good. I mean, someone I know! You don't think something like that'll happen. I feel all woozy.'

'Let me help you back to bed,' Daisy offered, filled with guilt. She had thought Wanda as hard as nails, or she would never have broken the news so abruptly.

The distress was obviously genuine. Wanda was actually shaking as Daisy supported her over to the bed. Was she really ill, not just seasick?

'Shall I ask Dr Amboyne to look in on you?'

'No, it would only worry Dickie. I just want to get to sleep. I've got some powders somewhere. Baines'll know, and tell her I want a hot water bottle, will you?'

'Right-oh,' Daisy said obligingly. It seemed to be her day for summary dismissals. 'I hope you get a good night's sleep and feel better in the morning.'

She went to look for Alec and met him coming away from Pertwee's cabin.

'What luck?' they asked simultaneously, and both shook their heads.

'Wanda's not at all well,' said Daisy, 'and easily upset. She cried like anything when I told her Pertwee is dead, so I'm sure he was one of her admirers though I never did get an answer out of her.'

'You didn't get the name of the second admirer?' Alec asked.

'No, but it strikes me, darling, that Pertwee probably knew whoever it was quite well or they wouldn't both have approached her at the same time. It wasn't Welford?'

Alec shrugged. 'Welford denies knowing anything about Pertwee, but he was too sick to be communicative. Of course, supposing they were in league to cheat at cards, he wouldn't want the connection known. If so, they were careful. The steward never saw them coming or going together.'

'That in itself sounds fishy. You'll have to ask Chester Riddman who his poker partners are. Were.'

As they talked, Alec had led the way to their own cabin. Taking off his jacket, he said, 'It's going to be ticklish. Get me out my evening togs, will you, love? You say Lady Brenda told you Riddman lost a lot of money. The Purser says he's known to have played poker with Pertwee. You saw Riddman on deck shortly after Pertwee was shot – assuming, as I must, that he *was* shot. Obviously Riddman is a prime suspect.'

'So you can't just march up to him and start asking questions without putting him on his guard.'

'Precisely. At least I'll talk to his steward first, see if I can get a description of the other man or men he gambled with. What did the second stage-door Johnnie look like? Damn this collar! I hate stiff collars.'

'They're as silly as bustles or Grecian Bends,' Daisy agreed. She noticed with pleasure his use of "damn", equating it to Gotobed's lapses into pure Yorkshire. After just over a fortnight of marriage, Alec was no longer afraid the odd swear word might injure her delicate aristocratic sensibilities. 'Let me do the studs for you, darling. Johnnie Number Two was utterly nondescript. All I can remember about him is that he was shorter than Number One – Pertwee. What's Welford like?'

'As I only saw him under the bedcovers by the light of the night-lamp, I couldn't describe him to save my life. He did emerge in the end, but when I realized his objective was the basin on the floor, I scarpered. I got the impression of a smallish man with a bald spot.'

'He can't be ruled out as Number Two then. Gosh, darling, it's just dawned on me that Pertwee might have been more to Wanda than simply another admirer. If he had been her lover, it would explain why she was so upset.'

Alec stopped with his waistcoat half on. 'It certainly would,' he agreed, 'and that opens up all sorts of possibilities. For instance, did he follow her in order to blackmail her?'

'I don't think so,' Daisy said doubtfully, holding the waistcoat for him to put his other arm in. 'They looked quite chummy. All she seemed concerned about afterwards was that Gotobed shouldn't find out.'

'Which suggests that there was something to find out,' said Alec. He buttoned his waistcoat and reached for his dinner jacket. 'She told you she didn't want him reminded of her career on the stage?'

'Yes, though come to think of it, he's never shown the least reluctance to talk about it. But if she's sensitive about it, she probably assumes he is.'

'Very likely. On the other hand, she'd have every reason to fear his finding out that her lover was aboard.'

'Even if Pertwee is still . . . was still her lover, I can't see why he came on the *Talavera.*' Daisy straighted Alec's black tie, a wifely gesture in which she took great pleasure.

'It would be easier and safer to resume their liaison when she gets back to England.'

'Failing a deathless passion and resultant refusal to be parted, I'd guess he was living on Gotobed's unknowing largesse,' Alec said cynically as they left the cabin. 'She would find it difficult to pass on large sums so early in the marriage, so he'd have to remain nearby.'

'But he's been winning at poker. Oh, but Brenda said Riddman's cheques hadn't been cashed. I think he told her the winner promised to hold them till New York. Darling, I bet Brenda knows the names of the men who played poker with Riddman! Shall I have a little heart-to-heart with her? If you try to pump her, it's bound to get back to him and warn him of your suspicions.'

'Daisy, I haven't forgotten Riddman,' Alec said, 'but you do realize, don't you, love, that if Pertwee was Wanda's lover, the man with the best motive for putting him away is Gotobed?'

# CHAPTER 13

Daisy stopped dead with her hand on the companion-way rail. 'Gotobed?' she said, horrified. 'Impossible!'

Alec groaned, recognizing the symptoms. Whenever Daisy got herself mixed up in one of his cases, or mixed him up in one of her entanglements, she sooner or later took one of his suspects under her wing. Thereafter, she refused to credit the possibility of that person's guilt.

Sometimes she was right, and sometimes she was painfully wrong. The trouble was, she could no longer view the case objectively. Her theories and opinions, which Alec ruefully admitted were occasionally useful, tended to exculpate her favourite. She would fail to report odd snippets of information. Alec was convinced – well, fairly certain – she did not do so on purpose; it was more like an unconscious refusal to see their significance.

'He was standing right beside Pertwee,' Alec reminded her, 'actually reaching into his pocket.'

'For matches, not a pistol. We would have seen if he had pulled out a gun.'

'Would you? I don't think I would, not at that moment.'

'Well, perhaps not. At that particular moment I was more concerned with catching the rail and not going overboard myself. But Gotobed couldn't have known we wouldn't be watching. He knew we were right there.'

'True. It would have to have been the decision of a split second when he saw our attention elsewhere. He could hardly miss at that range.'

'And he was carrying a pistol around on the off-chance?' Daisy said sceptically.

'Why not, if he knew about his wife and Pertwee?'

'Which is pure speculation in the first place,' she scoffed. 'Besides, if he'd shot Pertwee, he'd hardly have reported to the Captain that he'd been shot. No one would have known.'

'He couldn't be sure the body wouldn't be recovered,' Alec pointed out. 'If Pertwee had been hauled out with a bullet in him, and Gotobed was known to be standing beside him and had said nothing, it would have looked extremely fishy.'

'Maybe, but – Oh, sorry!'

They were blocking the way, still standing at the bottom of the companion-way where Daisy had come to a halt. She moved aside to let another couple pass and then started upwards. Alec followed.

'But?' he asked.

'Gotobed's no fool. If he wanted to bump off Pertwee, which I don't believe, he wouldn't have done it in such a public place when he was the only one near him.'

'Not if he had planned the murder, I agree. But we've only Gotobed's word for it that Pertwee asked for a light. Pertwee must have known who he was. What if he actually revealed his affair with Wanda at that moment, and Gotobed reacted without thinking?'

'In that case, Gotobed didn't know before, so why was he carrying a gun?' Daisy asked reasonably. 'And why would Pertwee reveal the *affaire*, thus killing the goose that laid the golden eggs?'

Alec was sure there must be answers to both questions, but he couldn't think of any. His head was distinctly muzzy after twenty-four hours without nourishment; not the best state in which to confront witnesses, let alone suspects. He still couldn't face food. Yet now that he was on his feet, he could not leave the investigation to Daisy, especially since she was determined to defend Gotobed.

She could help elsewhere though, and it would distract her. As they reached the entrance to the Grand Salon, he said, 'You're right about Lady Brenda, love. Will you see what you can find out from her, without being too obvious? Do not, for instance, ask if she was with Riddman when Pertwee was shot.'

'Right-oh, darling.' She scanned the room and Alec followed suit.

Tonight, two-thirds of the space was occupied by small tables – half of each dining table having been removed – and groups of easy chairs, all bolted down. Passengers were chatting, reading, playing cards, chess, or backgammon. On the small dance floor, several couples gyrated.

Alec noticed uneasily that the dancers' movements were frequently interrupted by unorthodox steps dictated by the ship's motion, affording them a good deal of amusement. The *Talavera* was skipping about like a drunken lamb. However, his stomach seemed to have settled, more or less, and he had begun to adjust automatically for the irregular movements as he walked. Nonetheless, he quickly averted his gaze from the dance floor.

'Brenda's dancing with Riddman,' Daisy said in surprise. 'Doesn't that suggest that he's lost his poker partners, one dead and one seasick?'

'Or he's come to realize he owes his fiancée some attention. Leave her be this evening. You may not need to talk to her at all if I get the information from Riddman's steward. He probably has a manservant aboard, but I'd rather keep him in the dark if possible. Ah, there's Gotobed.'

'Darling, he . . .'

'You know I have to have a first-hand description of what he saw when Pertwee went over.' He headed for the table where his quarry sat with Arbuckle and Miss Oliphant.

In spite of the cottonwool in his head, Alec easily manoeuvred matters the way he wanted them. The gentlemen rose when Daisy arrived . . . of course. As they all exchanged greetings, Alec seated her in the fourth chair. Then he laid his hand on Gotobed's sleeve and indicated a nearby empty table with his head. The two of them moved over to it. Alec felt Daisy's reproachful gaze following him.

'Sorry to drag you away, sir.'

'That's quite all right.' Gotobed appeared neither surprised nor alarmed. 'You'll be wanting to hear about it for yourself, Chief Inspector.'

'Please, Fletcher will do. Yes, I do need the story from the horse's mouth. You are the only eyewitness, as Daisy and I weren't looking at that moment.'

The Yorkshireman's lips twitched. 'So I gather. I see you have found your sealegs. I only wish Wanda would try Miss Oliphant's simples.'

'They do seem to have helped,' Alec said cautiously, 'especially the ginger. Will you describe, please, exactly what happened?'

Gotobed ruminated for a moment. 'To begin at the beginning,' he said, 'I went up to the boat deck to smoke a pipe. I don't care for the Smoking Room, and a bit of bad weather doesn't bother me. In fact, I rather like a good, boisterous blow. You're a townsman, I believe?'

'Born and bred. I can see the attraction of a blustery wind though. I know Daisy finds it invigorating.'

'Aye, there's a lass after me own heart,' Gotobed observed, lapsing momentarily into Yorkshire. He resumed in standard English: 'I found a sheltered nook to light my pipe then went over to the rail. It was just a few minutes later that I turned and recognized you and Mrs Fletcher under a pair of sou'westers.'

'Daisy's almost swallowed her,' said Alec, with a reminiscent grin, reflected on Gotobed's face. Alec was finding it damnably difficult to remember the man was a suspect. He was just too likeable. 'They were lent us by the first officer. I was talking to him about Denton.'

'The fellow who went overboard last night? How is he?'

'In a bad way, I'm afraid.'

'I'm sorry to hear it. This doesn't seem to be a lucky voyage, does it?' Gotobed sighed. 'And it started with such high hopes.'

'Seasickness plays havoc with one's plans,' Alec commiserated tactfully. 'But to continue, Daisy and I started towards you.'

'And before you reached me, that fellow . . .'

'Excuse me,' Alec interrupted, 'you don't know his name?'

'You haven't discovered yet who he was? I'm afraid I can't help you. I'd never spoken to him before, though I'd seen him about once or twice.'

Gotobed appeared to be perfectly sincere. Alec reminded himself that no man makes a million before he's forty without possessing a certain talent for dissimulation.

'Oh, we know who he was. A Mr Pertwee, Curtis Pertwee.' Though he watched narrowly, Alec did not see so much as a flicker of an eyelid at the name. 'I simply wondered why he approached someone with whom he was unacquainted.'

'I wondered the same thing myself. I suppose he saw I was smoking. He waved a cigarette at me and asked for a light. Naturally I reached for my matches, though I didn't think there was much sense trying to strike one in that wind and rain. In fact, now I recall thinking I'd have to lend him the box to take to a sheltered corner.' If Gotobed was making up the story, he certainly had the details pat.

'Safety matches?' Alec asked, on the off-chance of confusing him.

'I wouldn't carry any others in my pockets. I had my hand in my pocket when the ship cut a caper. I lost my balance and stepped back, mebbe twisted round a bit, but I kept my eyes on the fellow – Pertwee. He did a sort of hop towards me, and I wasn't sure but that he was going to crash into me. I imagine it was to avoid doing so that he twisted aside, with his back to the rail.'

'Ah, he was facing away from the rail when it happened?'

Gotobed nodded. 'Suddenly a look of horror came over his face. He raised his hand towards his shoulder, and I saw blood welling there. At the same time, he spun round. He pitched over the rail before I could react. I blame myself greatly for not catching him. An old man's reflexes are not what they were,' he added heavily.

'I doubt many men would have reacted fast enough or been able to hang on once he started to topple. The look of horror came first, did it?'

'No, not really. It all happened so fast.' Gotobed shrugged helplessly. 'I saw his expression, the blood, the movement of his hand, and his turning virtually simultaneously.'

'And you knew he'd been shot.'

'No, no. I was too shocked to think at all. Throwing the lifebelt was automatic, not a reasoned action. Then that possibility dawned on me. I believe I blurted it out to Mrs Fletcher immediately, but it was after she ran off to inform the bridge – What a cool head in an emergency! You must be very proud of her.'

'She has a good deal of common sense,' said Alec, with vicarious modesty. He hadn't realized Daisy had been responsible for stopping the *Talavera*, but he might have guessed. She had been the one to take charge when Lady Brenda turned hysterical after Denton fell overboard. Dammit, he *was* proud of her, and he ought to tell her so.

'It was not until she had gone,' Gotobed went on, 'that I really thought about it, and I could come up with no other explanation which fitted what I had seen.'

'You are familiar with firearms?'

'Not with their use, though I do know something of the metals involved in their manufacture. I was too old to fight in the war, of course, but I trust the details I was able to provide about Germany's pre-war imports of special steels may have been of some small assistance. And though a countryman, I am not, as you know, a country *gentleman.* The nearest I've come to shooting as a sport was earning a few shillings as a beater in my youth. Any poaching I may have been guilty of – and I admit to nothing, mind you! – was a matter of snares, not shotguns.'

He was convincing. Alec's suspicions veered towards Chester Riddman, but he asked, 'You did not hear a shot?'

'No. The wind noise up there was tremendous, as you may recall.'

'Nor see anyone leaving in a hurry or throwing something overboard which could have been a weapon?'

'My entire attention was on the unfortunate victim. Pertwee, you said? Has he relatives aboard?'

'Apparently not. Thank you, sir, I appreciate your cooperation. Perhaps I might beg a favour? Since I haven't my usual facilities for investigation, would you be so kind as to write down your recollections, while they are fresh in your mind, in the form of a formal statement?'

'Certainly. I shall let you have it tomorrow,' Gotobed promised. 'I'm afraid I haven't been very helpful.'

'You have been very clear, which few witnesses manage.

And without your report, no one would have known a crime had been committed.'

Gotobed showed no sign of wishing he had kept it to himself 'I hope you catch t'bugger as did it,' he said, standing up, his gaze fixed on something behind Alec.

Alec glanced back. Phillip and Gloria Petrie had joined Arbuckle and Miss Oliphant. Petrie was standing with his hand on the back of his wife's chair, and beside him stood Chester Riddman. Both were tall, sleek, and dressed in the finest evening get-up Savile Row could produce. Petrie looked as usual amiable and rather fatuous. In comparison, the younger American had a reckless, dissipated air.

'Riddman?' Alec asked Gotobed.

'Nay, lad, I've no call to be naming names.'

'I'll be asking Mr Riddman a few questions. But probably not tonight,' he added, spotting Daisy and Lady Brenda heading for the door to the ladies' lounge. With any luck, Daisy would provide him with some ammunition with which to face Riddman in the morning.

What luck! Daisy thought. Chatting with Arbuckle and Miss Oliphant, she had been wishing she could overhear Alec and Gotobed. Then the music stopped. Phillip and Gloria were next to Riddman and Brenda on the dance floor, and the two girls spoke to each other. Still talking, Gloria started towards her father's table, and Brenda drifted along with her. Phillip naturally followed, after exchanging a word with Riddman. Riddman in turn, after an indecisive moment, had reluctantly drifted along with Phillip.

Introductions took several minutes, after which Brenda announced that she was going to powder her nose.

'I'll come too, Birdie,' said Daisy, so here she was with her quarry, making for the ladies' lounge, that haven for confidences.

When Brenda emerged from the inner room, Daisy was seated at one of the long mirrors, studying her face critically.

'Freckles,' she observed as Brenda sat down on the stool next to her and took her powder-puff from her evening bag. 'Five minutes of sunshine, even at this time of year, and a whole new crop appears. It's a good job Alec doesn't mind them. I was pleased to see Mr Riddman dancing with you this evening.'

Brenda glowed. 'Yes, isn't it marvellous? Chester's a frightfully good dancer and such fun when he's in a good mood.'

So much for Second Officer Harvey, whom Daisy had spotted sadly watching Brenda and Riddman dancing. 'Has he turned over a new leaf?' she asked.

'I hope so. But I don't know. The men he plays poker with didn't turn up after dinner.'

'What, none of them?'

'Neither; there are just two regulars. Daisy, you said they sounded like card-sharps. Do you really think they've been cheating him?'

'I don't know. Maybe not both. Have you met them? Or has he described them to you? Tell me about them.'

'I've met them.' Brenda didn't look as if it had been an enjoyable experience. The name she next uttered was no surprise to Daisy. 'Pertwee's the one who found Chester's wallet on the quay and returned it. Chester always carries loads of cash, and it was all there so Pertwee must be honest, don't you think? He's rather common, though quite good looking in a flashy sort of way. Actually, he's just how you might imagine a card-sharp to be.'

'I'd have thought card-sharps do their level best not to look like what they are. Did he win a lot from Chester or was it mostly the other one?'

'I think it was mostly Pertwee. In fact, yes, I remember Chester saying the other chap was a sore loser.'

'Hmm.' Daisy couldn't work out exactly what had been going on, but it sounded fishy. The Purser might be able to shed some light on the working methods of sharps. 'What was the other man like?' she asked.

Brenda looked blank. 'Just ordinary. Not quite top drawer but not an absolute outsider. Rather quiet, I think. He didn't make much impression actually. I can't even remember his name.'

Blast! thought Daisy. That was the one scrap of information she had wanted most, apart from Riddman's whereabouts at the time of the shot, which she must not ask after Alec's categorical prohibition. 'Big or small? Young or old?' she persevered.

'Oh, just medium. I can't see what that has to do with whether he cheated at cards though, as long as he wasn't a midget who couldn't fit an ace up his sleeve. He seemed too dull to be a crook, but you just said a card-sharp would try not to look like one.'

'And you said he was losing anyway. Were he and Pertwee friends?'

'I haven't the foggiest. Daisy, *do* you think one or

both of them has been cheating Chester? Should I warn him?'

'Would he take any notice if you did?' Daisy countered. She sighed as Brenda's face fell. 'Sorry, Birdie! I honestly don't know, but I'll see if I can find out any more and tell you, all right? So if you remember the second man's name, let me know. It'd help.'

'Right-oh, and thanks. It's jolly decent of you.'

'I can't promise a definite answer.' She hadn't many answers for Alec either. She could have promised Brenda that Pertwee, at least, would never play poker again, but that would lead to questions about how she knew what was not yet general knowledge. 'Shall we go back?'

They returned to the Grand Salon and made their way towards the table where they had left the others. Only Alec, Gotobed, and Phillip were there.

'Where's Chester?' Brenda wondered in an apprehensive tone, scanning the room. 'Oh, he's dancing with Mrs Petrie! Gosh, maybe he's going to start being fun again.'

Because he imagined he had wiped out his gambling debts by bumping off the man who held his cheques? Daisy was sure it would not be so simple. Somewhere Pertwee must have heirs, who would receive all his effects, including the cheques.

As Riddman swung Gloria into an impressive turn, Daisy saw that his smile was strained. He did not look as if he was having fun – unlike the couple nearest them. Arbuckle and Miss Oliphant were obviously having the time of their lives. Daisy recalled Wanda's snide suggestion that the witch was on the catch for a wealthy husband. Could it be true?

'If so, good luck to her,' Daisy murmured to herself as she and Brenda reached the table.

Phillip sprang up. 'Lady Brenda, would you like to dance? I know you won't mind, old thing,' he said to Daisy. 'It's not your sort of dance.'

'Not at all,' Daisy heartily agreed, observing again the cavorting on the dance floor. Sitting down with Alec and Gotobed, she added, 'I've been dashing *up and* down companion-ways all day. I'll have to beg or borrow some more of Miss Oliphant's salve, or I shan't be able to move tomorrow.'

'She's a grand dancer,' sighed Gotobed. 'I didn't think it would be right, dancing when Wanda's ill abed. I ought to go down and see how she's feeling.'

'I did stop in earlier,' Daisy told him. 'She said she was going to take a powder to help her sleep, so there's no point in your going down.'

He frowned. 'I wish she wouldn't take those powders. There are herbs which aid sleep without any possibility of dangerous overdosing, Miss Oliphant was telling me. Camomile and valerian, I believe.'

'I expect they're safe enough,' said Alec, 'like mint and ginger. But there are also many plant preparations which are dangerous if not used properly.'

'Speaking of mint,' said Gotobed, signalling to a passing steward, 'can I get you a *crème de menthe*, Mrs Fletcher? Or something else, perhaps? What will you have, Fletcher?'

'I think I'd better stick to seltzer, thanks. I might venture on a few plain biscuits.'

'Bravo, darling! I'd like to try the ginger wine tonight, Mr Gotobed.'

Under cover of Gotobed's giving their orders to the steward, Alec asked in a low voice, 'Anything from Lady Brenda?'

'Pertwee did play poker with Riddman, and he was the big winner. She can't remember the other player's name, said he was utterly unmemorable, which sounds just like Johnnie Number Two.'

'And any number of others.'

'At least it doesn't rule out Welford,' Daisy pointed out.

'No. I must go and talk to Riddman's cabin steward. I was just saying, sir,' he added as Gotobed turned back to them, 'that I shall shortly have to – in official parlance – proceed to pursue my enquiries.'

'You'll stay and eat your biscuits first,' Daisy said sternly.

'I'm actually quite looking forward to them,' Alec admitted.

The digestive biscuits and seltzer were scarcely consumed when the dance ended and the three couples returned to the table. In the bustle as the Petries, Brenda, and Riddman took over a nearby empty table, Alec gave up his seat to Miss Oliphant and slipped away. Daisy sadly abandoned half her ginger wine to follow him. If he should decide to go up to the bridge to report to the Captain, she was determined not to let him go alone. Too many people knew he was investigating the two 'accidents'.

Most people aboard were still under the impression that Denton and Pertwee had fallen overboard by accident. Glancing back from the door, Daisy saw a scene of tranquil enjoyment. How that would change if everyone found out the truth!

# CHAPTER 14

Turning back down the wide, first-class passageway, Alec saw Daisy waiting for him at the corner.

'Don't scowl like that,' she admonished. 'I'm being discreet. I didn't ask to attend that interview, did I? What did Riddman's steward have to say?'

'That passengers get plenty of warnings about sharps aboard, and it's not his place to warn silly young chubs who think they know better. That Pertwee ordered a great deal of whisky but drank little and paid for less, the rest going down Riddman's throat and on Riddman's account. That the third chap was a quiet gentleman who lost more than he won. The others didn't pay him much mind, but in his – the steward's – opinion, he was the brains of the outfit.'

'And his name?'

'He couldn't rightly remember.' Alec grinned at her disappointed face. 'A name as commonplace as his appearance. Fordham, was it? Or Bidwell?'

'Welford!'

'It seems likely, doesn't it?'

Daisy did a hop and a skip to compensate for a sudden jolt from the *Talavera.* Alec caught her arm, pleased by his own steady stride. 'Where are you going?' she asked. 'To see Welford?'

'No, to the Purser first, to find out whether there is a Fordham aboard or a Bidwell.' He turned towards the nearest companion-way. 'If not, then it looks as if our friend Welford wasn't altogether frank when he told me he didn't fraternize with his cabin-mate.'

'In that case, they must have been in league for some fishy purpose. Except that, darling,' she continued with one of her lightning changes of viewpoint, 'perhaps he was just too ill to understand your questions properly. You should sympathize.'

Alec thought back to the absurd interview in the dark cabin. He could not have made notes had he wanted to, and he had had no chance since to write down what he recalled, but his memory was good. 'Mostly he just answered 'No' to my questions, which he could quite well have done without understanding them. But he did say something on the lines of not having to associate with Pertwee just because they were stuck in a cabin together.'

'Not quite a lie,' said Daisy thoughtfully, preceding Alec up the stairs as two women came down towards them, 'if that's how he worded it.'

'Something to that effect, I'm sure, but I'm not at all sure he was thinking clearly enough to work out the fine line between a lie and the truth. If he and Pertwee were in league, Pertwee's death must have rattled him.'

'Gosh, yes! Maybe he wasn't sick at all. On top of losing his colleague, he'd have to worry that Riddman might come after him next.'

They came to Timmins's office, where his assistant checked the passenger list for them: neither Fordham nor Bidwell, but a Mr and Mrs Fordyce and a Mr Welbeck. Alec groaned.

'They'll have to wait till tomorrow. Will you give me their cabin numbers, please, as well as Welford's Christian name, and his and Pertwee's home addresses?'

The assistant purser obliged. 'That's off their passports, sir,' he added, as Alec copied down the information, 'so there's no funny business. As you know, we hold them in the safe, so that no one loses theirs and gets refused permission to land.'

'Thanks.' Both addresses in the same part of London, Alec observed, closing his notebook and turning away. Ernie Piper, his detective constable, would have known exactly how far apart they were. He had a gift for that sort of thing. Alec wished he had Piper and Tom Tring with him now. Daisy was keen and did her best, but he could not rely on her as he could on his trained team. She was too apt to follow the beat of her own drummer.

Perhaps, he thought irrelevantly, that was why she would never be the dancer Joan had been.

'Couldn't they have false passports?' Daisy asked as they left the Purser's office.

'Good copies of British passports are expensive and pretty difficult to come by. Only within reach of the highest class of crook, which I suspect our two are not.'

'Where to now?'

'The bridge.'

'I *knew* it! If I hadn't come along, you'd have gone out alone. You promised not to.'

'I'd have come to fetch you.' He meant it, not because he was afraid that the murderer might attack, but because he didn't want Daisy worrying. It warmed him to know she worried about him. On one notable occasion, her concern had saved his life.

Impulsively, he caught her to him for a kiss. She responded enthusiastically.

'No sense of decency, these modern young people,' snapped an acid voice. A large woman in too many diamonds surged past them into the Purser's office, followed by a small man with an air of permanent apology.

Daisy burst into peals of laughter. 'Darling,' she gasped, 'how do you like being considered a modern young person with no sense of decency?'

'I suppose it's better than being an old fogy with antiquated notions,' Alec said wryly. 'Let's go. You'd better get your coat.'

'I left it in the ladies' lounge earlier, just in case. I shan't be a minute.'

She dashed off, and returned still buttoning her green tweed. The years since her father's death had made her thrifty. She had refused to buy a new coat just because she was getting married, when the old one was not so very old and perfectly good. As she had been wearing it when Alec fell in love with her, he had a fondness for it.

Hand-in-hand, heedless of decency, they walked along to the forward door. Alec inched it open. A biting wind whistled through.

Daisy held out her gloveless hand to the blast. 'No rain, thank heaven. Let's hurry.'

They stepped out to the open deck. The wind slammed

into them, its icy blasts veering and backing at random, never battering from the same side for more than a moment. The limitless darkness ahead accentuated the *Talavera*'s irregular motion. She seemed to play hopscotch across the waves, now and then skittering sideways. Daisy clung to Alec's arm.

'They've strung a rope across to the companion-way,' he pointed out. He shouldn't let her go with him, but he didn't have the strength for the ensuing battle if he tried to make her go back. 'You'll be safer hanging on to that. I'll be right behind.'

'I *feel* safer hanging on to you, but then you can't hang on.'

She moved ahead. He followed, one hand on her shoulder, the other sliding along the rope. Raising a foot to take a step seemed a venture fraught with peril, so he copied her shuffling gait. The few lamps left burning in the enclosed promenade shone through the glass to cast a wan light on her honey brown curls, tossing and tangling in every direction.

As they reached the base of the companion-way, a ship's boy came running down with infuriating ease, not even touching the rail. He glanced at Daisy, now clearly illuminated by the light at the top of the steps, then peered at Alec.

'Ma'am.' He saluted. 'Mr Fletcher, sir?'

'That's right.'

'Captain's compliments, sir, and he'd be glad to see you on the bridge at your earliest convenience. I'll tell him you're on your way, shall I?'

Effortlessly, he ran back up the ladder-like steps.

'I suppose it's just a matter of practice,' Daisy sighed, gripping the rail with both hands and plodding upwards.

'And youth,' Alec muttered to himself.

Reaching the boat deck, Daisy turned. 'What I still don't understand, darling,' she bawled through the booms and shrieks of the wind in the superstructure, 'is what connection there can possibly be between Pertwee and Denton.'

'This is not the place to discuss it,' Alec bawled back, as though he had ideas on the subject. He hadn't. Denton had no place in any of his theories about Pertwee's murder. In fact, unless the poor old fellow recovered consciousness and claimed to have been tipped over, his fall was bound to be written off as an accident, Lady Brenda's story notwithstanding.

Another rope led them to the bridge. Captain Dane came eagerly to meet them – to meet Alec, at least. He utterly ignored Daisy.

'Glad to see you on your feet, Fletcher. I hoped you'd be up and about now we're past that bit of rough weather.'

'Past it, sir? You wouldn't call this rough?'

'Rough?' The Captain laughed heartily. 'There's a bit of a chop, but nothing to signify. So you've come to report that spot of bother's all cleared up, eh?'

'I'm afraid not, sir. I was on my way to request the use of your wireless facilities. I want to ask Scotland Yard for information about a couple of men. I would not have disturbed you, but since you are here I'll report the results of my investigations so far.'

'Pshaw! All I want to hear is that there's a perfectly innocent explanation for both accidents, with no blame accruing to ship, crew, or company.' Gloomily, Dane turned away, with a backwards wave which Alec took as permission to make use of the wireless.

The three doors off the bridge led respectively to the Captain's quarters, the chart-room, and the wireless room. The last, Alec found, was little more than a cupboard, filled almost to bursting with equipment and the operator's chair, now unoccupied. Alec assumed the narrow door on the other side led to the operator's quarters.

Daisy was at his elbow. 'Sorry, love,' he said, 'no room.'

'You mean you're going to abandon me to Captain Dane's tender mercies?' she hissed.

'I have no doubt whatever of your ability to survive.' He stepped in and firmly shut the door.

He had to push the chair under the desk to get past. A knock on the far door brought a sleepy 'Coming!' A rumpled young man in crimson-striped silk pyjamas appeared, fumbling with his spectacles. The cabin behind him was no wider than his workroom and scarcely long enough for his bunk.

Settling his wire-rimmed glasses on his nose, he looked at Alec in surprise. Presumably he was usually called to duty by a ship's boy.

'Detective Chief Inspector Fletcher,' said Alec. 'I'm investigating the men overboard for Captain Dane. I need to send a message.'

'Oh, right-oh. Just let me get a jersey on.' He ducked back into his closet.

Alec took out his notepad and started to write down his message. The operator returned a moment later, his head stuck inside a navy blue jersey which appeared to have caught on his glasses. 'Damn,' he said in a muffled voice.

When Alec had helped him untangle himself, he saluted and said shyly, 'Kitchener, sir. I don't usually tie myself in knots like that, sir, only I'd just got to sleep. I was up all night last night trying to find out the extent of that storm.'

'Sorry to wake you. I want my sergeant at Scotland Yard to get on to this first thing in the morning, and we're several hours behind by now.'

'Scotland Yard! Aye, sir!' On hearing the magic words, Kitchener became not merely ready but eager to please. 'Do you want it sent in cipher, sir?'

'I hadn't thought about it.'

'If it's just in Morse, sir, anyone who picks it up can decode it.'

'I don't want that.' Alec frowned. 'Unfortunately, as I didn't expect to be involved in an investigation on board, I didn't arrange a cipher before I left.'

'That's all right, sir,' said Kitchener earnestly. 'We'll use the company cipher. It goes straight to a confidential clerk at the head office in London. I'll put in a couple of lines telling him what to do with it, and he'll see it gets to Scotland Yard. You can trust him, sir.'

Not having much choice, Alec agreed. He finished writing his message to Sergeant Tring – as an afterthought adding Mrs Gotobed's name to Pertwee's, Welford's, and Denton's to be investigated – and handed it to Kitchener to encode. 'I suppose I'd better let the Super know what I'm doing,' he muttered to himself. Knowing Daisy was aboard, Crane would be more resigned than surprised.

Alec scribbled a second, briefer message. The young operator was poring over his code book, slowly and painstakingly turning the first message into a mess of gibberish. The contrast when he turned to his apparatus was amazing. His finger flickered on the key, sending out the dots and dashes much too fast for Alec to follow, though he had learnt Morse code in the war.

When Kitchener began to encode Superintendent Crane's message, Alec said, 'I'll leave you to it. Thanks. Let me know when there's an answer, will you?'

'Aye, sir. Uh, sir, if it comes at four in the morning? The day after tomorrow, that'll be nine o'clock in London.'

'Then it can wait until breakfast. The only good thing about being on board ship is that my suspects have nowhere to go.'

Going out to the bridge, Alec found Daisy being lectured on the use of the sextant by an extraordinarily genial Captain Dane. She turned, with an appeal in her summer-sky blue eyes.

'As soon as the sky clears,' said the Captain, 'I'll give you a demonstration. You can take a sight yourself, why not?'

The appeal became desperation. 'Too kind,' Daisy faltered. 'Darling, Captain Dane has been showing me how to work out our position.'

'Oh, there you are, Fletcher. I didn't know your wife had an interest in navigation.'

'Daisy is interested in many aspects of science, sir. She recently wrote an article on the work of the scientists at the Natural History Museum.'

'Old bones!' The Captain looked at Daisy with considerably diminished respect. 'Not at all the same thing.

Get young Kitchener to show you his wireless telegraph. Now there's something worth writing about! Sent off your messages all right, Fletcher?'

'Yes, thank you, sir. Mr Kitchener was most helpful. It's a bit late to do anything else tonight, but I'll be pursuing my enquiries in the morning.'

On that official note, Alec and Daisy departed. When they reached the shelter of the enclosed promenade, Alec said, 'You had him almost eating out of your hand for a moment there.'

'I had to say *something* when you deserted me. I didn't know the blasted thing was a sextant, but it looked complicated enough to keep him going for a while, if he deigned to speak to me at all. You only just got back in time. He was starting to talk maths at me.'

Alec laughed. 'Since you have his permission, though, I think you should take a look at the wireless apparatus. It was interesting.'

'Permission!' said Daisy. 'I thought it was an order. I'm ready to collapse, darling. May we go to bed now?'

'Yes, let's.' He put his arm around her waist and gave her a quick hug, dropping a kiss on her tangled curls, but his mind was still on murder. 'If Riddman is our man, he'll get cocky thinking he's not suspected. With luck I'll take him off guard in the morning, give him a shock and perhaps get something useful from him.'

'I think he must have shot Pertwee. But why should he have chucked Denton overboard?'

'Why should Gotobed? Why should anyone? I'll have a word with Mrs Denton tomorrow, but until I can talk to Denton or Tom turns up something at home, there's not much else to be done on that case.'

'You asked Sergeant Tring to investigate Denton?'

'Who knows what passions seethe in a Suffolk village? There may be something perfectly obvious that Mrs Denton didn't want or just didn't think to tell you. Pertwee and Welford take precedence, of course.'

'Let's pop in and see how Denton's doing,' Daisy suggested.

The doctor's waiting room was deserted. From the sickbay came a low murmur of voices, but Alec didn't feel justified in knocking to ask for news. They went on to their cabin.

Daisy awoke next morning cosily wrapped in Alec's arms in the narrow berth. She snuggled back against his chest, feeling secure, protected against the world. Though she had never lacked self-confidence, being married added a new dimension. Now she was part of a whole. She could rely on Alec's support – at least when he was not lambasting her for meddling.

He had needed her help yesterday, though, poor darling. And even if he had really found his sea legs, his usual assistants were far away, so she could still be useful. He had better not try to shut her out now!

Daisy stiffened militantly, drawing a muttered protest from her husband. 'Move, woman,' he grunted. 'My arm's gone to sleep.'

A cautious rearrangement of bodies led to another delightful facet of matrimony. Afterwards, Alec went back to sleep but Daisy was wide awake.

Musing on marriage, her thoughts drifted to Mr Gotobed. He might have been much happier married to someone like Miss Oliphant, but he obviously adored Wanda in spite of her faults. Yet, however jealous he might be of her past lovers, Daisy refused to believe he would have murdered Pertwee.

Chester Riddman made a much more convincing murderer. He had a filthy temper, according to Brenda. He apparently owed Pertwee large sums of money, and his all-powerful grandfather disapproved of gambling. But could he have failed to realize that his cheques would not vanish with the death of the payee, that sooner or later they would come home to roost?

Who else might have wanted Pertwee out of the way? If only they knew more about him. The only others with whom he had any known contact were Wanda, who had been under her maid's eye all day, and his cabin-mate and presumed colleague, Welford.

Welford – a squabble amongst thieves? Welford was the brains of the pair. He had deliberately lost at poker, to avert suspicion, so Riddman's cheques were in Pertwee's name. Suppose they quarrelled and Pertwee refused to hand over Welford's share of the loot? Welford was probably quite capable of forging Pertwee's signature to cash the cheques.

Of course, like Wanda, Welford had been confined to his cabin by seasickness. Or had he? He had no servant to give him an alibi. But he *had* spent plenty of time alone in the cabin with Pertwee's belongings since Pertwee's death.

Daisy sat up and shook Alec's shoulder. 'Darling, I have a frightful feeling we may have shut the fox in with the chickens!'

# CHAPTER 15

'Nothing!' said Alec, gazing round at the shabby belongings heaped on the berths in the unoccupied cabin. 'No cheques, no marked cards, no spare aces, no love letters from Mrs Gotobed, no papers at all. Which tells us precisely nothing. Welford had plenty of time to abstract any evidence before I told the steward to move Pertwee's baggage.'

'Or Pertwee had that sort of stuff in his pockets when he went overboard,' Daisy proposed.

'So there was absolutely no need for you to drag me out of bed for this, as I'd have realized if I'd been more than half-awake.'

'Sorry, darling!' She grimaced at the battered cabin trunk which stood in the corner, reeking of mothballs. 'Must we repack everything?'

That would be quite a job, though the trunk had been only half-full. Daisy guessed Pertwee had bought it secondhand for the voyage, mostly for show. His best clothes, those he had worn on board, they had found in a large Gladstone bag, unmothballed. His one decent spare shirt, carefully folded, was accompanied by several detachable collars. Curtis Pertwee seemed to be altogether mostly for show.

'Whatever he won from Riddman, in general he can't have done very well for himself gambling,' Daisy said.

'On shore, individuals find it difficult to compete against the clubs. That's why the big liners are popular. He may have had other tricks in the confidence line, none strikingly successful.'

'Do you think these are all his worldly possessions?'

'Very likely. One of the stewards can repack. It's breakfast time and I'm ravenous.'

They went out to join the trickle of passengers heading for the Grand Salon. The ship had resumed a steady pitch and roll, interrupted occasionally by a violent hiccough which made everyone grab for the rails.

Though the sea was still restless, up on the promenade deck sunlight shone in through the long windows, obscured now and then by scudding clouds. From one of these fell a dark column of rain. Daisy stopped to watch its approach. A flurry of drops beat wildly against the glass, then passed on.

Daisy shivered, glanced round to make sure no one was close enough to hear, and said, 'You'll have to search Welford's bags next.'

'I'll have to have some evidence that he's involved before I even apply for a search warrant – or in this case ask the Captain's permission, I suppose. Until I hear from Tom Tring, the best I can do is try to eliminate Fordyce and Welbeck.'

'Can't you arrange for one of Riddman's stewards to take a peek at Welford? If he doesn't come to breakfast, the steward could pop into his cabin, saying he has to make a safety check or something. I bet Welford wouldn't even notice it was the wrong man. Most people only notice the uniform.'

'Good idea! My brain cells must be working slowly for lack of nourishment. I'll see what I can do.'

When they reached the Grand Salon, Alec consulted the Chief Steward, who went to consult the Purser, and returned with his consent to Daisy's plan.

'I'll see to it at once, sir,' he said in a conspiratorial voice. 'Enjoy your breakfast, madam.'

Remembering all yesterday's stairs, Daisy ate heartily. Alec consumed several buttered rolls, though he still could not face eggs, far less bacon, ham, or kidneys; and instead of his usual coffee, he opted for tea, which he drank by the gallon.

'No Arbuckle, no kippers, thank heaven,' he muttered to Daisy.

Wanda, too, was still missing. Overhearing Gotobed consulting Miss Oliphant, Daisy gathered that he thought his wife's indisposition might be as much nervous as physical. She still refused to see him, but Baines had reported that she was agitated and weepy.

'I'm afraid she feels out of her depth,' he said. 'I ought not to have . . .'

Daisy missed a bit as Phillip asked jocularly how the sleuthing was getting along. Alec told him about sending wireless messages to Scotland Yard, neatly diverting him from the progress of the investigation to the wonders of modern technological inventions.

The next thing Daisy heard of the other conversation was Miss Oliphant saying, 'If you wish.'

'Ee, lass, that's grand of you.'

'But even if she will see me, which I must consider unlikely, I cannot help her unless she is willing, which is still less likely.'

'It niver hurts to try,' said Gotobed philosophically.

Looking up, Miss Oliphant caught Daisy's eye and gave her a slight, wry smile. 'I am happy to see Mr Fletcher has recovered,' she said. 'Mr Arbuckle still suffers, I fear.'

Gloria heard her and turned to say, 'Poppa's not real sick, Miss Oliphant. He was okay last evening, remember? He just couldn't face a whole roomful of people eating, but he'll be up later.'

'That is excellent news, my dear.'

A bespectacled young man appeared just then at Alec's elbow. He wore ship's uniform, not a common seaman's but with less gold braid than the officers and by no means as spruce. His round, ingenuous face beamed as he reported, 'A wireless for you, sir.'

Alec took the paper he held out. 'Thanks, Kitchener. If there's a response, I'll come up to you.'

The wireless operator saluted and started to turn away.

'I say, old chap,' said Phillip, 'don't dash off. I'd like to take a dekko at your apparatus some time.'

'Sorry, sir, passengers aren't allowed in the wireless room.'

'Poppa'll fix it,' Gloria said confidently.

'My father-in-law arranged for me to see the engines.'

'Right-oh, sir, I'll be happy to oblige, but I'll need Captain Dane's say-so.'

Daisy said smugly, 'Captain Dane advised me to ask you to show me the wireless telegraph, Mr Kitchener.'

'Dash it, Daisy!' Phillip exclaimed. 'The Captain's known as a regular Tartar. How the deuce did you manage it?'

'Sheer charm, old thing.'

Gloria, Gotobed, and Miss Oliphant laughed. Phillip shook his head in admiration of her gall, if not her charm. Alec, folding his message after scanning it, was heard to mutter something about misleadingly guileless eyes. Kitchener expressed his enthusiastic willingness to demonstrate his precious apparatus for her pleasure at any hour she cared to name.

'Later this afternoon? And not just for pleasure,' she informed him. 'I'm writing an article about the ship.' At least, she was supposed to be, if she could ever find time to sit down and get on with it.

After breakfast, Daisy used work as an excuse when Gloria invited her to the Arbuckle suite to consult about costumes for the Fancy Dress competition that evening.

'You choose something for me,' she said. 'As long as it isn't positively indecent, I'll wear it, and write about it, too.'

'Okay, I'll see what I can do,' Gloria promised.

Daisy caught up with Alec, who had stopped to speak to the Chief Steward. 'Welford's still in his cabin, claiming sickness,' he told her, 'but the steward managed a good look at his face. He's the third poker player all right.'

'I was sure he must be. I'm glad he's still alive. What did the telegram say, darling?'

Wordless, he held it out to her.

Superintendent Crane's wireless message conveyed the agreement of the Commissioner of the Metropolitan Police and the Chairman of the Wellington Line to put Alec in charge of the investigation. Detective Sergeant Tring had been seconded to follow up his queries and would report to him directly, through the Wellington cipher clerk.

The telegram ended with words which must have puzzled that clerk and Kitchener: 'She's done it again!'

'Beastly man!' Daisy said indignantly. 'It wasn't even my choice to go to America! He should blame Mr Arbuckle. Are you going to see Riddman, darling? I noticed he wasn't in the dining room, but I don't think he ever does appear for breakfast.'

'Not an early riser. With this authority from London. though, added to the Captain's orders, I shan't hesitate to interrupt his beauty sleep.'

'Do be careful, darling. If he killed Pertwee . . . Still. I suppose he's not likely to attack you in his own cabin. But gosh! He might attack Welford in *his* cabin if he's guessed he was in league with Pertwee.'

'Yes, I thought of that last night and arranged for a discreet watch to be kept on Welford's cabin. My brain didn't entirely cease to function.'

'Of course not, darling,' Daisy said soothingly, and they parted.

Daisy went first to the sickbay to enquire after Denton. For the first time, Dr Amboyne was hopeful. The farmer had briefly opened his eyes and seemed to recognize his wife. His temperature was down a degree. He was breathing a littie easier, though by no means had he breath to spare for answering questions.

'I can't allow Mr Fletcher to see him, but I do believe. barring a relapse, he'll pull through. A tough chap. I'd not have given a farthing for his chances.'

Delighted, Daisy fetched her papers from the cabin and

went up to the library, where she sat staring at her notes and wondering how Alec was getting on with Chester Riddman.

'Who's there?'

'Your steward, sir. Gentleman to see you.'

'Can't see anyone. I'm not well.' Riddman echoed Welford's words of the clay before, but his voice was truculent instead of shaky.

'I'm sorry, Mr Riddman,' said Alec, 'but I am under the Captain's orders. I'm afraid I must insist on speaking to you.'

The steward let him in. The smell of stale whisky and cigar smoke made Alec's gorge rise. He controlled the reaction with an effort.

The cabin was not only far more spacious than Welford's, with room for a table and several easy-chairs, but much better lit. Though the curtains were closed, the brightness outside seeped around and through, showing a heap of clothes on the floor and their owner, raised on one elbow, glaring bleary-eyed from the bed.

Alec flung open the curtains and turned. Riddman had closed his eyes to bloodshot slits. He was a revolting sight, his chin dark with stubble, his crimson-striped silk pyjamas creased, the rumpled bedclothes suggesting an uneasy sleep.

'Judas Priest,' he groaned. 'Whaddaya want?'

'Detective Chief Inspector Fletcher, Scotland Yard,' Alec introduced himself. 'I'm sorry to disturb you, sir.'

'What's the big idea? I'm an American citizen,' Riddman protested. 'You Limeys can't . . .'

'You're on a British ship, sir.'

'Look, I know gambling on board is against your rules, but there's no need to make a federal case of it. It was just a friendly game with a couple of pals.' He reached for the wallet on the bedside table. 'Can't we just . . .'

'I must advise you not to complete that sentence.' Alec put steel in his voice, his gaze frigid.

'Jeez, just a little contribution for the widows and orphans fund,' the American said feebly. 'Forget it.'

'I shall, sir. Your gambling is not my affair, except insofar as it may bear upon the death of one of your "pals".'

Riddman closed his eyes and sank back, his thin face screwed up. 'Oh punk, it *was* Pertwee, then!' He looked very young. To Alec's dismay, a couple of tears squeezed out from beneath his eyelids.

Alec had met with enough weeping witnesses, suspects, and criminals in his professional life for his mother always to pack several extra handkerchiefs when he travelled. Feeling in his pocket, he hoped she and Daisy between them had made sufficient provision. He had not expected to come across witnesses, suspects, and criminals on this trip. Accompanied by Daisy, he ought to have known better.

'I didn't mean to do it!' Riddman cried.

Daisy could not concentrate on her work for thinking about Alec and Riddman. In the end, she decided to kill two birds with one stone and go to talk to the Purser about gambling on board ship. Besides understanding the situation more clearly, she might be able to fit the subject into her article.

Catching Mr Timmins in a rare moment of leisure, Daisy explained her dual purpose and hinted that she needed the information as much for Alec as for herself.

'We don't get boatmen on the *Talavera*,' Timmins said defensively.

'Boatmen?'

'That's what we call professional gamblers who regularly go to sea. They can get away with it on the big liners with thousands of passengers, but we spot 'em pretty quick. As I told your husband, we had Pertwee marked as possibly one of the fraternity. There's not much we can do though, unless the mark complains, and most of 'em are too embarrassed. Gambling's against company rules, though we'd have to put half the passengers in irons to enforce it and most of the crew. We put up signs warning against gambling with strangers.'

'I've seen them,' Daisy agreed. 'Apparently, Pertwee found Mr Riddman's wallet on the quay and returned it intact, a convincing display of his honesty.'

Timmins nodded knowingly. 'He'll have a confederate who's a "file", an expert pickpocket. They have any number of tricks. One fellow I know of dresses as a clergyman and makes friends with children. Often they let the mark win until they go ashore, then fleece him in one final game.'

'I gather Riddman lost and kept playing in hopes of his luck changing. Pertwee promised not to cash any of his cheques before New York.'

'And hasn't done so. They'd have let Riddman win in the end, so he had no cause for complaint, then pretended to tear up the cheques. A good file would have no trouble substituting worthless paper before his eyes. Then they'd rush to a bank as soon as they landed and cash them before he got a chance to put on a stop order.'

Daisy didn't have a current account. She had heard of stopping payment on a cheque, but it had not crossed her mind in relation to Riddman. No doubt Alec, the son of a bank manager, had worked it out long since.

'Since Pertwee is dead,' she said slowly, 'Riddman has all the time in the world to stop payment before his heirs try to cash them.'

The Purser met her eyes and winced. 'I'm afraid so,' he agreed.

'Thank you, Mr Timmins. You'll keep this to yourself, won't you? I'll be sure to put a bit in my article warning of the dangers of gambling with strangers.'

'You do that, Mrs Fletcher.' With a shrug he added sadly, 'But they all think they're too clever to be caught.'

And the same applied to murderers.

Daisy returned to the library, hoping that Alec would be waiting there for her. He wasn't.

He'd be furious if she went to check that Riddman hadn't done him in and stuffed his body out through the porthole. She decided to go and see Wanda. Perhaps Miss Oliphant had succeeded in persuading the blooming bride to give her medicines a try.

Baines opened the door. With a nervous glance towards the bedroom, she whispered, 'I'm sorry, madam, but madam already has a visitor.'

'I'll wait.' Daisy stepped in.

The bedroom door was shut. Daisy heard raised voices and recognized them, though she could not make out the words. Wanda and Miss Oliphant were at it hammer and tongs.

'Oh dear, perhaps I shan't wait!'

'Might be best not, madam. It takes madam awhile to settle down after she's got herself excited.' The maid flinched as Wanda's voice rose in a screech.

What on earth could the mild Miss Oliphant have said to rouse such fury? Curiosity, Daisy's besetting sin, warred with discretion. She was dithering when the bedroom door flung open and the witch stalked out.

Miss Oliphant's round, normally placid face was bright red, her mouth set in an inflexible line. She closed the door behind her with a deliberate restraint as expressive as a violent slam.

Seeing Daisy, she let her rigid shoulders relax a bit. 'Mrs Fletcher,' she said, 'I fear Mrs Gotobed and I have had a severe disagreement. Perhaps you can convince her that my mind is not to be changed by shouting, even if it were not a matter of principle. I am sorry,' she added, turning to Baines, 'to have put your mistress out of temper.'

'If it wasn't you, madam, it'd be something else.' The maid shrugged. 'What can't be cured must be endured.'

'A very sound sentiment,' Miss Oliphant said warmly, and with a slight bow to Daisy she left.

Daisy lapsed into vulgarity: 'Whew! If that was a disagreement, I wouldn't want to hear them quarrel.'

Baines gave her a perfunctory smile and started towards the bedroom. 'I'd better see if madam wants anything.'

'Don't go and put your head into the lion's mouth. I expect I can calm her down a bit.'

Wanda was in bed, sitting bolt upright and glaring at herself in a gold-backed hand mirror. She glanced up as Daisy entered. In the bright daylight pouring through the porthole, her face was blotched, her eyes small and hard within circles of puffy flesh.

'Oh, it's you,' she said flatly. 'That bloody woman's made me look a perfect fright. What a bitch! And I was going to let Dickie come in today.'

'You must be feeling better then. I'm so glad. I expect you can repair the damage.'

'S'pose so.' Wanda threw back the bedclothes and slipped her feet into high-heeled, pink mules adorned with fluffy marabou feathers dyed to match. The quilted silk bed-jacket she wore over her pink satin nightdress was similarly trimmed. She threw it off and wrapped herself in an embroidered kimono before sitting down on the stool at the dressing table. 'I was only sick first thing in the morning yesterday,' she said, with a sly glance at Daisy, who, since she had not been thrown out, had found herself a seat.

'First thing?' Daisy absorbed the information, watching Wanda open bottles and jars and start dabbing creams and lotions on her face. 'And today?' she asked cautiously.

'Today, too. It wore off an hour ago. You know what that means, don't you?'

'Y-yes.' Daisy was rather surprised that morning sickness would develop so soon. Wanda had only been married for a week or so. However, she was no expert, though she hoped to learn by personal experience one of these days.

Then she recalled that Arbuckle had assumed Wanda to be Gotobed's mistress before they married, so time was irrelevant. Or was Gotobed not the father? Had Curtis Pertwee been Wanda's lover, as Daisy had surmised?

She had been silent long enough to be noticeable.

'Cripes, you are the innocent, aren't you?' Wanda sneered, watching Daisy in the looking glass while continuing to mess about with her cosmetics. 'Do you know where babies come from? Well, I've got a bun in the oven, if you'll excuse the expression. And that old bitch, that witch, won't help me get rid of it!' she added, with sudden venom.

'Miss Oliphant?' Startled, shocked in spite of her past residence in Bohemian Chelsea, Daisy understood the herbalist's outrage. 'No, I'm sure she wouldn't.'

'Bloody self-righteous old bag. Never had a man of her own. What does she know about it?'

'I expect Mr Gotobed will be delighted,' Daisy ventured.

'Don't tell him! Gawd, Daisy, swear you won't tell him. I'm not going through with this, starting having kids at my age!'

'I won't tell him,' Daisy promised reluctantly. 'But there's no need to have more than this one, you know. When you get back to England, go to Marie Stopes's clinic in Holloway, and they'll explain how to avoid conceiving scientifically, not in the old hit-or-miss ways.'

Before Daisy's wedding, Lucy had insisted on her going to the clinic started by Marie Stopes – Mrs Roe as she was since her second marriage. 'You don't want to get preggy right away,' she had argued. 'Get settled first, get things sorted out with Mrs Fletcher. You *are* going to ask me to be godmother to your first, aren't you, darling?'

Daisy was glad she had complied. She wouldn't have wanted to be traipsing around America suffering from morning sickness. Thus far, she sympathized with Wanda. And she could comprehend not wanting to start a family at her age. Wanda had looked nearer forty than thirty when Daisy came in a few minutes earlier.

By now, her face in the mirror had taken on its accustomed painted pulchritude. She did not answer Daisy because she was tilting her head back to put some drops in her eyes, a delicate task requiring concentration. When she turned, her eyes were once more large, dark, and lustrous.

'I'm not going to argue about it,' she said. 'Send Baines in to do my hair, will you? And if you see Dickie about, say I'm dying to see him.'

Whatever her social inadequacies, Wanda had perfected the art of the indirect dismissal. Daisy departed.

She wondered briefly whether Wanda had succeeded in extracting a promise from Miss Oliphant not to tell Gotobed about her condition or her request. But a spinster of that vintage was probably virtually incapable of broaching such a subject with a man, and Wanda was canny enough to know it.

On her way back to the library, Daisy saw neither Gotobed nor Miss Oliphant. In the sporadic sunshine, the deckchairs on the port side of the promenade deck were in demand, in spite of the icy draught every time some hardy soul opened a door to go out to the open deck or came in, wind-blown and red-nosed. Among the latter were Brenda, Gloria, and Phillip – Daisy had just reached the library when she saw them enter together by the far door. She was going to wave to draw their attention when Mr Harvey followed Phillip.

She ducked into the library. With the second officer present, she couldn't very well draw Brenda aside and attempt to prepare her for the shock in case Alec arrested her fiancé.

# CHAPTER 16

'My dear . . . chap' – Alec had nearly said 'boy', but decided it would not be well received – 'you're by no means the first young man, and you won't be the last, to go off on his travels and end up in trouble. I doubt that the Prodigal Son was the first! They had the right idea in the eighteenth century. Any English gentleman sending his son on the Grand Tour of Europe provided a bear-leader to keep him on the straight and narrow.'

'A bear-leader?' Riddman was momentarily distracted from his woes.

'To lick a rough cub into shape. Usually a clergyman; military men too often led their charges into bad company.'

'Jeez, you're not like any American cop I ever tangled with! But it's all very well talking. My grandfather won't care a damn that some sap-head boob raised merry hell two hundred years ago. Stand by to watch the fur fly when little Chester gets home!' Riddman shivered, reached for the cigarette case lying beside his wallet, and waved it at Alec.

'No, thanks.' Alec considered lighting his pipe. This looked like being a long interview, though for a moment he had thought he had a confession. However, he doubted his stomach was yet fit to cope with smoking, and a pipe implied a degree of relaxation which he was not ready to concede.

The confession had turned out to be no more than a lament for money lost and retribution expected, but that did not necessarily mean Chester Riddman had not shot Pertwee. Time to stop playing the Dutch uncle and get down to brass tacks.

'Do you own any firearms, Mr Riddman?'

'I have hunting guns and a couple of pistols back home. I heard about your Limey gun laws, though, so I didn't bring any.' He drew on his cigarette with quick, nervous puffs. 'Anyway, I'm not in such a funk I'm gonna shoot myself.'

'I'm less concerned with your shooting yourself than with whether you shot Pertwee.'

Riddman gaped, aghast. 'Shot him? Why would I do such a fool thing? I didn't know he wasn't on the level till you told me just now. Croaking him'd just've wrecked my chances of winning back what I lost.'

'I hope I've convinced you that's a mug's game, even if you're playing with honest men.' Finding himself side-tracked yet again, Alec returned to the main point with a blunt question. 'You were seen on deck shortly after he fell overboard. Where were you before that?'

'After lunch? I was in the Smoking Room. I had a shot of rye and smoked a cigar. I was chewing the rag with some guys about the mileage auction pool. They'll remember me,' Riddman said eagerly. 'Someone came in and said a boat had been lowered to fish out another man overboard, and we all went out on deck together. I can give you their names.'

With a deep internal sigh, Alec wrote down the names.

If he'd just asked that one question right at the beginning, he'd have averted half an hour of alternating between father confessor and nanny. Still, he might have done the boy some good.

'If these gentlemen confirm your story,' he said, 'well and good. If not, I'll be back with more questions.'

'Yes, sir. I'm gonna stick close as a burr to Birdie now. She's my only hope of bringing my grandfather around.'

Alec was far from certain that Daisy would approve of a rapprochement between Riddman and Lady Brenda. She favoured Harvey. Still, it was up to the girl to choose between them. Dismissing the matter from his mind, Alec went in search of the two gentlemen named by Riddman.

'So Riddman's out of it,' Alec told Daisy, neatly catching her fountain pen as it rolled off the desk.

'Bother.' She wrinkled her nose. 'I rather fancied him as the villain. That leaves Welford.'

'And Gotobed. Or someone not yet in the picture,' he added hastily as she frowned at him. 'Welford isn't in his cabin. The chap watching didn't have instructions to stop him leaving, as I was then thinking in terms of protecting him. I set a couple of stewards who know him to hunt for him, but they haven't spotted him.'

'He can't go far, after all. And assuming he killed Pertwee because they quarrelled, he has no reason to attack anyone else.'

'No, but I want to talk to him before I have to tackle Gotobed about his wife's connection with Pertwee. I'd hate to upset him if there's nothing in it.'

'Gosh, yes. Or supposing there is something in it, if he doesn't know, which I'm sure he doesn't.' Daisy debated internally whether to tell Alec about Wanda's pregnancy and decided it was irrelevant. Wanda would never have informed her husband, and Miss Oliphant would probably rather die than mention it. 'Ah, elevenses, spiffing!'

A deck steward entered the library carrying a tray. The bouillon sloshed about in the half-filled mugs, and the biscuits were served in a bowl, as they might have slid off a plate. The *Talavera* was dancing a jig across the waves, constant, restless, unpredictable motion with an occasional wild hop, skip, and jump.

Daisy was pleased to see Alec helping himself to a handful of digestive biscuits. He even held out his mug for more bouillon when the steward returned with a fresh, hot jugful. Admittedly his mind was not on the food, but that he was concentrating on murder rather than his stomach was – in its way – a great improvement.

At length Daisy interrupted his meditations. 'Darling, I went to enquire after Denton earlier. Dr Amboyne says he's improving, though he can't talk yet.'

'Great Scott, I'd forgotten him, I'm afraid. I still can't for the life of me see where he fits into the puzzle.' Alec sank into his musings again.

Having no useful suggestions to offer, Daisy returned to her writing. The article was beginning to shape nicely, but her thoughts tended to wander, from Gotobed – surely not a murderer! – and his obnoxious wife to the unhappy triangle of Riddman, Brenda, and Harvey.

Alec took out his notebook and started to make lists. Daisy guessed he missed being able to discuss the case with

Tom Tring. She wished she could supply his lack, but she knew her partisanship limited her usefulness to him. When she liked someone, as she liked Gotobed, she tended to see the arguments in his favour and to disregard any evidence against him.

'I'm not getting anywhere,' Alec said in disgust. 'I think I'll leave it for the moment and come back to it fresh after lunch. I'm going to go up and take a look at hiding places for sharpshooters up on the boat deck. Coming?'

'No, I think not, darling. I *must* get on with this.'

Alec was not gone for very long. 'Phew, it's cold out, in spite of the sun.'

'What did you find?'

'There are at least half a dozen places up there a man could have lurked unseen with a good view of the place where Pertwee and Gotobed were standing,' he told her gloomily. 'All scoured clean by wind and rain. No proof of Gotobed's story, and no disproof either.'

On his way back, he had fetched the stack of information he had to master for his job in Washington. Side by side, they worked steadily until lunchtime.

Arbuckle turned up at lunch, cautious about what he ate, but cheerful. Gotobed reported happily that he had seen Wanda and she was much better, though not yet ready to reappear in public. Miss Oliphant did not join in the general, if not quite sincere, wishes for her rapid recovery.

The wishes for Denton's recovery were entirely sincere when Dr Amboyne took his place at the head of the table and announced that his patient was at last out of danger.

Glancing at the second officer's table, Daisy saw Brenda laughing at something Riddman had said to her. They were seated at the far end of the table from Harvey. The officer was being polite to the ladies next to him, his monkey-face showing nothing of his feelings about the situation.

Again the meal was interrupted by the arrival of a wireless message for Alec, this time delivered by a ship's boy. Apologizing, Alec read it, then passed it to Daisy. It was from the Wellington Line: They had gone through their records and found that Pertwee and Welford had booked together just three days before the *Talavera* sailed.

'It would have been helpful earlier,' Daisy whispered, 'before we worked out that they must have been confederates.'

Sighing, Alec nodded. 'I wonder if Tom's coming up with anything useful.'

After lunch, he took Amboyne aside. Daisy, waiting, saw the doctor shake his head. When Alec rejoined her with a long face, she said, 'No luck, darling? Let's go for a brisk walk out on deck to blow the cobwebs away.'

'Good idea.'

A number of passengers were strolling around the promenade, walking off their lunch. Most of the deckchairs on the sunny side were filled now. Arbuckle's reserved seats were occupied by himself and Miss Oliphant, and Phillip, Gloria, Riddman, and Brenda. Riddman started to rise as Alec and Daisy approached.

'These here are your chairs, aren't they?'

'That's all right,' Daisy assured him. 'You and Birdie stay. We're going out.'

Arbuckle chuckled. 'Hang on to her, Fletcher.'

'Phillip and I went out,' said Gloria, 'and came back

pretty quick. It's dead calm one minute and a howling gale the next, and mighty cold, too, in spite of the sun.'

'You'll blow away, old bean,' Phillip confirmed. 'Better stay in.'

Being told what to do by Phillip was enough to make Daisy determined on the opposite. 'We'll need our coats, darling,' she said to Alec.

His grin was understanding and sympathetic, but he said, 'I'm not sure I'm ready for this. No one else is out there. Hold on a minute, love, while I stick my nose out.'

He opened the nearest door, took several steps outside, and stopped, apparently admiring the sparkling waves and racing clouds. Then suddenly he staggered backwards as if he had been struck on the chest. His trouser legs flapped wildly. He managed to stop and turn, and practically ran back to shelter with the wind gust behind him. When he opened the door, a gale entered with him.

'Whew! We'll promenade inside, Daisy!'

'Yes, that was enough fresh air for me. I suppose I'd better send a message to the wireless man to say I don't think I'll get up there this afternoon.'

They walked aft. As they approached the after door, Gotobed came up the companion-way from below. He was obviously intending to go out, bundled up in his ulster, a grey-and-white muffler dangling round his neck, and his fore-and-aft cap in his hand.

'You'd better tie your hat on tight,' Daisy advised, 'and your scarf. There are gale-force gusts blowing.'

'It comes up suddenly,' Alec said. 'Don't let down your guard.'

'I'll take care.' Gotobed wound the scarf around and

knotted it, then put the cap on his head, let down the ear-flaps, and tied the string beneath his chin. 'Ready for owt, I am!' Out he went.

Though he was in the lee of the enclosed deck, the cape of his topcoat billowed like a parachute as cross-currents caught it. Expecting the wind, he was braced for it and battled his way – uphill as the ship rolled – towards the companion-way to the boat deck. Daisy and Alec stopped to watch, as did several other indoor walkers.

The wind died as suddenly as it had arisen. Gotobed took a side-step, momentarily compensating for a force no longer there. Grinning, he turned and waved to them. He grabbed the handrail and started up the steps.

Daisy and Alec were turning away to continue their walk when another man, his face hidden by a woollen balaclava, crossed the deck outside. Again everyone paused to watch the brave soul who ventured where they dared not. For the moment unhampered by wind, he scurried to the companion-way and began the climb. They saw his legs through the gaps between the steps.

'I hope someone warned him about the gusts,' Daisy said, as they set off again. 'He looked less hefty than Gotobed.'

She had scarcely spoken when a figure tumbled backwards down the steps and landed on the deck with an ominous thud, audible through the windows.

'Stay there!' Alec was already in motion. He dashed to the nearest door. Wind blasted in as he wrenched it open.

The ship rolled to starboard. The limp body began to slide. Alec ran towards it, but as the tilt steepened, the *Talavera* did a skip and a hop, throwing him off balance.

In a horribly boneless way, the man in the balaclava slithered inexorably down the slope, under the rail, and into the frothing waves.

Captain Dane sat with his head in his hands. His tiny sitting room was crowded, with Alec and Gotobed seated, the second mate and an able seaman standing.

Harvey held what looked like a rounders bat or a policeman's truncheon. 'A.B. Foster here found it in the scuppers, sir, on the promenade deck.'

Alec reached for it. No hope of dabs after the sailor and the officer had handled it, even if he had had a fingerprint kit with him. It was much heavier than it looked, weighted towards the thicker end.

'It seems to be an ordinary bat, hollowed and filled with lead to make a bludgeon. A dangerous weapon.' And surely an unlikely weapon for an elderly millionaire to carry about with him. 'How long could it have lain there without being spotted?'

'The scuppers are cleaned out at dawn, sir,' said Harvey, 'before any passengers are about. So, hours but not days.'

Alec nodded. 'Thank you. I may want a word with you later, Foster.'

The seaman saluted and departed. Dane raised his head and looked at Harvey.

'The Purser has gathered all the passengers in the Grand Salon, sir, except those who can't leave their cabins. The cabin stewards are checking those. Mr Timmins will have the missing man's name any moment. He wondered whether you want to address the passengers, sir.'

'I suppose I must.' The Captain heaved himself to his feet. 'I'll tell 'em we have a Scotland Yard man aboard; that should reassure 'em. If that's all right with you, Fletcher?'

The question was perfunctory. Alec gave the only possible answer: 'Certainly, sir, as you wish. I doubt it's much of a secret any longer. However, all most people are aware of is an unfortunate series of accidents. Perhaps you might advise passengers not to go out on deck until the wind drops and the sea calms.'

Dane nodded acquiescence. 'Make use of this room for the present,' he said, and went out with Harvey in attendance.

Alec turned to Gotobed. The Yorkshireman was solemn but seemed unperturbed by his invidious position. Consciousness of innocence? Or confidence that proof of even the fact of murder would be virtually impossible?

'I hope you understand the Captain's concern, sir,' Alec said, 'passing the buck' in Arbuckle's useful phrase. 'Twice, now, you have been the only person close by when a man fell overboard. Would you mind telling me again exactly what you observed on both occasions?'

Gotobed complied. Patiently he described his encounter with Pertwee and then moved on to the recent incident. 'You saw me go out. The wind was terrific until I reached the companion-way, then it dropped. Nonetheless, I held on to the rail as I climbed. I came to the top, took a step or two to my left, and stopped, still holding the rail, to look at the view.'

'You saw no one else on the boat deck?'

'Not a soul, but I was hardly paying attention. The sea

and sky were spectacular. I had no eyes for aught else. I started to turn to face forward, and as I turned, the wind struck. If it was fierce down below, it was brutal up on the exposed boat deck, as you can imagine. Its onslaught flattened me against the rail. That was when I saw the man in the balaclava helmet toppling backwards down the steps, arms and legs flailing. The poor fellow hadn't a chance.'

'He fell from the top of the steps?'

'Pretty near, though I couldn't swear he had reached the top. He was already falling when I first caught sight of him. He cannot have been holding the rail or not tight enough. Perhaps he was already off balance, in the act of taking a step forward, poised on one foot, when the gust hit.'

Alec hefted the bludgeon. 'And this?'

Gotobed shrugged. 'If for some reason he was carrying it, the weight might have thrown him further off balance. It seems to me more likely it has nothing to do with him.'

'Possibly,' Alec conceded. The story was plausible. He might have swallowed it whole if not for Pertwee's prior demise. 'Perhaps we'll have a better idea when we get his name.'

'Do you think . . . ?'

Harvey opened the door and stuck his head in. 'Sorry to interrupt, but Mr Timmins thought you'd want to know at once, Mr Fletcher. The missing man is Henry Welford.'

'Thank you.' The answer was more than half expected. 'Please ask the Captain, before everyone disperses, to request that anyone acquainted with Welford or Pertwee give his name to the Purser.'

Harvey saluted and hurried off.

After the second officer's first few words, Alec had

looked not at him but at Gotobed. No flicker of recognition crossed the Yorkshireman's face. Either he already knew who had fallen, or he had never heard Welford's name before.

In either case, there was little point in continuing to question him at present. If he had carried the bludgeon to an appointed meeting on the boat deck, then he had his story well prepared and he was far too canny a customer to be shaken by interrogation.

'The name Henry Welford means nothing to you?' Alec asked, for form's sake.

'Nowt,' said Gotobed, his lapse into Yorkshire a sign that he had relaxed his previous tension. Deliberately? 'O' course, he mebbe took passage under a false name. Who knows but what I'd ha' recognized the fellow if I could've seen his face?'

'It's conceivable,' Alec conceded. He stood up. 'I'm sure you'll understand, sir, that in view of your presence at two deaths, I must ask you to keep to your suite until the situation is resolved. I have no authority to confine you. This is a request, for your own safety as much as anything else.'

'Aye, lad,' Gotobed said heavily, rising. 'You've your duty to do, and there'll be no grudge borne.'

'Thank you, sir. I'm sorry it's come to this. We'll go down together – I must speak to Mrs Gotobed.'

'She's not well. I know I can trust you not to upset her.'

'I'll do my best, sir.' Alec was not prepared to promise. He had some pretty upsetting questions to put to the blooming bride.

# CHAPTER 17

Daisy paid little heed to the grim-faced Captain's fulmination on the subject of avoidable accidents and his request that people should stay inside until the sea calmed. She was watching the stewards deliver their lists of names to the Purser, watching Timmins check the names against his master list.

She had been on her way to talk to Wanda when she was herded, along with everyone else, into the Grand Salon. The fruitless search for the missing man was over. The boats had not been out for long. No one who saw him fall could think there was the slightest chance of finding him alive, and the Captain had not wanted to risk his men unnecessarily in the wild seas. When Captain Dane, Alec, and Gotobed went off together, Daisy decided that Wanda, however little she liked her, ought to be warned that her husband was suspected of murder.

Daisy did not want to believe Gotobed was a murderer. The Captain *must* be right when he spoke of accidents. Yet she had to admit Alec was justified in looking askance at the Yorkshireman. Twice he had been right there on the spot when a man fell overboard and drowned.

It was fishy, to say the least, and it would look even

fishier if the latest victim turned out to be Welford. Daisy edged closer to the Purser.

Timmins put down his pencil with a sigh, looked up, caught Daisy's eye, frowned. He wrote a few words on a bit of paper, which he folded and gave to a steward. The steward took it to Harvey, who was standing just behind Captain Dane. Harvey read the brief message and started for the door.

Daisy intercepted him. 'Welford?' she whispered.

He nodded. She went out with him, past the stewards with orders to stop passengers leaving before the Captain finished his peroration. Outside he told her, 'The Purser thought Mr Fletcher would want to know at once. You're joining him?'

'Not just now. Actually, I'm going to see Mrs Gotobed, but there's no need to bother him with that while he's busy.'

'Do you think that's wise?' Harvey asked worriedly.

'She's not a suspect. She's been stuck in her bedroom with her maid always on call in the sitting room.'

'That's not quite what I meant. Do you think you ought to talk to her without the Chief Inspector's knowledge?'

'I've helped Alec with several cases,' Daisy said with airy unconcern, 'and this time he hasn't got his sergeant with him or hordes of constables on call. In fact, I've already done quite a bit while he was laid up with seasickness.'

'Ye-es, but . . .'

'He'll be anxious to know that it was Welford. You'd better hurry.'

Daisy went on down to the Gotobeds' suite. Though she had dismissed them, Harvey's doubts had made her reconsider. She decided she had better leave it to Alec to inform Wanda that her husband was not merely on his little list but at the top in capital letters – with no names below. She probably already knew that a third man had fallen overboard. The steward checking the cabins would have told Baines, who surely had passed it on to her mistress.

If Wanda asked outright who had drowned, Daisy would tell her. Otherwise, she'd just wait for Alec to turn up, which he was bound to do, and attempt to sit in on his interview with Wanda.

The blooming bride, still in her kimono, was pacing the sitting room. When Baines admitted Daisy, Wanda came towards her eagerly.

'They say someone else has fallen in, but they won't tell me who. Oh, Daisy, it isn't Dickie, is it? Tell me it's not Dickie!'

'It's not Dickie – Mr Gotobed.'

Wanda dropped into the nearest chair, her head bowed over hands clenched in her lap. After a moment she said in a shaky voice, 'Are you sure? You're not just trying to let me down easy?'

'I said it isn't him. I meant it. I wouldn't say that if it wasn't true, even to break it to you gently.'

'Then why didn't he come and tell me he's safe?' Wanda demanded, raising an angry face. 'He must've known I'd be ever so worried.'

'The stewards were herding all the passengers they could find into the Grand Salon,' Daisy evaded, sitting down, 'to listen to Captain Dane pontificating on the dangers of going out on deck in rough seas and turbulent winds. I just managed to escape.'

'Clever you. Baines, do stop skulking in the corner like a tailor's dummy. Go away. I'll send for you when I need you. Daisy, if it wasn't Dickie who fell overboard, who was it?'

'No one recognized him. It's jolly cold outside, and he was all muffled up.'

'You're absolutely certain sure it wasn't Dickie? He came down after lunch and put on that awful old coat and hat of his, with a huge, great muffler round his neck, to go and smoke outside.'

'Honestly, Wanda, it was not Mr Gotobed. I saw him afterwards.'

'Oh.' After a moment's silence, Wanda asked, 'What happened? Did you see?'

'The man was climbing the steps to the boat deck. There are terrific wind gusts with calm in between, and I suppose he wasn't holding the rail when a gust hit. He fell down the steps to the promenade deck and slid under the rail into the sea before Alec could catch him. It was beastly!'

'You were right there, then, when it happened.'

'Not exactly,' Daisy said cautiously.

Before she had to decide how much to reveal to the chief and only suspect's wife, Gotobed came in, followed by Alec.

Wanda rushed to her husband, wailing, 'Dickie-bird, I've been ever so worried!'

He folded her in his arms, patting her back, and murmuring soothingly, 'There, there, love, there's nowt for you to fret your pretty head over.'

Meanwhile, Alec scowled at Daisy, his dark brows meeting over icy eyes. Undaunted, she went to him. 'I didn't tell her who it was,' she whispered, 'nor that they were alone together when he fell.'

'I suppose you'd better stay,' Alec said resignedly. 'He's less likely to make a fuss about leaving her to my tender mercies.'

'Fletcher wants to ask you one or two questions,' Gotobed was saying to Wanda.

'Why?' she asked in alarm. 'What about?'

'We'll come to that in a moment, Mrs Gotobed,' said Alec. 'Sir, I'd prefer you to wait in the bedroom, if you don't mind.'

'I'll stay with Wanda, Mr Gotobed,' Daisy offered.

'But . . .'

'Oh, go, Dickie, do!' Wanda made impatient shooing motions. 'I haven't done anything wrong. I don't need you to hold my hand.'

She watched him trudge to the bedroom door. When he glanced back, she blew him a kiss, as if in recompense for her sharpness. He lifted one hand briefly in acknowledgement, then closed the door behind him. Daisy thought sadly that, for the first time since she had met him, he looked his age.

'What's going on?' Wanda asked apprehensively, taking a seat as far as possible from the bedroom door. The light from the porthole shone over her shoulder, making it difficult to see her expression clearly. Daisy could see, however, that she was as taut as a bowstring.

Daisy and Alec sat down, and Alec said, his voice low enough not to be heard by Gotobed, 'Does the name Henry Welford mean anything to you, Mrs Gotobed?'

For a moment, Wanda was quite still. Then she quavered, 'W-Welford? It sounds vaguely familiar. Why?'

'Because Welford was an associate of Curtis Pertwee, and Pertwee was an admirer of yours.'

'Oh. Oh yes. I think that was the name of the bloke who was with Curt . . . Mr Pertwee when he came up to me the other day.'

'You were acquainted with Pertwee before he approached you on board the *Talavera.*' Alec made it a statement, not a question.

'I . . . Yes, he was at the stage door sometimes, after a performance. After all, that's why they call them "stage-door Johnnies".'

'I dare say he brought you flowers, took you out to dinner now and then?'

'I don't remember,' Wanda said quickly. 'I was quite in demand, you know. Can't remember all of 'em, can I?'

'Mrs Gotobed, I'm sorry to be so blunt, but I must ask you whether Curtis Pertwee was ever your lover.'

The shock, horror, and disgust crossing Wanda's face were obvious in spite of all her cosmetics and the poor light. Surely she was not a good enough actress to fake that swiftly changing expression. 'Never!' she declared adamantly. 'Here, what's all this about?'

'I'm afraid there has been another fatality, as I gather you are aware. The missing man is Henry Welford, and your husband was alone on deck with him when he fell to his death.'

Appalled, Wanda gasped, her face blanching. 'No!' she cried. With a visible effort she pulled herself together enough to go on: 'He didn't know I knew them. Unless Daisy told –'

Gotobed burst into the room. 'That's enough, Fletcher! I know you're just doing your job, but I won't have her upset. Anything else you have to say can be said in my presence.'

'Very well, sir.' Alec turned back to Wanda and said bluntly, 'Mr Gotobed has been the person closest to the victim in two unnatural deaths. As the only police officer aboard, and with Captain Dane's concurrence, I am confining him to this suite for the rest of the voyage. The Captain is offering you the use of an unoccupied cabin if you wish to move.'

His heart in his eyes, Gotobed gazed at Wanda. With consummate grace, she rose and went to him, holding out her hands. 'Of course I'll stay. I don't know what's reelly happened, but Dickie wouldn't ever harm me, would you, Dickie-bird?'

Alec exchanged a glance with Daisy and gave up. The Gotobeds did not appear to notice their departure.

'I've misjudged her,' said Daisy remorsefully. 'I'm sure Pertwee wasn't her lover, and I didn't think she was so fond of Gotobed. She was really upset over your suspecting him.'

His finger to his lips, Alec nodded at the sailor lounging against the wall on the opposite side of the short passage leading to the suite. A large, tough-looking man, he sketched a salute and winked as they passed.

'You didn't tell Gotobed about seeing Wanda with Pertwee and Welford, did you?' Alec asked.

'I haven't breathed a word to anyone but you. You *must* be wrong about him.'

'Someone else saw them and told him then.'

'Maybe.' Daisy sighed.

'Jealousy is a powerful emotion. He wouldn't need

proof that they were lovers to give him a motive for doing away with Pertwee.'

'But what about Welford?'

'Blackmail is the obvious answer,' Alec pointed out, 'which would explain their meeting on the boat deck, too. Welford could have threatened to tell me that Gotobed killed Pertwee because he suspected he was Wanda's lover.'

'It's a bit convoluted, but I suppose it's possible.' Daisy sighed again and wrinkled her nose at him. 'Darling, we're going to have to tell Arbuckle what's going on.'

'Will you do that, Daisy? Sorry to abandon you, but I'm hoping other acquaintances of Pertwee or Welford have come forward who might shed some light on this affair.'

'Right-oh. Just as well, I expect. We can all sit around and abuse you.'

'At least explain the basis for my actions,' Alec begged.

As she was on the cabin deck, Daisy went first to Arbuckle's suite to see if he was there. He was not, but Gloria and Brenda were, giggling together over their costumes for the Fancy Dress Ball. They greeted Daisy with cries of joy and made her try on the suit of cardboard armour they had contrived between them and painted with silver paint from the boatswain.

'Because you came to the rescue last summer when I was in trouble,' Gloria explained. 'I've told Birdie all about it.'

'Here's your shield,' said Brenda, producing a round tea tray covered with a Union Jack. 'The steward gave us a broom handle for a lance, but we're still working on it.'

Resignedly, Daisy tried on the armour. There was one good thing about it: encased in cardboard and carrying lance and shield, she could not be expected to tango. She was glad, too, that the two girls were having fun, apparently unaffected by the unpleasant events around them.

'What are you going as, Birdie?' she asked.

'A bird, of course. One of the stewardesses gave us a feather boa a passenger left behind on the last voyage. And Gloria's going to be a Glow-worm, only we're having trouble fixing the electric torch inside her caterpillar costume.'

'I rather think glow-worms are actually beetles.' She had learnt that when writing her Natural History Museum article.

They stared at her in dismay. 'Gee whiz!' said Gloria. 'It's too late to change. Never mind, I guess not many people know that.'

'Hardly anyone, I should think,' said Daisy, sorry she had spoken. 'But if the torch won't work, make a hookah and you can be the caterpillar in *Alice in Wonderland.* I must go. Thanks for my costume – it's spiffing. And thanks for not making me be a daisy, which is what I always ended up as when I was little. Gloria, do you know where your father is?'

'Poppa and Phil came for their coats; they were talking about going outside for some fresh air. There haven't been any wild gusts in a while, and the ocean's calmed some, too. But if you go after them, take care.'

On the way to fetch her coat, Daisy realized that the *Talavera* was once again forging steadily through regular swells. Their mischief done, wind and wave had subsided, or the ship had escaped beyond the patch of unruly weather. The thrumming of the engines held an urgent note. Captain Dane was doubtless trying to make up for lost time.

It was chilly outside, but the wind had died completely, and the only white froth on the sea was the wakes. Quite a few passengers had taken advantage of the improvement to go out on deck. Daisy found Arbuckle taking a turn around the boat deck in Miss Oliphant's company, while Phillip had coerced Riddman into a game of deck tennis. Chester Riddman actually appeared to be enjoying himself.

As expected, Arbuckle was highly indignant to hear his friend had been confined to his suite. 'Gotobed wouldn't hurt a fly! What in tarnation's got into Fletcher's head?'

Miss Oliphant said not a word, but her tightly folded lips expressed her feelings. Daisy hastened to remind them of Gotobed's proximity to two men now dead.

'But unless he's a homicidal maniac,' Arbuckle exploded, 'why the heck would he wanna hump them off?'

'I would take my oath that Mr Gotebed is not a maniac of any kind,' said Miss Oliphant quietly.

Daisy looked around. No one seemed to have noticed Arbuckle's outburst. 'If he did it, which I don't believe any more than you do, he had a reason,' she said. 'I can tell you, but only if you give me your word not to talk about it, even to each other. Because if he *doesn't* know, then finding out would at best upset him, at worst just might really lead to murder.'

'Whatever it is, I do not wish to know,' Miss Oliphant declared. 'I am prepared to trust Mr Fletcher's judgement that there may be good and sufficient reason. I believe I shall go in now. No doubt I shall see you both later.' With a slight bow, she turned towards the nearest companion-way.

Daisy was quite certain the witch had guessed that the imbroglio in which Mr Gotobed found himself was at least partly his wife's fault.

'I honour the lady for not prying,' growled Arbuckle, 'but dam it, Gotobed's my pal and I can't defend him if I don't know what's what. I want you to give me the low-down. You have my word I won't spill the beans.'

'I saw her talking with Pertwee and Welford the day after we sailed. Maybe flirting a bit, that's all. There's no evidence that there was ever anything more. But Pertwee was a good looking chap in a way which might appeal to Wanda. Gotobed could easily misinterpret the situation. *I* never breathed a word to him, of course, nor to anyone but Alec; but as Alec says, other people must have seen them and someone might have mentioned it to him.'

'Gotobed wouldn't kill a guy for making sheep's-eyes at his wife!'

'But you must see that Alec couldn't just ignore it,' Daisy argued.

'I guess not,' Arbuckle conceded.

'And he's not resting on his laurels. He's still investigating, and so is Sergeant Tring at home. There's no proof Gotobed did in Pertwee and Welford, nor is there likely to be any; but with the circumstantial evidence, he simply can't be allowed to go about as usual.'

'I guess not. Waal, you've given me plenty to think about, Mrs Fletcher. I can go and see him, can I?'

'Oh yes. But do be careful what you say. And I shouldn't go just yet if I were you. When we left them, they were being rather lovey-dovey.'

'Don't sound to me like he thinks she's been two-timing him!' Arbuckle exclaimed.

'Ah, but he knows he has her all to himself now.'

Daisy left him looking unhappy but thoughtful. She hoped he would come up with a way to exculpate Gotobed. Even if nothing was ever proved, having the suspicion of murder hanging over one for the rest of one's life would be perfectly beastly.

In spite of the two fatal 'accidents' aboard, the Fancy Dress Ball was to proceed as planned. When Daisy met Alec in their cabin to change for dinner – costume was not to be donned until after the meal – he refused categorically to wear his uniform as a Detective Chief Inspector of the Metropolitan Police, which he had brought in case he needed it in Washington.

'It's not fancy dress,' he said.

'Most passengers don't know that,' Daisy argued, working on his collar studs.

'They do now, since I interviewed the three who admitted having met Pertwee and Welford.'

'Oh yes, what did they say?'

'Nothing useful. One had chatted with them in the Smoking Room. The others had each played a game or two in Riddman's suite and decided the stakes were too high. Ouch! I'll tell you what, I'll go as a plumber, in my shirt-sleeves and *no collar*!'

'And the old boots and old trousers we brought for country walks, with string around the knees. Good idea! I bet Gloria will know where to get hold of a plumber's wrench.'

Gloria did. She came to the ball with a torch hung around her neck and dangling inside her bright green caterpillar costume. Brenda had feathers sewn all over her frock, with wide feathered sleeves to flap and a cardboard beak protruding from her forehead. Arbuckle wore chaps, fringed buckskin vest, and what he called a bolo tie, acquired on a trip to the Wild West.

Miss Oliphant turned up in a borrowed ship's boy's uniform jacket and cap, worn over matching bloomers, announcing herself as a ship's girl. She did not win a prize from the master of ceremonies, but Arbuckle awarded her a bottle of ginger wine.

Phillip and Riddman were the official winners of the group. They were a pair of charwomen, wrapped in bright, flowered overalls, with carpet slippers on their feet, flowered hats on their heads, and mops and buckets in hand. As they returned to their seats after accepting their prizes – a half-bottle of Scotch each – walking tipsily and pretending to swig from the bottles, the fog-horn's mournful blast boomed out.

There was a sudden silence in the Grand Salon, followed by a collective groan.

'What next?' Arbuckle shook his head. 'Storms, gales, people falling overboard and drowning. I'm beginning to think Gotobed's right and I should invest in airplanes. What next?'

'Icebergs?' Brenda said with a shiver.

'Wrong season,' Arbuckle assured her. 'The *Titanic* sailed in April, when the Arctic ice starts breaking up.'

'Wasn't it the *Republic* which collided with another ship in a fog and sank?' Phillip asked tactlessly. Gloria pinched him, and he added hastily, 'All souls on board saved, as I recall. I must have been fourteen or fifteen, and I remember the excitement when the radio operator, Binns, got back to England. He was the hero of the hour.'

'He remained at his post on the sinking ship, guiding the *Baltic* to the rescue,' Miss Oliphant reminisced.

'I don't suppose young Kitchener will get his chance to show equal heroism,' Alec said dryly. 'The sea is wide and ships are small, and we are outside the usual shipping lanes because of avoiding that storm. Have you seen the wireless apparatus yet, Petrie?'

Phillip had visited Kitchener in his den, but Daisy had not, what with the weather and the events of the day. She resolved to go next morning, come hail, snow, hurricane, or iceberg – not to mention murder or mayhem – or it would be too late to fit it into her article.

The *Talavera* glided snail-like through a white nothingness. Up on deck, her throttled-back engines were no more than a whisper of vibration. The tops of the masts were invisible, the funnels wreathed in shifting veils. When Daisy looked over the side, she saw the tops of the swells emerging from the fog, one by one, dark and glassy as obsidian.

Every two minutes, the fog-horn wailed its warning. It reminded country-bred Daisy of a cow which had lost its calf – a very large cow. The sound reverberated, seemed to echo back off the all-enveloping fog. Presumably it penetrated at least far enough to warn off any vessel close enough to pose a danger.

The sound died away into a hushed stillness without a

breath of wind, then once again blared forth. The damp cold seeped into Daisy's bones. She went on to the wireless room.

Kitchener was delighted to see her and pleased to answer her questions, though because of the fog he never doffed his earphones. At intervals he tapped out the ship's identification and position, but his fingers performed this exercise almost automatically, without interrupting the interview.

Now and then, the young wireless operator fell silent, listening intently for a minute or two. He explained that in bad weather a regular period was left clear of other messages to allow for emergency transmissions.

Daisy asked him about the sinking of the *Republic* in 1909. He was telling her the story of CQD Binns – CQD being the old emergency call letters, standing for Come Quick, Danger – when suddenly he stopped and held up his hand.

'SOS,' he hissed. He listened a moment longer. 'Sorry, miss, you'll have to go. I think we're the nearest ship.'

# CHAPTER 18

The *Talavera* altered course and inched open her throttles. The first officer told the passengers, again herded into the Grand Salon, that they were heading for the spot where a freighter had holed the *Garibaldi*, an Italian emigrant ship.

Captain Dane had not ordered full speed ahead on the grounds that if his vessel came to grief, he could be of no service. Several hours must elapse before the *Talavera* reached the position of the disaster. However, the *Garibaldi* was sinking slowly, and its surviving passengers and crew were being transferred by lifeboat to the freighter, the *Mary Jane.*

'The *Mary Jane* is apparently seaworthy, but she has considerable damage to her bows, and of course she has no accommodations for passengers. We haven't a great deal,' the first mate continued ruefully, 'but at least we can give them all shelter from the elements. I understand there are over one thousand. All passengers who are willing to share their space are requested to give their names and cabin numbers to the Purser.'

'A thousand!' Daisy exclaimed. 'And the *Talavera* has cabins for two hundred, most occupied. I suppose someone could sleep on the floor between our berths, darling.'

'At a pinch,' Alec agreed, and went to join the queue at the Purser's table.

Arbuckle was first in line. Of course, he and the Petries had a sitting room. So did the Gotobeds, neither of whom was present. Daisy decided to go down and ask whether they would be willing to put up some of the *Garibaldi*'s unfortunate passengers.

As she had rather expected, Gotobed was eager to do everything possible to help, while Wanda pouted and complained but gave in.

'I know you don't feel very well, my dear,' Gotobed apologized, 'but think of those poor souls, cold, very likely soaked to the skin, having lost all their possessions and nearly lost their lives. It is the least we can do.'

'I said all right, didn't I? I'm going to lie down for a bit in the other room while we've still got some privacy. Daisy, can I have a word with you?'

Daisy followed her. Wanda sat down on the chaise longue, kicked off her shoes, and lay back. 'Give us a fag,' she requested.

'Sorry, I don't smoke. I didn't think you did.'

'Dickie doesn't like women smoking. It's my nerves. I hardly slept a wink last night. Dickie doesn't like me to take my powders.' She jumped up and started to pace in stockinged feet. 'I can't sit still.'

'Do you want to move to another cabin, after all? Or have Mr Gotobed move? I'm sure it could be managed, even with . . .'

'No, no, I'm not afraid of Dickie. Daisy, is Miss Oliphant really hot under the collar?'

'She's pretty upset with you,' Daisy said candidly.

'Why? Do you want her to give you something to help you sleep? I should think she might.'

'Will you ask her to come and see me? You can tell her I want to say I'm sorry and I've changed my mind about you know what, if you think that'll help.'

'I'll ask her to come.' She was not prepared to pass on what she suspected to be an insincere repentance.

In the sitting room, Gotobed started to rise as she returned. He looked old and disheartened. She waved him back to his seat: 'I'm just passing through. Wanda wants to consult the witch.'

His face brightened. 'That's grand. I have great faith in Miss Oliphant.'

As Daisy expected, Miss Oliphant bridled at Wanda's request, but she softened when she heard of Gotobed's confidence in her and agreed to go.

Daisy had found her with Arbuckle sitting in deckchairs in the enclosed promenade. Many passengers were there, their numbers increased by those who had emerged from their cabins with the return of calm seas. Others were outside, standing at the rail, peering fruitlessly into the fog.

'Gloria and Phillip are out there,' Arbuckle said to Daisy as Miss Oliphant left them, 'with Lady Brenda and Riddman. That young fella seems to have gotten his act together some.'

'Yes, he's pulled his socks up since Alec's heart-to-heart, and Brenda seems as keen on him as ever. I wonder whether their quarrel was a storm in a teacup or if there's trouble ahead.'

'Don't you worry your head about it, honey.'

'I don't, not really. I'm just sorry for Mr Harvey. I suppose his duties kept him from spending enough time with her to win her over.'

'He's better off without her,' said Arbuckle cynically. 'She's an expensive and flighty young lady.'

'I expect you're right. Do you happen to know where Alec is?'

Arbuckle shook his head. 'I can tell you where he isn't: in the Grand Salon. It's off limits. They're preparing it to house twelve hundred unexpected passengers.'

The *Talavera* carried few spare mattresses and no great stock of blankets. Many passengers had volunteered to give up a blanket or two and bedspreads, and all the clean sheets and towels in the ship were added to the collection. The Purser had sent out an appeal for clothes. Daisy went down to the cabin and sorted out a few things she thought she and Alec could spare. She made sure they all had laundry marks, in case there was a chance they might be returned.

She had just started folding everything neatly when Alec came in. He looked at the small heaps on the bunks and said, 'For the shipwreck victims? Good. Give them all my stiff shirts and collars. I'll buy new shirts with attached soft collars when we get to New York. Riddman tells me they're all the rage.'

'You'd better keep a shirt and a couple of collars for extra special occasions, darling,' Daisy said judiciously, 'like the Captain's dinner, though I suppose that will have to be cancelled.'

'Dane will be delighted. Oh, and you can give them that maroon cardigan. It's warm but I can't stand the colour.

I've been looking for an excuse to get rid of it for years, only Mother knitted it.'

'I know, that's why I didn't put it out. Right-oh, all in a good cause, as long as when she asks where it's gone you make it plain it wasn't my idea. You've been talking to Riddman?'

'Just to see if he remembered anything else about Pertwee or Welford, which he doesn't. Nor do the three men who admitted to having met them – or Pertwee at least – and a fourth has come forward who is no more helpful.' He sat down on a berth and watched Daisy folding. 'If Tom doesn't come up with something useful, I'm stymied.'

'You mean you'll have to let Gotobed go?'

'I haven't really much excuse for holding him now. Opportunity, yes. As for means: yes in Welford's case – it would only have taken a good shove; but no proof he had a gun or any other means to cause Pertwee to fall. Motive: I'm inclined to believe Wanda that Pertwee was never her lover, so it comes down to the pair having been admirers, a decidedly feeble motive even if I had evidence that Gotobed knew.'

'Which you don't.'

'Which I don't.' Alec stood up. 'I must go and talk to both of them again before chaos descends upon the ship. I'll give you a hand carrying those up first.'

They delivered the clothes to the Purser's office. Alec rejected Daisy's offer to assist at the interviews with the Gotobeds, so she went to write up her wireless room notes and add a bit about preparations for receiving vast numbers of refugees.

Then it was just a matter of waiting. Lunch was served to all first-class passengers in their cabins – Daisy and Alec joined Arbuckle and the Petries in their suite. A few others ate in the library at the desks, and everyone else balanced their plates on the arms of deckchairs.

The rest of the voyage was not going to be comfortable. Fortunately, in spite of the many delays, the *Talavera* was expected to dock in New York just two days hence.

By mid-afternoon, the majority of the passengers were outside standing at the bows or the front rail of the boat deck. The lifeboat crews gathered by their boats, ready to lower away. The fog had thinned since Daisy was out in it, or rather, it was now intermittent. Long patches, sometimes several hundred yards, were clear, with the sun just visible through a haze. The *Talavera* crept along, cutting through the sable waves. If the sinking ship was wallowing in the fog-bank ahead, Captain Dane was not risking his vessel running into it, errand of mercy or no.

'Hush!' someone shouted, and the chattering crowd grew still. 'I thought I heard a foghorn.'

The *Talavera*'s foghorn hooted deafeningly just above them. Everyone laughed, then fell silent again, straining their ears. Faintly through the still air came a distant answer.

A moment later, the *Talavera* replied. At the same time she altered course slightly. As she steamed on, the far-off call grew gradually more distinct. Second Officer Harvey came running down the companion-way from the boat deck and made the passengers move back from the bows, just as they plunged again into heavy fog.

Arbuckle stopped Harvey. 'What's the chance of us hitting one of those two ships?' he asked bluntly.

'Very little, sir. As you can tell, we are moving very

slowly, but the Captain must take obvious precautions. The *Garibaldi* has been abandoned and the *Mary Jane* has no wireless, so our only contact, our only fix on their position now is the foghorn.'

'No wireless,' Phillip exclaimed, 'in this modern age!'

'Many freighters don't, sir. Excuse me, I must get back to the bridge.'

The fog began to turn to drizzle, seeping down from the invisible sky. Many of the passengers headed indoors. Daisy was tempted, but the *Mary Jane*'s foghorn was so clear now that the meeting was obviously imminent. She turned up her collar, wishing for a sou'wester.

The *Talavera* slid through the unravelling fog and suddenly emerged. Through the rain the intent watchers saw a small, broad-beamed ship, stern on. Every inch of its deck was crammed with people. When they saw the *Talavera*, a shout went up.

'Why, it's nothing but a tramp steamer!' Arbuckle cried, as the *Talavera* abruptly reversed engines.

The crowd moved back to the rail. 'Looks like a regular rust bucket,' said Riddman.

'Gee, those poor folks must be soaked to the skin,' Gloria commented.

'And freezing,' Daisy said with a shiver.

'I wonder whether anyone has thought to prepare hot drinks.' Miss Oliphant trotted off.

'Where's the *Garibaldi*?' Brenda asked.

Alec pointed. Little more than superstructure, funnels, and masts was visible. The stricken vessel lay tilted, half of its upper deck under water, the rest awash. They regarded the sobering sight in silence for a moment.

Arbuckle shook his head sadly and said, 'The Eyeties build those emigrant ships outa tinfoil. Fletcher, one of these days I wanna word with you about airplanes.'

'I merely flew them, sir.'

'So you can tell me about that side of things.'

'Look,' said Phillip, 'there's a couple of boats put off from the *Mary Jane*.'

The *Talavera*'s boats were swinging out and down. Soon the sea between the two ships was crawling with small craft. As the first boats from the freighter – one of her own and three of the *Garibaldi*'s – reached the side, *Talavera* crewmen saw their wretched cargo up the ladders. At the top, stewards helped them over the rail and hurried them inside. Then the pace of arrivals quickened. The stewards were busy settling people, and passengers started to lend a hand.

Alec and Arbuckle stationed themselves at the head of a rope ladder. As each exhausted, shivering Italian reached them, they lifted them aboard. Every now and then a sailor swarmed up one-handed with a baby or small child under his arm.

Daisy's knowledge of Italian was just enough to greet them, ask them to wait a minute, and then tell them to go with her. As soon as a small group gathered, she would escort them to the Grand Salon. It was there that she first saw Gotobed. His guard must have answered the call for all hands.

He saw her and came over to her. 'I thowt happen I'd be able to help,' he said.

'You speak Italian, don't you? I'd forgotten. If they don't need you here —'

'A couple of the stewards know enough to cope.'

'– then I'm sure you'd be useful on deck. These poor people arrive so confused and disorientated, just having someone speak their language would ease their minds.'

He went with her. Thereafter, she saw him everywhere, tirelessly translating, reuniting separated families, holding babies or crouching to blot the tears of little children. What a pity Wanda did not want children!

The thought made Daisy wonder where Miss Oliphant was. Probably dispensing tea somewhere, perhaps with one of her remedies added to the warming brew.

Daisy lost count of the number of groups she had led inside. They were still coming, an unending stream as the little boats plied back and forth. Several injured people were hoisted up in slings and carried below to the unoccupied cabins, where Dr Amboyne could tend them.

Gotobed approached Daisy again. 'I'm afraid Wanda will take on, but it's time to give up our sitting room. It's getting right crowded in the Grand Salon. Would you mind, lass, going and warning her I'll be sending summun down?'

Daisy's fingers and toes were growing numb, and the drizzle, though light, was beginning to soak through her coat. She was glad of a respite, an excuse to stay in the dry and warm for more than a couple of minutes at a time. After delivering her next group, she went on down to the Gotobeds' suite.

Her knock went unanswered. After a moment, she opened the door and went in. The door to the bedroom was ajar. From within came Wanda's furious voice.

'I've wrecked two bloody nails trying to open the bloody porthole. I don't give a damn what the bloody stewards are busy with, you get one in here right this minute.'

'But, madam,' Baines protested.

'*Now*, d'you hear me? And bring me some more seltzer water. Get a move on!'

Baines sped through into the sitting room. As she closed the door behind her, something crashed against it. Her lips tightened in her set face.

Seeing Daisy, she burst out, 'I won't put up with it! She's never been easy, but this is the last straw. Soon as we get to New York, I'm leaving, and I'll forfeit my wages 'stead of notice. There're plenty of American ladies on this very ship've asked me if I'd like to work for them. And I'm sorry to let Mr Gotobed down, who's as nice a gentleman as can be, but I won't put up with being thrown things at!'

'I don't blame you,' Daisy sympathized, wondering whether there was any point in continuing with her errand with Wanda already in a terrific bait. 'Perhaps I can open the porthole for her, at least.'

'Shouldn't think so, madam, it's ever so difficult without the steward's special key. She says she's too hot and she's been drinking water like a whale.'

'Oh dear, does she look feverish?'

'She's red in the face, madam, but I put it down to temper.'

'I dare say you're right. I'd better ask her if she'd like me to send the doctor along, though.'

'Upon your head be it, madam. I'll go and fetch her seltzer, but she'll have to come out here to get it. I'm not going back in there to be thrown things at.'

The maid left. Daisy went to the inner door, knocked, put her head around the door, and said quickly, 'Wanda, it's Daisy. Would you like me to ask Dr Amboyne . . .'

With a scream of rage, Wanda flung something at her. Daisy ducked and slammed the door shut. She heard whatever it was shatter against the wood.

Not a good moment to send down a distressed Italian family, and so she told Gotobed, not quite explaining that his wife was in the middle of a royal tantrum. Daisy was no keener than Baines on 'being thrown things at', but Gotobed had troubles enough without hearing about it.

Dusk was closing in, an hour or so later, when he again approached Daisy. This time he shepherded a wet and weary youngish couple with two handsome and still lively boys of about Belinda's age and a younger girl.

'Mr and Mrs Ferelli and the children will sleep in my suite,' he said. 'Will you be so kind as to show them the way, Mrs Fletcher? Please tell Wanda I'll be down shortly, and ask her to make them comfortable – if you feel there's any chance she might,' he added wryly.

'I'll take them down,' Daisy agreed. She did not promise to speak to Wanda, half intending to show them in and flee. But when they reached the suite, Baines was peacefully sewing in the sitting room, so Daisy went in.

'Madam's asleep,' said the maid.

'Good! I'm sure it'll do her good.' In a mixture of Italian and sign language, Daisy explained the situation to the Ferellis, warning them to keep quiet. She asked Baines to fetch them towels and hot drinks and do anything else she could for them. 'Mr Gotobed will be down very soon. The last two boatloads are on their way. Can you manage till he comes?'

'Certainly, madam.'

'I'll just peek in and make sure Mrs Gotobed is sleeping soundly.' Turning to the Ferellis, Daisy put her finger to her lips. She tiptoed to the bedroom door, inched it open, and looked in. Wanda, sprawled untidily on the bed amid rumpled blankets, did not stir. Her tantrum must have worn her out.

Daisy was pretty worn out, too. Deciding she had done her bit, she went along to the cabin. A harassed-looking stewardess was just coming out.

'Oh, Mrs Fletcher, madam, I'm that glad you've come. Maybe you can do something with her.' She hoicked a thumb over her shoulder. 'Her name's Loochiya Crochet, or something like. I've got her into dry clothes, but she won't do anything but cry.'

Daisy suppressed a sigh. She had forgotten that she and Alec had volunteered to take someone in. Squaring her shoulders, she went in.

Lucia Croce was small, plump, and scarcely more than a child. In donated tweeds too large for her and utterly inappropriate for her olive-skinned southern prettiness, she huddled on one of the fold-down seats, a steady stream of tears flowing down her cheeks. As a first step, Daisy gave her a hankie.

Asking what was the matter stretched Daisy's Italian. From the passionate flood of words which followed, she managed to extract two, frequently recurring, '*mio marito*.'

Obviously Lucia, who looked far too young to be married, was worried about her husband. Daisy assumed they had been parted in the exodus from the *Mary Jane.* Her heart sank at the prospect of trying to find one young man amongst the crowds. But what if she had guessed wrong, if Mr Croce awaited his bride in New York and she was only concerned for his feelings when he heard the *Garibaldi* had sunk?

Gotobed could find out. Telling Lucia to come with her, Daisy headed back to the Gotobeds' suite.

Gotobed opened the door. Behind him was a lot of excited chatter, including the shrill voices of the boys. No sign of Wanda, though, Daisy was relieved to see. She explained her problem and Gotobed asked Lucia a question. He listened intently to the ensuing flood. The Ferellis gathered around, making soothing noises.

'Her husband was hurt in the collision,' Gotobed explained to Daisy. 'Since she has not been reunited with him, she's afraid he is dead.'

'Oh, poor thing! He'll be in one of the spare cabins, under Dr Amboyne's care.'

'I think I'd better take her along to find him. Mrs Fletcher, I can't wake Wanda and I'm a bit concerned. Would you take a look at her for me?'

'Of course, but I expect she's just taken one of her powders. Perhaps she took what Miss Oliphant gave her, too, and they've reinforced each other. Thanks for dealing with Lucia.'

Wanda was still sprawled on the bed in much the same position. No doubt her husband had been too gentle with her, trying to wake her by talking to her. Daisy had no objection to giving her a good shaking, but she started by calling her name. No reaction, not so much as the flicker of an eyelid.

Daisy sat on the edge of the bed and took Wanda's hand. It was hot and dry, as was her forehead. Her breathing seemed unnaturally rapid. Beginning to worry, Daisy felt for a pulse in her wrist. That too, when at last she found it, seemed too fast and weak.

On the bedside table stood an empty tumbler. Beside it lay a ship's stationery envelope and a torn paper, the kind used to hold medical powders, with a few white grains clinging to it. Alarmed now, Daisy picked up the envelope. Inside was greenish stuff which looked like chopped-up leaves, like one of Miss Oliphant's remedies. She sniffed and decided it smelt just like the lemon balm tea she had drunk a few days ago.

But she could not forget what Wanda had said about the witch being out to catch a husband.

'Baines, will you come and sit with Mrs Gotobed? I'm afraid she's ill, and I don't want to leave her alone while I go for the doctor.'

Daisy headed for the doctor's office. If he was not there, as seemed likely, she ought to be able to find out where he was. On the way, she came across Alec and Miss Oliphant talking together in the corridor.

As soon as he saw her face, he asked, 'What's wrong, Daisy?'

'Darling, I'm so glad I found you. I may be making a mountain out of a molehill, but . . .'

'I'll leave you,' said Miss Oliphant tactfully.

'Oh no, please stay. You may be able to help. Wanda seems to be in a sort of stupor – I can't wake her. I'm pretty certain she's taken at least one of her powders, and she may have taken lemon balm, too, if that's what you gave her, Miss Oliphant.'

'I told her not to mix them!' exclaimed the witch. 'Lemon balm on its own is entirely harmless, but one can never be sure of the effects of untested combinations of medications. Fetch Dr Amboyne. I shall go to her at once.' She set off at a near trot.

'Is Wanda alone?' Alec asked.

'No, Baines is with her. I was just going for Dr Amboyne.'

'Where's Gotobed?'

Daisy explained about Lucia Croce. 'So he's probably with the doctor now. He'll come straight back when he hears about Wanda. He was already concerned about her.'

'I've been wondering whether she takes something else, whether she's addicted to hashish or cocaine. Have you noticed her dilated pupils?'

'I think that's from the eye-drops she uses. Alec, you don't suppose Miss Oliphant gave her the wrong stuff? By mistake, of course.'

'Of course. Go and get the doctor.' Alec strode swiftly after Miss Oliphant.

# CHAPTER 19

Alec was damp to the skin and tired from the unaccustomed exertion of hauling the *Garibaldi*'s passengers over the rail. With the last of them brought aboard, he had gone down to change. When he'd met Miss Oliphant, he'd stopped for a moment to exchange impressions of the rescue. He had been about to go on, hoping to find Daisy in their cabin, when she had arrived looking disturbed.

Now, dampness and fatigue forgotten, he hurried towards the Gotobeds' suite, considering the hint Daisy had reluctantly voiced.

Miss Oliphant as murderess? Surely she had not shot Pertwee, and she had certainly not pushed Welford down the companion-way. Could she have deliberately poisoned Wanda? The animosity between them was as obvious as the sympathy between Miss Oliphant and Gotobed. Daisy had told him of Wanda's accusations that the old maid was husband-hunting and would not turn up her nose at a millionaire, American or English.

Wanda was inclined to speak without taking into account the effect of her words. Had she said something to Gotobed which had led him to believe she was romantically involved with Pertwee? Or had Gotobed seen them together and reached his own conclusions?

Either would explain Pertwee's murder – which still left the puzzles of Welford's fatal and Denton's near-fatal plunges.

In any case, Gotobed was the obvious villain where Pertwee was concerned and the only possible murderer if Welford had been murdered. But would he poison his wife, whom he seemed genuinely to love in spite of her faults? Or had Miss Oliphant given her some dangerous herb?

Always supposing she had in fact been poisoned. Alec hoped it was a false alarm, a mountain created by Daisy out of a molehill. More than likely, Wanda had simply taken too many of her sleeping powders.

At that point in his reflections, Alec caught up with Miss Oliphant at the door of the suite.

'I knocked, Mr Fletcher. There is no answer.'

'We'll go in. This is no time to stand on ceremony.' He opened the door. 'Great Scott!'

Five pairs of dark eyes stared at him.

'I'd forgotten Gotobed offered to take in a family.'

'I speak a little Italian,' said Miss Oliphant. 'I shall endeavour to explain our presence. You had better go straight to Mrs Gotobed. Call me if matters appear urgent.'

Alec went through to the bedroom. Wanda lay on the bed with the counterpane spread loosely over her. The lady's maid stood up.

'Mrs Baines?' It never hurt to give a woman a courtesy title, however she was normally addressed, and Mrs, if wrong, was less likely to give offence than Miss. 'I'm Alec

Fletcher. Has Mrs Gotobed's condition changed since my wife left?'

'It's Miss Baines, sir. She hasn't changed, not so's you'd notice. But then, I'm not a nurse. She hasn't moved a muscle, that I can tell you.'

'Thank you.' Alec checked Wanda's pulse and found it weak and fast but steady. Deciding to take advantage of Miss Oliphant's being delayed, he picked up a scrap of paper from the bedside table. 'Can you tell me what this is?'

'It looks to me like she took one of her powders, sir, to help her sleep. She was in a bit of a state earlier. I s'pose she thought a good nap would set her to rights.'

'No doubt. And this?' He held up the envelope.

'That's what Miss Oliphant gave her, sir. I don't think she can've had any of that, because she'd've had to send me for hot water, which she didn't. It's a sort of herbal tea. There's no teapot nor cup and saucer like the steward would have brought, either, besides them all being so busy with those poor shipwrecked souls.'

'And you didn't bring her the glass of water for the powder?'

'No, sir, she must've got it from the washstand. She sent me to get seltzer water; ever so thirsty she was this afternoon. It took ever such a long time, what with everyone being busy, and when I came back, she was already asleep. Truth to tell, I was relieved.' Baines hesitated. 'D'you think she's taken too many powders, sir?'

'Have you seen any papers other than this?' Alec countered.

'No, sir. I looked under the bed and in the wastepaper basket, too.'

'Good for you. You won't be offended if I take a look around for myself? You may have heard that I'm a police officer. I'm trained to see things that other people miss.'

As he searched, his eye was caught by the array of gold-topped pots on the dressing table. Finishing the search, without finding any papers, he went over to regard them with a frown.

'Which of these would be her eye-drops? No, don't touch, please.' Damn, he thought, no fingerprint kit, but on glass he might be able to bring up dabs with flour. The bottle Baines indicated was nearly empty. 'Do you know what it is?'

'Belladonna,' said Miss Oliphant, coming in. 'I warned her to stop using it. It is a highly dangerous preparation. It has its uses medically, but I never touch it.'

'Deadly nightshade,' Alec said. He turned to look down at Wanda, lying motionless. 'Could it produce this effect if too much was introduced into the eyes?'

'I don't believe so, but you must ask Dr Amboyne.' She sat down on the edge of the bed and took Wanda's wrist in her fingers. Her hands were square and strong, with shortcut nails. 'I see she has taken some lemon balm,' she said, noticing the envelope on the table.

'That's what you gave her? You couldn't have got it mixed up with something else?'

'Not possibly,' Miss Oliphant said sharply. Nonetheless, she reached for the envelope and sniffed at the contents. 'Baines, fetch some hot water, please. I shall drink a cup myself to prove it harmless.'

'I didn't mean to imply . . .' Alec began, rather less than truthfully.

'I shall drink a cup. It is soothing to the nerves, and after the various occurrences of this voyage, I find my nerves in need of support.'

'I should never have guessed it, ma'am,' Alec said sincerely, as Baines went out. 'Am I to take it that you consider Mrs Gotobed's life to be in danger?'

'I am not qualified to pronounce a prognosis, Mr Fletcher. If she has taken two or three of her powders, I doubt it. If, on the other hand, she has ingested belladonna, I fear she is unlikely to survive. Immediate treatment can save victims, usually children who have eaten the sweet berries, but coma is the last stage before death.'

Alec stood looking down at Wanda. He didn't like her, but she didn't deserve to die. 'Where's the doctor?' he said irritably, turning towards the door.

As if in answer, Amboyne hurried in, black bag in hand. 'What's up? What's up?' he asked equally irritably. 'I have a great many patients at present. What seems to be the matter, Miss Oliphant?'

'What's wrong?' An agitated Gotobed came in behind the doctor. 'Is Wanda ill? Seriously?'

Amboyne swung round. 'I don't know yet, and it will be easier to find out if you will please wait in the other room. I shall inform you as soon as I have a diagnosis, I assure you.'

'You too, Daisy,' said Alec, seeing her behind Gotobed.

Swallowing a protest, Daisy took Gotobed's arm and gently led him out. He slumped into a chair, looking dazed. The Ferellis gathered around him, asking questions, chattering in sympathetic tones. The little girl climbed into his lap, and he put his arm around her.

Daisy took a chair at what little distance the room allowed. She was glad of the Ferellis' concern. She did not want to have to try to answer Gotobed's questions.

A couple of minutes later, Alec entered and came over to her. 'Tired, love?' he asked.

'Yes! What's the verdict?'

'Amboyne can't tell yet,' he said loudly enough for Gotobed to hear, then went on more quietly, 'He needs more information. Do you happen to know of any symptoms she suffered before she fell asleep?'

'Baines said she was very thirsty and her face was rather red. It sounded to me as if she might be running a fever.'

'You didn't see her yourself?'

'No, she was in a filthy temper. In the end I put down the red face to sheer spleen. Alec, I feel dreadful. I ought to have done something straight away.'

'It might have been sheer temper, and if not, you couldn't possibly have guessed, love. I must go back. Send Baines right in when she returns, will you?'

'Oh, darling, perhaps you'd better tell Dr Amboyne that when I went in later, after she fell asleep, the bedclothes were all tumbled and tangled as if she'd tossed and turned like mad. If she took a powder, wouldn't she have fallen asleep at once?'

'Unless she took it because she couldn't fall asleep. I'll tell him anyway.' Alec dropped a quick kiss on Daisy's cheek, straightened to see all the Ferellis staring, blushed, and fled back to the bedroom.

'*Mio marito*,' Daisy informed the smiling Italians.

Gotobed jumped up, the child still in his arms, and

started towards the bedroom door. 'What did Fletcher say? Is Wanda . . . ?'

'Dr Amboyne is examining her,' Daisy said firmly, standing up to bar his way. 'You will only delay him if you . . .'

Alec came back. 'Amboyne thinks it's belladonna poisoning.' He watched Gotobed's face as he spoke, as did Daisy. She saw nothing but shock. 'He wants to take her to the sickbay immediately. Daisy, will you please go and find the nurse and have her bring a couple of men with a stretcher.'

'A stretcher!' cried Gotobed. 'If it is urgent to get her there, surely we can carry her. It's not far.'

'I'll see what he says. But in the meantime, Daisy . . .'

'I'm on my way.'

Daisy met the nurse – as starched as ever despite the influx of patients – just bustling out of the surgery door to the passage, with a trayful of medicines.

'Oh, Mrs Fletcher, you'll be wanting to know about that Mrs Crotchy. The gentleman that brought her along said she's assigned to your cabin; but you needn't worry, she won't leave her husband, poor lamb, not that he's as bad off as some.'

'I'm glad.' Daisy had forgotten Lucia. 'But actually I've come with a message from Dr Amboyne.' She explained the urgent need of a stretcher.

As she spoke, the nurse turned back into the surgery and set the tray down on the doctor's desk. 'Mostly pink pills, to keep them happy,' she explained briefly, 'and the rest can wait; but we won't wait to find a pair of men, never there when they're wanted. If you'll just give me a hand with this, madam.'

She opened a cupboard and took out a rolled-up stretcher. Carrying an end each, they manoeuvred it out of the surgery. It was more awkward than heavy.

The nurse locked the door and they set off along the corridor. They hadn't gone far when they came across a couple of stewards and roped them in to do the donkey-work. Nurse and Daisy followed.

And all the while, Daisy was thinking. Belladonna? The eye-drops of course. Suicide? Why should Wanda commit suicide? She didn't seem the type, besides having a rich and adoring husband ready to cater to her every whim. But if not suicide, surely not murder? Daisy could not bring herself to believe the adoring husband had deliberately poisoned his bride.

Miss Oliphant? The lemon balm seemed innocent enough, but could the herbalist have given Wanda something else as well? Yet surely the principles which had made her refuse to help abort a foetus would not permit her to kill the mother carrying that foetus.

It *must* have been an accident.

Daisy failed to see how an accident could have happened. She had just reached this unsatisfactory conclusion when the procession reached the Gotobeds' suite. The two Italian boys were on the watch. They ran in, calling out to 'Signor Gottabetta'.

Wanda was moved on to the stretcher. The procession wended back, led by doctor and nurse. Gotobed and Miss Oliphant followed the stretcher, and Daisy and Alec brought up the rear, several paces back.

'I don't know,' said Alec softly, shaking his head. 'I just don't know. If he only had a stronger motive. He says she seemed perfectly well after lunch, quite cheerful, in fact. She actually encouraged him to go up on deck to help, when they discovered the guard had left his post. But then, Amboyne says the symptoms of belladonna poisoning normally take several hours to develop. He had a case when he was a country GP, a child who ate deadly nightshade berries.'

'Did he save the child?' Daisy asked.

'No. And he doesn't hold out much hope for Wanda.'

'Oh, darling!'

'He agrees with Miss Oliphant that she's reached the last stage before death. What she already had in her system from the eye-drops may have speeded things up.'

'It looks as if she took it at lunchtime?'

'It seems probable. I'll have to get a description of the meal from Gotobed and talk to the steward who served them, see if their stories match. I'm sure Gotobed is too clever to be caught out. I doubt I'll ever find proof that it wasn't accident or suicide, which of course it may be. Why should he have killed her? If you marry a chorus-girl, you must surely expect admirers from her past to bob up now and then.'

'Sir! Mr Fletcher, sir!'

They turned to find Kitchener hurrying after them. The wireless operator was waving several sheets of paper.

'Ah, from Scotland Yard?'

'Yes, sir. It came in awhile ago. I'm awf'ly sorry, I just haven't had a moment to decode it till now, what with all that's been going on. It's . . . It looks to me rather nasty, sir.'

Alec gave him a stern look. 'You're to forget what you have read. Not a word to *anyone*.'

'My lips are sealed, sir, honestly.'

'Good. Thank you, Kitchener. You have been most helpful.'

There were three sheets covered in Kitchener's sprawling writing. As Alec scanned them, Daisy heard his sharply indrawn breath, and then he exclaimed, 'Great Scott!'

'What is it?' she asked, trying to read the scrawl upside down. 'Darling, what has Tom Tring discovered?'

'Motive enough for any man,' he said grimly. He read on to the end, while Daisy bobbed about on tiptoe in her efforts to see over his shoulder. Folding the papers, he thrust them into his pocket.

'Alec!'

'Pertwee and Welford were well known as petty con men,' he told her, 'though nothing was ever proved against them. Welford was the brains of the pair and used his public school background to good effect, while Pertwee brought in marks attracted by those flashy good looks. But more to the point: Tom sent Ernie Piper to Somerset House to search the Births, Marriages, and Deaths records. It turns out Pertwee was Wanda's brother . . .'

'What!'

'And Welford was her husband.'

# CHAPTER 20

'Bigamy!' breathed Daisy, looking stunned.

Alec put his arm around her shoulders. 'It's one possibility which never crossed my mind,' he admitted.

'Nor mine. Blackmail?'

'I imagine so. If Gotobed repudiated Wanda or didn't pay up, the press would have a field day. He'd be held up to public ridicule. Can you imagine what that would do to a man like him?'

She shook her head, but said stubbornly, 'I believe he's strong enough to get over it. And anyway, he might not have known.'

'Come now, love, a pair of confidence tricksters would hardly be likely to ignore such a marvellous opportunity. In fact, I don't doubt that the marriage was planned and carried through with blackmail in mind.'

Alec hesitated. He could not be in two places at once, yet he was far from sure he ought to trust Daisy to observe and report impartially. If only Tring were here! But he had no choice.

'Daisy, I must talk to the steward who served the Gotobeds' lunch. Will you go along to the sickbay and keep an eye on things there for me? You won't mention anything about this, of course.' He touched the pocket where he had stowed the papers.

'Right-oh, darling. Gosh, I do hope Dr Amboyne manages to save Wanda!' She went off after the others.

It took Alec some time to run his quarry to earth. The steward, one Bailey, was perfectly willing to talk. He had gone to the Gotobeds' suite to set the table and take their orders. The gentleman had been writing, the lady painting her fingernails. They consulted the menu cards together while the steward dealt with napery, silver, and glass.

'I bet I can tell you exactly what they had, sir. Soup oaks onions first, it was, for both of them. Fillet der sole twice for the fish, oh burr and citron – that's a lemon-butter sauce, and very nice, too. Then, lessee, they both had the beef, turnydose chaser, with new potatoes and petty peas. They didn't neither of them want salad. 'That's for rabbits,' said Mr Gotobed, I recall. He finished up with cheese and biscuits, and madam had the fruit compôte with cream.'

'Very comprehensive, thank you. Wine?'

'Nah. He had a beer, and she only had water, seltzer water. Always talking about slimming, she was.'

'Did you stay there to serve the meal?' Alec asked, without much hope.

'Not me, sir. Nipping in and out, I was. I had to fetch everything from the kitchens, and all my passengers was eating in their cabins on account of the Grand Salon being otherwise engaged, you might say.'

'When you were in the Gotobeds' suite, you didn't notice anything out of the ordinary?'

'Not a thing, sir. Wait, I tell a lie.'

'Yes?' Alec asked eagerly.

'Oh, nothing much. Only most people when they sit down to lunch, they stay put, like. But one time when I went in, Mr and Mrs Gotobed was in the bedroom. I heard 'em.'

'What did you hear?'

'I don't listen at doors,' Bailey protested. ''Sides, I was too busy. Run off my feet, I was. I heard 'em talking, but I couldn't tell what they was saying.'

'Pity.' Still, if Wanda had gone out first, that was the opportunity Alec had sought for Gotobed to poison her food without her seeing.

Means, motive, opportunity, the unholy trinity; he had them all. It gave him no pleasure.

Daisy had found Gotobed and Miss Oliphant in the doctor's waiting room. Gotobed was alert, head cocked, listening for sounds in the sickbay. His face was tired and careworn. He glanced round as Daisy entered but did not appear to take in her presence, so intent was he. The witch sat quietly beside him, hands folded in her lap, head bowed. She looked up, rose, and came to Daisy.

'Camomile and linden, I think,' she said, her tone hushed but matter-of-fact. 'Will you stay with him while I fetch it?'

'Of course.'

*Could* Miss Oliphant have poisoned Wanda? Could she have claimed to have changed her mind about helping her end her pregnancy and given her a draught of belladonna, saying it was an abortifacient? But that would kill the child too – Daisy came round full circle yet again. At any rate, if the witch's aim was to marry Gotobed, she was not going to poison him.

When Miss Oliphant returned, she was followed by a steward with a tray holding a steaming teapot, three cups and saucers, a plate of biscuits, and a large book. She herself carried her medicine chest.

All the paraphernalia were set on the desk, and the steward enquired, 'Shall I pour, madam?'

'No, thank you, let it steep a little longer.'

'Very well, madam. What with everything at sixes and sevens, dinner tonight will be soup and sandwiches. Stewards will bring them around for passengers to eat wherever they wish.'

As he left, Miss Oliphant sat down at the desk and pulled the book towards her. 'This is my best reference book,' she explained to Daisy. 'Should Mrs Gotobed survive, I wish to be prepared to suggest appropriate stimulants to Dr Amboyne, though whether he will make use of them is another matter.'

'What a good idea. May I take a look at the contents of your chest?'

'Certainly, but please do not disarrange them. It is not locked.'

Daisy raised the lid. The blue glass jars and bottles nestled in their green plush niches, a place for everything and no space wasted. What interested her were the red labels that she recalled. Warning labels, she had presumed when she first glimpsed them.

But she found no foxglove, nor anything else she recognized as dangerous as well as therapeutic. Instead, the red-labelled containers held lemon balm, camomile, mint, calendula petals and calendula ointment, comfrey balm, rose water, eyebright, and other harmless-sounding preparations. Daisy decided that far from being a warning, the red was simply to make it easier to pick out frequently used items.

Miss Oliphant poured the tea and Daisy took a cup to Gotobed. He drank thirstily. Daisy sipped hers, feeling a soothing warmth spread through her. After a while she noticed that Gotobed had relaxed his tense posture. He still looked weary and deeply unhappy, but no longer overwrought.

Time passed. Occasionally uninterpretable sounds came from the sickbay, but for the most part the only sound was the turning of pages in Miss Oliphant's book. Daisy kept catching herself nodding off

Then Dr Amboyne came through, shoulders slumped, shaking his head. 'I've done everything I can. She's not going to pull through. If you'd like to go in, sir.'

Gotobed rose heavily and plodded into the sickbay. Miss Oliphant closed her book. Amboyne went over to her and they talked quietly. Daisy simply could not summon up the energy to move.

Alec came in a few minutes later. He looked even grimmer than last time she saw him. 'Where is Gotobed?' he asked curtly.

'With his wife,' said Amboyne. 'She may go at any moment. By the way, Denton is fit to answer questions at last.'

'Thank you. I shan't intrude now.' Alec sat down beside Daisy. In a low voice, he told her what the steward had said. 'So you see, there's the opportunity, the last piece of the puzzle.'

'You must hear his side of the story,' she objected.

'I shall, but I have Captain Dane's authorization to arrest him. When the *Talavera* sails back, he'll be taken back to England to stand trial.'

Daisy had no answer.

The doctor went off to see his other patients. Daisy, Alec, and Miss Oliphant sat in silence, waiting. How long they waited Daisy had no idea. It seemed like forever, yet when the nurse came in, she thought, 'Not already!'

'She's gone, poor lamb.' From the open door behind her came racking sobs. Miss Oliphant started up, her face twisting. The nurse shut the door. 'Mrs Denton's with him and maybe that's best, madam; she doesn't know anything but he's lost a loved one, nothing on her mind except to comfort him as best she can.'

Miss Oliphant subsided, looking distressed but conscious that she was by no means so disinterested.

'He's shattered!' Daisy said to Alec.

'That doesn't mean he didn't kill her. Which in turn doesn't mean his reaction is not perfectly sincere.'

Daisy unhappily acknowledged the possibility. Her heart went out to Gotobed, guilty or not.

'Why did Mrs Gotobed leave the room in the middle of the meal?' asked Alec.

'I left first.' Gotobed's face was alarmingly grey. He looked quite incapable of leaving the armchair where he drooped in the suite's sitting room, the Ferellis having been evicted. 'She asked me to fetch her a handkerchief. She said they were in a drawer in the dressing table, in a sachet on top, but I couldn't find them without pawing through her . . . things, which I didn't care to do. So I called her to come and look for herself.'

'And you went back to the table.'

'Not until she'd found the damned sachet. It was right at the bottom. She blamed Baines.'

Alec tried a different approach. 'At what stage in the meal was this?'

Gotobed thought. 'It must have been after the steward brought the main course. The tournedos were already on the plates, under covers, but the potatoes and vegetables were in serving dishes. He'd brought carrots instead of peas, which suited me fine, but Wanda insisted on peas. He went off to get them, and that's when she decided she wanted a handkerchief.'

'So she went into the bedroom to fetch one.'

'I went,' said Gotobed, shaking his head. 'I was happy to do such little errands for her. I loved her. That's why I married her. I would never have done anything to harm her.'

'Not even when you discovered that she was not really your wife?' Alec infused his voice with disbelief.

'What?' Gotobed sat up straight, a hint of colour touching his cheeks. 'What the devil do you mean by that, Fletcher?'

'There is irrefutable evidence that Wanda Fairchild – to start with her stage name – was born Wanda Pertwee and, some fifteen years ago, married Henry Welford.'

'Pertwee? Welford?' Gotobed gaped at him, angry colour rising. 'Poppycock!'

'Detective Constable Piper found the records at

Somerset House and obtained certified copies. There was no divorce.'

Alec jumped up as every vestige of colour fled from Gotobed's face. He seemed to crumple, looking old and ill. If it was a performance, it was a very convincing performance, Alec thought uneasily. Unless the shock was not the facts but having his motive discovered?

'Shall I fetch the doctor, sir?' As Gotobed shook his head, Alec went over to the small cabinet in the corner where his search of the suite had turned up a bottle of whisky. He poured half a tumbler, added a splash of water from a carafe, and took the glass to Gotobed.

'Thank you. Help yourself.' He took a gulp.

Alec hesitated, then poured himself a more modest drink and returned to his seat. He was no longer quite ready to arrest Gotobed. Yet what solution could there be other than that Gotobed had murdered Pertwee, Welford, and Wanda?

But that would not explain Denton's dive. Suddenly, Alec was very keen to interview the Suffolk farmer. He ought to speak to the steward again, too, to see if more thorough questioning brought to light any evidence that Gotobed had gone into the bedroom first. After all, Wanda might have been driven to suicide by the deaths of her husband and brother.

But if not Gotobed, who had killed those two?

'Not married!' Gotobed said in a tone of wonder. To Alec's relief, the Yorkshireman was reviving. He sat up straighter and there was a trace of his usual vigour in his voice when he went on, 'She deceived me, but happen I've been deceiving meself, too. Wishful thinking is a grand persuader. I thowt I knew her through and through. She had her little faults, to be sure, but which of us doesn't?'

'All too true, sir. I'll have more questions for you later, but I think you should have a bit of a rest now. Are you sure you wouldn't like me to send Dr Amboyne to see you?'

'No, no. But I believe I should like to consult Miss Oliphant, if she will be so kind. I suspect I may need one of her magic potions to help me sleep tonight.'

'I'll ask her,' Alec promised, and headed back to the sickbay.

Daisy was still in the waiting room, sitting with the nurse, Miss Oliphant, and Mrs Denton around the desk, drinking soup from mugs and eating sandwiches.

'Darling, have you eaten?' she cried, as Alec trudged in. 'You must be starving! Come and join us. There's plenty of sandwiches and half a jug of soup. You'll have to share my mug.'

Between bites and sups, Alec passed on Gotobed's message to Miss Oliphant. Uncharacteristically flustered, she went at once, taking with her some herbs from her medicine chest and a packet of sandwiches quickly wrapped by the nurse for Gotobed.

Daisy kept stuffing Alec with sandwiches until he swore he could not eat another crumb. 'I'd like to talk to Mr Denton,' he told the nurse. 'Dr Amboyne said he's well enough.'

'That he is, sir,' affirmed Mrs Denton, 'long as you don't make him talk too long. He didn't ought to get to coughing, Doctor says. But he were asleep when we come out. He needs his sleep, don't he, Nurse?'

'Always napping, and the best thing for him, but he doesn't usually sleep very long. I'll just take a peek and see if he's awake, Mr Fletcher. If he is, you can go right in, but you won't mind if I go too; it's my bounden duty to see you don't tire the poor lamb.'

If Nurse was going to be present at the interview, Daisy had no more intention of being left out than Mrs Denton had of letting her husband be questioned without her at his side. The four of them gathered around Denton's hospital bed. Wanda's body had been removed. Daisy didn't care to wonder where it was being stored for autopsy.

Denton's breathing was laboured, his weathered face sallow without the ruddiness of health, but his eyes were bright enough. Mrs Denton took his calloused hand and said, 'Well, Pa, here's folks come to see you. The gentleman wants to ask you some questions. He's a detective policeman from Scotland Yard.'

'Mr Denton, do you remember what happened? How you came to fall over the railing into the sea?'

'Aye, I mind well!' wheezed the farmer. He continued with frequent pauses to catch his breath. ''Tis not the sort o' thing a chap'd forget. There were I, leaning on the rail and a-smoking of me pipe, peaceable like. Moonlight 'twere, pretty as a picture. You should've bin there, Ma.'

'I wish I were!' lamented Mrs Denton.

'I were just wond'ring if our Albert was done planting the winter wheat, when I feels someone a-grabbing of me ankles and he gives a great heave, and over I goes, clean as a whistle.'

'Brenda was right,' Daisy mouthed at Alec.

'And I lost me pipe and the cap Ma got at the church jumbly sale,' Denton added in an aggrieved voice.

‘’Twere his fav’rite pipe,’ Mrs Denton explained, ‘and a fancy cap wi’ ear flaps to keep out the cold wind, as was Squire’s father’s in the old days.’

Daisy held her breath as Alec asked, with what she considered unnatural calmness, ‘Not a fore-and-aft cap? Did it have peaks both in front and at the back?’

Mrs Denton nodded. ‘That’s right, sir.’

‘Kep’ me neck warm.’ Denton’s voice was failing.

‘That’s enough now,’ said Nurse. ‘Time for your medicine and a nice nap, Mr Denton. I can’t let you ask the poor lamb any more tonight, Mr Fletcher, he’s had enough. It’d be as much as my job’s worth.’

‘One more question. Mrs Denton can answer it. Would you please describe your husband’s overcoat, ma’am?’

‘His coat?’ Mrs Denton asked, surprised. ‘’Tis quite ordin’ry, brown what they call tweed, with a cape to keep off the rain. That were Old Squire’s, too, from the bazaar. ’Twon’t never be the same again after that seawater ducking,’ she added sadly.

‘Thank you,’ said Alec. ‘Please accept my best wishes for your swift recovery, Mr Denton.’ He headed for the door.

Daisy followed, bursting with excitement. As soon as the sickbay door closed behind them, she exclaimed, ‘Someone took him for Gotobed!’

Alec smiled, but said, ‘Gotobed’s coat is grey.’

‘It was moonlight. Colours don’t show. Someone tried to kill Gotobed. I bet it was Pertwee, and he was going to try again, only that cross-wave threw *him* over.’

‘Try again in broad daylight, with people about?’ Alec asked sceptically.

‘Darling, you don’t *still* think Gotobed’s the villain?’

'Let's say my mind is considerably more open than it was a quarter of an hour ago, but we still have Wanda's death to account for. I must talk to the steward again.'

In spite of that 'we', he refused to let Daisy go with him and forbade her to go and see Gotobed lest she unwarrantably raise his hopes.

Disconsolate, she went along to Arbuckle's suite. Arbuckle had gone to see Gotobed, but she found Phillip trying to teach a card game – Racing Demon – to Gloria, Brenda, Riddman, and a young Italian couple. After Daisy's somewhat clearer explanation and a demonstration, they started playing. Several hilarious games kept Daisy from trying to work out what Denton's revelations led to and what Alec hoped to find out from the steward.

Arbuckle returned, looking puzzled. 'Fletcher wants us all to meet in Gotobed's suite tomorrow after breakfast,' he announced.

'What for, Poppa?'

'I'll be darned if I rightly know, honey.'

'Us too, sir?' Riddman asked. 'Birdie and I, that is.'

'Yes, both of you, but not our Eyetalian guests, of course. Do you know the low-down, Mrs Fletcher?'

'Not exactly,' Daisy temporized. 'And if I did, I shouldn't dare tell you. I'd better be getting along.'

She found Alec in their cabin, preparing for bed. Lucia Croce had not returned.

'Thank heaven,' Alec said.

'I dare say she'll stay with her husband.'

'I hope so. If she turns up in the middle of the night, I suppose as a gentleman I'll have to give up my berth to her and sleep on the floor. I'm much too tired.' He climbed into bed.

'It's been an endless day. Darling, what's this about a meeting in Gotobed's suite tomorrow morning?'

'You'll find out tomorrow morning. Come here.'

'You're much too tired,' Daisy teased.

'Not for some things. Come here.'

# CHAPTER 21

'Arbuckle and Phillip and Gloria,' said Daisy, as she and Alec made their way towards Gotobed's suite next morning, 'but why Brenda and Riddman?'

'Lady Brenda because she saw Denton's attacker. Riddman because he knew Pertwee and Welford better than anyone else.'

'Who else? Miss Oliphant?'

'Yes, Gotobed insisted. And Captain Dane's sending Harvey to represent him.'

'Harvey and Riddman? Oh dear!'

'Not my choice. Are they still rivals? I was under the impression that Lady Brenda had returned to her first love.'

'Or opted for money.' Daisy sighed. 'I shouldn't think they'll come to blows, but I'm sure the air will be thick with invisible daggers.'

Everyone else was already there when they arrived. A couple of extra chairs had been brought in so there were enough to go around, set out in a semicircle with one facing them. Harvey was seated at one end, Brenda at the other with Riddman beside her. Brenda looked uncomfortable. The two men studiously ignored each other.

Daisy took the only free seat in the circle. Alec chose to stand, leaning on the back of the chair facing the group.

'Thank you all for coming,' he began. 'The first thing I want to say is that we shall almost certainly never know for sure exactly what happened on this unhappy voyage. I have a theory which seems to me to tie all the loose ends together. Before you hear it, I must have an assurance from each of you that nothing you hear in here this morning will go any further, except, of course, Mr Harvey's confidential report to the Captain. Lady Brenda?'

'I shan't tell, I promise. I know you all think . . .'

'Lady Brenda,' Alec interrupted, 'if you had not held your tongue when asked, everyone on this ship would know what you saw the night Denton fell overboard. Mr Riddman?'

One by one, they all gave their word. Alec continued.

'You have all been involved in one way or another. You may be able to point out weaknesses in my theory, or you may have ideas of your own. If so, I want to hear them. But before we go any further, Mr Gotobed has something to say to you. Sir?'

Gotobed stood up and turned to face them. To Daisy, he looked rather like a Christian facing the lions.

'I'm telling you this.' he said heavily, 'partly because it'll help you understand Mr Fletcher's story, partly so you won't think too badly of me when you see I'm not mourning Wanda as a husband ought. It seems I niver was her husband.'

There was a surprised murmur, in which, Daisy noticed, Miss Oliphant did not join. Gotobed glanced at the witch, who gave him an encouraging smile. He continued with renewed confidence.

'They say there's no fool like an old fool. That's me. I knew Fairchild was Wanda's stage name, but I never enquired further, not even when that's how she signed the marriage certificate. Her real maiden name was Pertwee. And when I married her, she was already the wife of Henry Welford.'

A collective gasp this time, again not echoed by Miss Oliphant. Gotobed resumed his seat beside her, and she took his hand. Silently, Daisy cheered.

'Now it's your turn, Lady Brenda. Would you mind describing for those who haven't heard exactly what you saw that night?'

Clearly and briefly, Brenda described seeing Denton tipped overboard. 'You believe me now?' she asked.

'Mr Denton has confirmed your report,' Alec told her. 'He – or rather, his wife – has also described his clothes in more detail than you were able to make out in the dark. Not only was he smoking a pipe, he wore a fore-and-aft cap and a taped greatcoat.'

'Jeez!' Arbuckle exclaimed. 'In the dark, he'd be the spitting image of Gotobed!'

'By Jove, yes!' said his son-in-law. 'Hang it, old chap, d'you mean to say Mr Gotobed was the real target?'

'It seems probable,' Alec confirmed. 'I've been unable to dig up any reason why anyone should attack Denton, an inoffensive farmer. But Mr Gotobed had made a will in his presumed wife's favour. Others would have profited by his death.'

'Pertwee and Welford, I guess,' said Gloria, 'and Wanda herself. Golly gee!'

'I suspect either Pertwee or Welford attacked Denton in

the mistaken belief that he was Mr Gotobed. Does anyone have a cogent argument against?'

People looked at each other. Heads shook.

'Good. The next bit is more complicated, more of a leap of faith. Pure speculation, in fact. I'm assuming that our precious pair had no intention of giving up the battle after their unfortunate mistake, which, remember, nearly resulted in the death of a stranger.'

'Waal, now,' said Arbuckle thoughtfully, 'they wouldn't want to make the same mistake again, would they?'

'Exactly, sir.'

'So that's why Pertwee approached Mr Gotobed in broad daylight and spoke to him,' Daisy reflected. 'But surely he didn't plan to chuck him in then, darling, in front of everyone, including us?'

'Hardly. No, his part was to identify the victim and keep him standing in one place. In deference to the ladies, I shan't describe what Mr Gotobed saw and reported. What none of you know except Daisy and Second Officer Harvey – and Mr Gotobed himself – is that Pertwee apparently fell over the rail because he was shot.'

'So that's why you asked me about guns!' said Riddman. 'I thought you'd got a mite mixed up and forgot Pertwee drowned.'

'Drowning is probably what killed him, but he might have been saved if he hadn't been shot first. As I see it, Welford was concealed with a firearm somewhere in the superstructure. There are plenty of good hiding places, and my sergeant discovered Welford'd been a marksman during the war.'

'Alec, you didn't tell me!' Daisy cried indignantly. 'That's not fair.'

He grinned. 'Sorry, love. I told you what seemed to me at the time the vital part of the wireless message. I forgot that minor point, which I'd skimmed over when reading it, and didn't remember until I heard Denton's evidence and my viewpoint switched a hundred and eighty degrees. To return to our story: We have Welford hidden on the boat deck, Pertwee keeping Mr Gotobed occupied.'

'And then the cross-wave hit the ship,' said Gotobed. 'Either Welford was just pulling the trigger, or his finger jerked as he tried to keep his balance. Any road, his aim would be upset. And in the meantime, Pertwee and I danced our little jig as we tried to keep our balance.'

Harvey drew the obvious conclusion. 'So the bullet meant for Mr Gotobed hit Pertwee.'

'By Jove,' said Phillip, 'the fellow was jolly well done in by his own accomplice!'

'That's my guess,' Alec agreed.

'Welford must have been simply shattered.' Daisy could almost sympathize. 'I suppose he bunged the gun over the side right away, to get rid of the evidence. He couldn't know the body would not be recovered. But do you think he still wanted to kill Mr Gotobed, darling, or did he decide to try blackmail as he'd proved such an incompetent murderer?'

'Remember the bludgeon found in the scuppers. Perhaps by then a desire for revenge for his brother-in-law's death may have added to his greed as motive.'

'You mean he blamed Jethro,' – Miss Oliphant blushed, but continued with undiminished indignation – 'Mr Gotobed for Welford's demise?'

'Criminals are even more liable than the law-abiding to blame someone else so as to avoid accepting their own responsibility,' Alec said dryly. 'It tends to make them incautious, which is a great help to us. Let's move on. Now we have a rough sea, a violent and bitterly cold wind. Mr Gotobed is not deterred. He goes out and, during a lull in the wind, climbs the steps to the boat deck. Welford, who has been spying on him, hoping for a chance, follows.'

'We saw him,' Daisy said. 'Not his face. He was very well bundled up. He could easily have hidden a bludgeon under his coat.'

'At the head of the companion-way,' Alec resumed, 'Mr Gotobed has stepped aside and stopped to admire the view. Welford reaches the top, takes out his life-preserver . . .'

'Life-preserver?' Brenda asked uncertainly.

'Sorry, the bludgeon. He raises it, preparatory to bringing it down on his victim's head. It's heavy, weighted with lead. At that moment a tremendous gust strikes. With the weight high above his head, his balance is already disturbed.'

'If his hands had not been otherwise occupied,' Miss Oliphant said severely, 'he might have been able to grasp the rail.'

'I guess the wind and the waves were *your* life-preserver, Gotobed,' said Arbuckle.

'Aye, t'weather was on my side.'

'In a sense,' Alec concurred, 'though the villains' stupidity in failing to take conditions into account was also responsible for their ruin.'

'Now we come to the fourth incident. Mrs Gotobed, as she was then assumed to be – perhaps it's easiest if I refer to her as Wanda – Wanda, then, knew of the deaths of her brother and her actual husband. She knew Mr Gotobed was under suspicion in their deaths.'

'I assumed it was his being a suspect that was upsetting her.' Daisy recalled Wanda's horror. 'But it must have been her real husband's death.'

'Gotobed was suspected of killing Welford,' said Alec, 'yet when offered alternative accommodation she chose to remain in the suite with him.'

'I thought it proved she trusted him and really did love him in her way,' Daisy said mournfully.

'That was the obvious inference when we were unaware of her connection with the deceased. We'll never know her true feelings, though in view of her willingness to commit bigamy, I believe we can take it she was from the beginning part of the plot to commit murder.'

Daisy nodded. 'When Denton was tipped over, she knew Mr Gotobed had gone up to smoke his pipe. She probably alerted the others. But what I find terribly persuasive is that she was so sure it must be Mr Gotobed who had fallen in. At the time, I thought she was being either hysterical or theatrical, like Brenda.'

'I wasn't!'

'No, sorry, of course you weren't. But Wanda reacted exactly the same way when Welford drowned. Again she was convinced it must be Mr Gotobed who had fallen in. Yes, I'm sure she was in on the planning.'

'You betcha!' Arbuckle agreed with fervour. 'Heck, I always knew she was bad news; I just didn't know how bad.'

'The rest is pure conjecture. Presumably she realized Pertwee and Welford's bungling was responsible for their deaths, yet she may have held Mr Gotobed partly to blame because his luck had thwarted them. So again, revenge may have entered into the matter. In any case, there was still a fortune at stake.'

'If she wasn't really frightfully keen on her brother and her husband,' Brenda proposed, 'maybe she was glad she wouldn't have to share the filthy lucre.'

'Possibly. Whatever her reasons, she appears to have decided to proceed with the plan. The means she had to hand. The drops she used to make her eyes look larger and more lustrous are deadly when ingested.'

'In-whatted?' Phillip asked in puzzlement. Daisy wondered just what he thought one could do with eye-drops besides put them in one's eyes. She also silently wondered why Wanda had asked to see Miss Oliphant again. Had she hoped the witch might be blamed for Gotobed's death?

'Swallowed,' Alec explained to Phillip. 'A very small amount can be fatal if treatment is delayed, which is quite likely as symptoms don't appear for several hours. However, Wanda used most of the remaining contents of her vial, which, according to her maid, was nearly full.'

'She wanted to make absolutely sure,' said Daisy, 'but how did she come to take it, darling, instead of Mr Gotobed?'

'I'm getting to that,' Alec said patiently. 'Let's consider why she chose yesterday's lunch as the time to act.'

'Something to do with the *Garibaldi* sinking?' hazarded Brenda.

'Sure, baby,' said Riddman. 'I guess Mr Gotobed would've told her he was gonna take in some Eyeties.'

'I did.'

'Them being there'd put the kibosh on the whole deal.'

'And with the chaos attendant upon the rescue,' Miss Oliphant added, 'the chances of help being delayed until it was too late were vastly increased.'

'Besides which,' said Daisy, who had worked out another factor yesterday, when Alec told her he had to see the steward again, 'lots more passengers than usual were lunching in their cabins, so the steward serving lunch would be run off his feet and less likely to notice anything amiss.' She was beginning to think Alec was very clever to let everyone have their say. This way, they all had a stake in his theories and were more likely to ingest them wholesale.

'All good reasons,' Alec resumed, 'whether Wanda came up with one or all of them. Mr Gotobed, would you mind telling us exactly what you ordered for lunch?'

'We both had the same, except for afters. First French onion soup, then sole with lemon-butter sauce, then tournedos Chasseur with new potatoes and peas.'

'Exactly the same, sir?'

'The only difference up to that point was that I asked for plenty of sauce with the fish and beef, whereas Wanda wanted only a little. I expect you all know she watched her figure. The steward kindly brought a sauce-boat with extra for each course, and I took some of the lemon-butter, but as it happened the kitchens had poured as much as I cared for over the tournedos on my plate. Then I had a very nice Gruyere with water biscuits and Wanda had fruit compote, with cream, slimming notwithstanding.'

'And you drank?'

'I had a pint of bitter. She had seltzer water.'

'Hang on,' said Phillip. 'There's lots of things she could have put the stuff in, but wouldn't it taste beastly?'

'Belladonna berries,' Miss Oliphant informed the company, 'from which the eye-drops are prepared, taste sweet. Is it certain that she died of belladonna poisoning?'

'As certain as we can be without an autopsy. Dr Amboyne agrees with you that the observed symptoms are entirely consistent, and there is a good deal of the substance unaccounted for.'

'But I do not comprehend, Mr Fletcher, how Mrs . . . Welford could have introduced the poison into Mr Gotobed's food or drink without his noticing.'

'I would have liked to have the steward here to speak for himself. However, with all our extra passengers, the crew are still – as Daisy put it – run off their feet, so I'll give you the salient points. Everything was perfectly normal until at one point when Bailey went in, both the lady and the gentleman were in the bedroom. Mr Gotobed told me that Wanda had asked him to fetch her a handkerchief. He was unable to find it, so she went to look, too.'

'The steward would go in to take away dirty plates or to serve the next course,' said Daisy. 'He wouldn't have time to keep popping in to ask if everything was satisfactory. So there was no food on the table when Wanda was alone there. She must have put the poison in the beer. But why did she then drink it?'

'Your logic is impeccable, love. Mr Gotobed and Wanda were both at table when the steward took in two covered plates of tournedos, a gravy-boat with extra sauce, a dish of potatoes and one of carrots.'

'Peas,' Gloria corrected him. 'Mr Gotobed said he ordered peas.'

'He did. He would have accepted the carrots, but Wanda insisted on peas. The steward went off to fetch them.'

'Which was when Wanda asked me to fetch her handkerchief.'

'And then poured the eye-drops into the gravy-boat, I bet,' guessed Daisy. 'Liquid, highly flavoured, and intended for Mr Gotobed. But that still leaves the question of why did *she* take some?'

'We're nearly there. The dastardly deed done, she joined Mr Gotobed in the bedroom. The steward returned with the peas. He couldn't wait for them to come in, so he took the covers off the plates and served portions of vegetables and potatoes. He noticed that, as requested, the kitchens had poured plenty of sauce over one serving of beef, which he set at Mr Gotobed's place. The other plate, however, which should have had a small amount of sauce, as requested by Wanda, had none at all. Deciding it looked dry and unappetizing, he ladled some sauce from the boat over the meat.' His lips quirking at the collective gasp. Alec finished the story: 'Then, as Wanda and Mr Gotobed had not returned, he replaced the covers and left.'

'You know how deep the plates are,' said Gotobed, 'to stop the food sliding off in high seas. There was plenty of gravy on mine. I didn't take any extra, though Wanda reminded me twice that I'd ordered it. She ate everything on her plate.'

Daisy sighed. 'If she hadn't kicked up a dust and insisted on peas, the steward wouldn't have come back. In effect, she died because she wouldn't eat her carrots. My old nanny wouldn't have been a bit surprised.'

# EPILOGUE

On a sparkling clear day, the *Talavera* steamed across New York Bay, passengers crowding the rails. Up on the boat deck, Mr Arbuckle eagerly pointed out the sights to Daisy and Alec. Ahead towered the Statue of Liberty and the skyscrapers of Manhattan.

Daisy's attention wandered from the list of buildings with the number of floors for each. Looking down at the swarms of people on the promenade deck, she caught sight of Gotobed and Miss Oliphant. Gotobed had on his caped greatcoat, but he had given his fore-and-aft cap to Denton, to whom it had caused so much trouble. Daisy deplored the bowler hat he now wore.

'I'm so glad he has the witch to console him,' she said.

'What's that, Mrs Fletcher?' Arbuckle followed her gaze. 'Oh, Gotobed and Miss Oliphant. Waal now, I guess she's the sort of lady he ought to have had his eye on right from the start, a real nice lady. He's sweet on her, all right. I'm mighty glad you were clever enough to figure out what really happened, Fletcher, so he can start again without suspicion of murder hanging over him. If you'll excuse me, I'll go down and have a word.'

He went off. Leaning on the rail, Daisy said, 'He's right,

your theory was brilliant, darling. Everyone is quite sure you're right.'

'I'm not.' Alec sighed. 'It's the most likely explanation I could come up with. It's quite possible that Wanda committed suicide. It's possible Miss Oliphant killed her. It's possible that Gotobed killed her, or all three victims, though Denton's experience makes me very nearly certain they were trying to kill him, so it could he considered self-defence.'

'But nothing can be proved,' Daisy reminded him.

'No, and that's why it's best for all concerned if my story stands. Great Scott, Daisy, I'm just afraid I'm beginning to absorb your cavalier attitude towards the law!'

# Rattle His Bones

by Carola Dunn

ISBN: 978-1-84901-518-9
Price: £6.99

Has the unflappable flapper met her match?

As a grey drizzle descends upon the damp errand boys and busy omnibuses of London, Daisy Dalrymple is feeling rather cheerful and excited to be showing her nephew and future stepdaughter the glories of Kensington's Natural History Museum. But as closing time draws near, Daisy and co hear a tremendous crash and are horrified to discover one of the curators dead – horribly murdered – atop of a pile of dinosaur bones.

Together with her fiancé, Detective Chief Inspector Alec Fletcher of Scotland Yard, Daisy is soon investigating a baffling case of missing gems, dispossessed European gentry, fakery and fossils . . . and where professional grudges boil over into murder!

The eighth book in the Daisy Dalrymple series

'The honourable Daisy Dalrymple brings her usual style and flair to this eighth instalment. Dunn's witty prose shines in this light-hearted whodunit.' *Publishers Weekly*

# Styx and Stones

by Carola Dunn

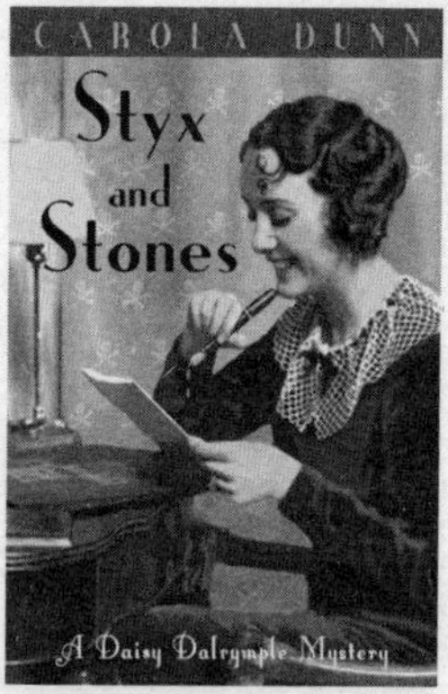


ISBN: 978-1-84901-492-2
Price: £6.99

When malice turns to murder . . . The hot summer heat is enough to put anyone on edge but to Daisy Dalrymple, it seems that her brother-in-law, Lord John Frobisher, is exceptionally tense – and with good reason. Someone with an evil sense of humour is sending him a series of poison pen letters that threaten to reveal racy secrets which could ruin him completely.

Promising to protect Lord John from public scandal, Daisy travels to his village in Kent only to discover it's teeming with enough gossip, resentment and intrigue to make everyone a suspect . . . or victim. Then a murder is committed, and Daisy is forced to find the killer before the ink dries on her own death warrant!

The seventh book in the Daisy Dalrymple series

'Daisy's newest adventure, like the others in the series, offers enough tart wit to engage the seasoned mystery reader.'
*Publishers Weekly*